THE PICKWICK PAPERS

Published by Priory Books,
© Peter Haddock Publishing,
United Kingdom, YO16 6BT.

THE PICKWICK PAPERS

CHAPTER 1

The First Day's Journey, and the First Evening's Adventures; with their Consequences

Mr Pickwick, with his portmanteau in his hand, his telescope in his great-coat pocket, and his note-book in his waistcoat, ready for the reception of any discoveries worthy of being noted down, had arrived at the coach-stand in St Martin's-le-Grand.

"Cab!" said Mr Pickwick.

"Here you are, sir," shouted a strange specimen of the human race, in a sackcloth coat, who, with a brass label and number round his neck, looked as if he were catalogued in some collection of rarities. Mr Pickwick entered all these observations in his note-book with a view to communicating them to the next meeting of the Pickwick Club. His entry was scarcely completed when they reached the Golden Cross. Down jumped the driver, and out got Mr Pickwick. Mr Tupman, Mr Snodgrass, and Mr Winkle, who had been anxiously waiting the arrival of their illustrious leader, crowded to welcome him.

"Here's your fare," said Mr Pickwick, holding out the shilling to the driver.

What was the learned man's astonishment, when that unaccountable person flung the money on the pavement, and requested to be allowed the pleasure of fighting him (Mr Pickwick) for the amount!

"You are mad," said Mr Snodgrass.

"Or drunk," said Mr Winkle.

"Or both," said Mr Tupman.

"Come on!" said the cab-driver, sparring away like clockwork. "Come on – all four on you."

"What's the row, Sam?" inquired one gentleman.

"Row!" replied the cabman, "what did he want my number for?"

"I didn't want your number," said the astonished Mr Pickwick.

"What did you take it for, then?" inquired the cabman.

"I didn't take it," said Mr Pickwick indignantly.

"Would anybody believe," continued the cab-driver, appealing to the crowd, "as an informer 'ud go about in a man's cab, not only takin' down his number, but ev'ry word he says into the bargain?" (A light flashed upon Mr Pickwick – it was his note-book).

"Did he though?" inquired another cabman.

"Yes, did he," replied the first; "and then gets three witnesses here to prove it. But I'll give it him, if I've six months for it. Come on!" and the cabman knocked Mr Pickwick's spectacles off, and followed up the attack with a blow on Mr Pickwick's nose, and another on Mr Pickwick's chest, and a third in Mr Snodgrass's eye, and a fourth, by way of variety, in Mr Tupman's waistcoat, and then danced into the road, and then back again to the pavement, and finally dashed the whole temporary supply of breath out of Mr Winkle's body; and all in half a dozen seconds.

"Where's an officer?" said Mr Snodgrass.

"You shall smart for this," gasped Mr Pickwick.

"Informers!" shouted the crowd.

"What's the fun?" said a rather tall, thin, young man, in a green coat, emerging suddenly from the coach-yard.

"Informers!" shouted the crowd again.

"We are not," roared Mr Pickwick, in a tone which, to any dispassionate listener, carried conviction with it.

"Ain't you, though – ain't you?" said the young man, appealing to Mr Pickwick, and making his way through the crowd by the infallible process of elbowing the countenances of its members.

That learned man in a few hurried words explained the real state of the case.

"Come along, then," said he of the green coat, lugging Mr Pickwick after him by main force, and talking the whole way.

"Here, No. 924, take your fare, and take yourself off – respectable gentleman – know him well – none of your nonsense – this way, sir – where's your friends? – all a mistake, I see – never mind – accidents will happen – best regulated families – never say die – down upon your luck – put that in his pipe – damned rascals."

And with a lengthened string of similar broken sentences, delivered with extraordinary volubility, the stranger led the way to the traveller's waiting-room, whither he was closely followed by Mr Pickwick and his disciples.

"Here, waiter!" shouted the stranger, ringing the bell with tremendous violence, "glasses round – brandy-and-water, hot and strong, and sweet, and plenty, – eye damaged, sir? Waiter! Raw beef-steak for the gentleman's eye – nothing like raw beef-steak for a bruise, sir; cold lamppost very good, but lamp-post inconvenient – damned odd standing in the open street half an hour, with your eye against a lamp-post – eh, – very good – ha! ha!" And the stranger, without stopping to take breath, swallowed at a draught full half a pint of the reeking brandy-and-water, and flung himself into a chair with as much ease as if nothing uncommon had occurred.

While his three companions were busily engaged in proffering their thanks to their new acquaintance, Mr Pickwick had leisure to examine his appearance. The green coat had been a smart dress garment, but had evidently adorned a much shorter man than the stranger, for the soiled and faded sleeves scarcely reached to his wrists. His scanty black trousers displayed here and there those shiny patches which bespeak long service, and were strapped very tightly over a pair of patched and mended shoes, as if to conceal the dirty white stockings, which were nevertheless distinctly visible. His face was thin and haggard; but an indescribable air of jaunty impudence and perfect self-possession pervaded the whole man.

"Never mind," said the stranger, "said enough – no more; smart chap that cabman – handled his fives well."

This coherent speech was interrupted by the entrance of the Rochester coachman, to announce that "the Commodore" was on the point of starting.

"Commodore!" said the stranger, starting up, "my coach – place booked, – one outside – leave you to pay for the brandy-and-water, – want change for a five."

Now it so happened that Mr Pickwick and his three companions had resolved to make Rochester their first halting-place too; and they agreed to occupy the seat at the back of the coach, where they could all sit together.

"Up with you," said the stranger, assisting Mr Pickwick on to the roof.

"Any luggage, sir?" inquired the coachman.

"Brown paper parcel here, that's all – other luggage gone by water – packing-cases, nailed up – big as houses – heavy, heavy, damned heavy," replied the stranger, as he forced into his pocket as much as he could of the brown paper parcel, which gave every appearance of containing one shirt and a handkerchief.

"Heads, heads – take care of your heads!" cried the stranger, as they came out under the low archway, which in those days formed the entrance to the coach-yard. "Terrible place – dangerous work – other day – five children – mother – tall lady, eating sandwiches – forgot the arch – crash – knock – children look round – mother's head off – sandwich in her hand – no mouth to put it in – head of a family off – shocking, shocking! eh, sir, eh?"

"I am ruminating," said Mr Pickwick, "on the strange mutability of human affairs."

"Ah! I see – in at the palace door one day, out at the window the next. Philosopher, sir?"

"An observer of human nature, sir," said Mr Pickwick.

"Ah, so am I. Most people are when they've little to do and less to get. Poet, Sir?"

"My friend Mr Snodgrass has a strong poetic turn," said Mr Pickwick.

"So have I," said the stranger. "Epic poem – ten thousand lines – revolution – composed it on the spot – bang the field-piece, twang the lyre. Sportsman, sir ?" abruptly turning to Mr Winkle.

"A little, sir," replied that gentleman.

"Fine pursuit, sir – fine pursuit. – Dogs, sir?"

"Not just now," said Mr Winkle.

"Ah! you should keep dogs – fine animals – sagacious creatures – dog of my own once – pointer – out shooting one day – entering enclosure – whistled – dog stopped – whistled again – Ponto – no go; stock still – called him – Ponto, Ponto – wouldn't move – dog staring at a board – looked up, saw an inscription – 'Gamekeeper has orders to shoot all dogs found in this enclosure' – wouldn't pass it – wonderful dog – valuable dog that – very."

"Singular circumstance that," said Mr Pickwick. "Will you allow me to make a note of it?"

"Certainly, sir, certainly – hundred more anecdotes of the same animal. – Fine girl, sir," (to Mr Tracy Tupman, who had been bestowing sundry anti-Pickwickian glances on a young lady by the roadside).

"Very!" said Mr Tupman.

"English girls not so fine as Spanish – noble creatures – jet hair – black eyes – lovely forms – sweet creatures – beautiful."

"You have been in Spain, sir?" said Mr Tracy Tupman.

"Lived there – ages."

"Many conquests, sir?" inquired Mr Tupman.

"Conquests! Thousands. Don Bolaro Fizzgig – Grandee – only daughter – Donna Christina – splendid creature – loved me to distraction – jealous father – Donna Christina in despair – prussic acid – stomach pump in my portmanteau – old Bolaro in ecstasies – consent to our union – join hands and floods of tears – romantic story – very."

"Is the lady in England now, sir?" inquired Mr Tupman, on whom the description of her charms had produced a powerful impression.

"Dead, sir – dead," said the stranger, applying to his right eye the brief remnant of a very old cambric handkerchief. "Never recovered the stomach pump – undermined constitution – fell a victim."

"Will you allow me to note that little romance down, sir?" said Mr Snodgrass, deeply affected.

"Certainly, sir, certainly – fifty more if you like to hear 'em – strange life mine – rather curious history – not extraordinary, but singular."

In this strain they reached the Bull Inn, in the High Street, where the coach stopped. Mr Winkle turned to Mr Pickwick, and murmured a few words; a whisper passed from Mr Pickwick to Mr Snodgrass, from Mr Snodgrass to Mr Tupman, and nods of assent were exchanged. Mr Pickwick addressed the stranger.

"You rendered us a very important service this morning, sir," said he, "will you allow us to offer a slight mark of our gratitude by begging the favour of your company at dinner?"

"Great pleasure – not presume to dictate, but broiled fowl and mushrooms – capital thing! What time?"

"Let me see," replied Mr Pickwick, referring to his watch, "it is now nearly three. Shall we say five?"

"Suit me excellently," said the stranger, "five precisely – till then – care of yourselves;" and lifting the pinched-up hat a few inches from his head, and carelessly replacing it very much on one side, the stranger, with half the brown paper parcel sticking out of his pocket, walked briskly up the yard, and turned into the High Street.

"Evidently a traveller in many countries, and a close observer of men and things," said Mr Pickwick.

"I should like to see his poem," said Mr Snodgrass.

"I should like to have seen that dog," said Mr Winkle.

Mr Tupman said nothing; but he thought of Donna Christina and the stomach pump; and his eyes filled with tears.

Punctual to five o'clock came the stranger, and shortly afterwards the dinner. He had divested himself of his brown paper parcel, but had made no alteration in his attire, and was, if possible, more loquacious than ever.

"Devil of a mess on the staircase, waiter," said the stranger. "Forms going up – carpenters coming down – lamps, glasses, harps. What's going forward?"

"Ball, sir," said the waiter.

"Many fine women in this town, do you know, sir?" inquired Mr Tupman, with great interest.

"Splendid – capital. Kent, sir – everybody knows Kent – apples, cherries, hops, and women. Glass of wine, sir!"

"With great pleasure," replied Mr Tupman. "I should very much like to go," said Mr Tupman, resuming the subject of the ball, "very much."

"Tickets at the bar, sir," interposed the waiter; "half-a-guinea each, sir."

Mr Tupman again expressed an earnest wish to be present at the festivity; but meeting with no response in the darkened eye of Mr Snodgrass, or the abstracted gaze of Mr Pickwick, he applied himself with great interest to the port wine and dessert, which had just been placed on the table. The waiter withdrew, and the party were left to enjoy the cosy couple of hours succeeding dinner.

The wine was passed, and a fresh supply ordered. The visitor talked, the Pickwickians listened. Mr Tupman felt every moment more disposed for the ball. Mr Pickwick's countenance glowed and Mr Winkle and Mr Snodgrass fell fast asleep.

"They're beginning upstairs," said the stranger.

"How I should like to go," said Mr Tupman again.

"So should I," said the stranger – "confounded luggage – nothing to go in – odd, ain't it?"

"I should be very happy to lend you a change of apparel for the purpose," said Mr Tracy Tupman, "but you are rather slim, and I am – "

"Rather fat – not double distilled, but double milled – ha! ha! pass the wine."

Mr Tupman passed the wine, coughed twice, and looked at the stranger with a stern intensity. "I was about to observe, sir," he said, "that though my apparel would be too large, a suit of my friend Mr Winkle's would, perhaps, fit you better."

The stranger took Mr Winkle's measure with his eye as he said, "Just the thing."

Mr Tupman looked round him. The wine, which had exerted its somniferous influence over Mr Snodgrass and Mr Winkle, had stolen upon the senses of Mr Pickwick.

"Winkle's bedroom is inside mine," said Mr Tupman; "I know he has a dress-suit in a carpet bag and supposing you wore it to the ball, and took it off when we returned, I could replace it without troubling him at all about the matter."

"Capital," said the stranger, "famous plan – fourteen coats in the packing-cases, and obliged to wear another man's – very good notion, that – very."

"We must purchase our tickets," said Mr Tupman.

"Not worth while splitting a guinea," said the stranger, "toss who shall pay for both – I call; you spin."

Mr Tupman rang the bell, purchased the tickets, and ordered chamber candlesticks. In another quarter of an hour the stranger was completely arrayed in a full suit of Mr Nathaniel Winkle's.

"It's a new coat," said Mr Tupman, as the stranger surveyed himself with great complacency in a cheval glass; "the first that's been made with our club button," and he called his companion's attention to the large gilt button which displayed a bust of Mr Pickwick in the centre, and the letters "P.C." on either side.

"'P.C.'" said the stranger – "queer set out – old fellow's likeness, and 'P.C.' – What does 'P.C.' stand for – Peculiar Coat, eh?"

Mr Tupman, with rising indignation and great importance, explained the mystic device.

Mr Tupman's new companion adjusted his dress, or rather the dress of Mr Winkle; and, accompanied by Mr Tupman, ascended the staircase leading to the ballroom.

The door was thrown open, and Mr Tracy Tupman and the stranger entered the ballroom. The musicians were securely confined in an elevated den, and quadrilles were being systematically got through by two or three sets of dancers. The finale concluded, the dancers promenaded the room, and Mr Tupman and his companion stationed themselves in a corner to observe the company.

"Charming women," said Mr Tupman.

One of the most popular personages, in his own circle, was a little fat man, with a ring of upright black hair round his head, and an extensive bald plain on the top of it – Doctor Slammer, surgeon to the 97th. The doctor chatted with everybody, laughed, danced, made jokes, played whist, did everything, and was everywhere. To these pursuits, the little doctor added a more important one in paying the most devoted attention to a little old widow, whose rich dress and profusion of ornament bespoke her a most desirable addition to a limited income. Upon the doctor and the widow, the eyes of both Mr Tupman and his companion had been fixed for some time, when the stranger broke silence.

"I'll dance with the widow," said the stranger.

"Who is she?" inquired Mr Tupman.

"Don't know – never saw her in all my life – cut out the doctor – here goes." And the stranger crossed the room; and, leaning against a mantel-piece, commenced gazing with an air of respectful and melancholy admiration on the fat countenance of the little old lady. The stranger progressed rapidly; the little doctor danced with another lady; the widow dropped her fan; the stranger picked it up, and presented it – a smile – a bow – a curtsey – a few words of conversation. The stranger walked boldly up to, and returned with, the master of the ceremonies; a little introductory pantomime; and the stranger and Mrs Budger took their places in a quadrille.

The stranger was young, and the widow was flattered. Doctor Slammer was paralysed. He, Doctor Slammer, of the 97th rejected! Impossible! It could not be!

A few seconds after the stranger had disappeared to lead Mrs Budger to her carriage, he darted swiftly from the room with every particle of his bottled-up indignation effervescing, in a perspiration of passion. The stranger was returning, and Mr Tupman was beside him. He spoke in a low tone, and laughed. The little doctor thirsted for his life.

"Sir!" said the doctor, in an awful voice, producing a card, "my name is Slammer, Doctor Slammer, sir – 97th Regiment – Chatham Barracks – my card, sir, my card." He would have added more, but his indignation choked him.

"Ah!" replied the stranger coolly, "Slammer – much obliged – not ill now, Slammer – but when I am – knock you up."

"You – you're a shuffler, sir," gasped the furious doctor, "a poltroon – a coward – a liar – a – will nothing induce you to give me your card, sir!"

"Oh! I see," said the stranger, half aside, "liberal landlord – very foolish – lemonade much better – hot rooms – elderly gentlemen – suffer for it in the morning – cruel – cruel;" and he moved on a step or two.

"You are stopping in this house, sir," said the indignant little man; "you are intoxicated now, sir; you shall hear from me in the morning, sir. I shall find you out, sir; I shall find you out."

"Rather you found me out than found me at home," replied the unmoved stranger.

Doctor Slammer fixed his hat on his head with an indignant knock; and the stranger and Mr Tupman ascended to the bedroom of the latter to restore the borrowed plumage to the unconscious Winkle.

Seven o'clock had hardly ceased striking on the following morning, when Mr Pickwick's mind was aroused from the state of unconsciousness, in which slumber had plunged it, by a loud knocking at his chamber door.

"Who's there?" said Mr Pickwick, starting up in bed.

"Boots, sir."

"What do you want?"

"Please, sir, can you tell me which gentleman of your party wears a bright blue dress-coat, with a gilt button with 'P.C.' on it?"

"It's been given out to brush," thought Mr Pickwick, "Mr Winkle," he called out, "next room but two, on the right hand."

"Thank'ee, sir," said the Boots, and away he went.

"What's the matter?" cried Mr Tupman, as a loud knocking at his door roused him from his repose.

"Can I speak to Mr Winkle, sir?" replied Boots from the outside.

"Winkle – Winkle!" shouted Mr Tupman, calling into the inner room.

"Hallo!" replied a faint voice from within the bed-clothes.

"You're wanted – some one at the door;" and, having exerted himself thus much, Mr Tracy Tupman turned round and fell fast asleep again.

"Wanted!" said Mr Winkle, hastily jumping out of bed, and putting on a few articles of clothing; "who on earth can want me?"

"Gentleman in the coffee-room, sir," replied the Boots, as Mr Winkle opened the door and confronted him; "gentleman says he'll not detain you a moment, sir, but he can take no denial."

"Very odd!" said Mr Winkle; "I'll be down directly."

He hurriedly wrapped himself in a travelling-shawl and dressing-gown, and proceeded downstairs.

An officer in uniform was looking out of the window. He turned round as Mr Winkle entered, and made a stiff inclination of the head.

"Mr Winkle, I presume?"

"My name is Winkle, sir."

"You will not be surprised, sir, when I inform you that I have called here this morning on behalf of my friend, Doctor Slammer, of the 97th."

"Doctor Slammer!" said Mr Winkle.

"My friend, Doctor Slammer, requested me to add that you were intoxicated during a portion of the evening, and possibly unconscious of the extent of the insult you were guilty of and that he will consent to accept a written apology, to be penned by you, from my dictation."

"A written apology!" repeated Mr Winkle, in the most emphatic tone of amazement possible.

"Of course you know the alternative," replied the visitor coolly.

"Were you entrusted with this message to me by name?" inquired Mr Winkle, whose intellects were hopelessly confused by this extraordinary conversation.

"I was desired to identify the wearer of a very uncommon coat – a bright blue dress-coat, with a gilt button and the letters 'P.C.'"

Mr Winkle actually staggered with astonishment as he heard his own costume thus minutely described. Mr Winkle's first impression was that his coat had been stolen.

"Will you allow me to detain you one moment?" said he.

"Certainly," replied the unwelcome visitor.

Mr Winkle ran hastily upstairs, and with a trembling hand opened the bag. There was the coat in its usual place, but exhibiting, on a close inspection, evident tokens of having been worn on the preceding night.

"It must be so," said Mr Winkle, letting the coat fall from his hands. "I took too much wine after dinner, and have a very vague recollection of walking about the streets, and smoking a cigar afterwards. I was very drunk; – I must have changed my coat – gone somewhere – and insulted somebody – I have no doubt of it; and this message is the terrible consequence." Saying which, Mr Winkle retraced his steps in the direction of the coffee-room, with the gloomy and dreadful resolve of accepting the challenge of the warlike Doctor Slammer, and abiding by the worst consequences that might ensue.

Besides, he reflected, if he applied to Mr Snodgrass to act as his second, that gentleman might possibly communicate the news to Mr Pickwick, who would certainly lose no time in transmitting it to the local authorities, and thus prevent the killing or maiming of his follower. Such were his thoughts when he returned to the coffee-room, and intimated his intention of accepting the doctor's challenge.

"Shall we say – sunset this evening?" inquired the officer, in a careless tone.

"Very good," replied Mr Winkle, thinking in his heart it was very bad.

"You know Fort Pitt?"

"Yes; I saw it yesterday."

"If you will take the trouble to turn into the field which borders the trench, I will precede you to a secluded place, where the affair can be conducted without fear of interruption."

"Fear of interruption!" thought Mr Winkle.

"Nothing more to arrange, I think," said the officer.

"I am not aware of anything more," replied Mr Winkle.

"Good-morning."

"Good-morning;" and the officer whistled a lively air as he strode away.

That morning's breakfast passed heavily off. Mr Tupman was not in a condition to rise, after the dissipation of the previous night; Mr Snodgrass appeared to labour under a poetical depression of spirits; and even Mr Pickwick evinced an unusual attachment to silence and soda-water. Mr Winkle eagerly watched his opportunity: it was not long wanting. Mr Snodgrass proposed a visit to the castle, and as Mr Winkle was the only other member of the party disposed to walk, they went out together.

"Snodgrass," said Mr Winkle, when they had turned out of the public street. "I want your assistance, my dear fellow, in an affair of honour," said Mr Winkle.

"You shall have it," replied Mr Snodgrass, clasping his friend's hand.

"With a doctor – Doctor Slammer, of the 97th," said Mr Winkle, wishing to make the matter appear as solemn as possible; "an affair with

13

an officer, seconded by another officer, at sunset this evening, in a lonely field beyond Fort Pitt."

"I will attend you," said Mr Snodgrass. He was astonished, but by no means dismayed.

"The consequences may be dreadful," said Mr Winkle.

"I hope not," said Mr Snodgrass.

"The doctor, I believe, is a very good shot," said Mr Winkle.

"Most of these military men are," observed Mr Snodgrass calmly; "but so are you, ain't you?"

Mr Winkle replied in the affirmative; and perceiving that he had not alarmed his companion sufficiently, changed his ground.

"Snodgrass," he said, in a voice tremulous with emotion, "if I fall, you will find in a packet which I shall place in your hands a note for my – for my father."

This attack was a failure also. Mr Snodgrass undertook the delivery of the note as readily as if he had been a twopenny postman.

"If I fall," said Mr Winkle, "or if the doctor falls, you, my dear friend, will be tried as an accessory. Shall I involve my friend in transportation – possibly for life!"

Mr Snodgrass winced a little at this, but his heroism was invincible. "In the cause of friendship," he said fervently, "I would brave all dangers."

How Mr Winkle cursed his companion's devoted friendship. "Snodgrass," he said, stopping suddenly, "do not give information to the local authorities – do not obtain the assistance of several peace officers, to take either me or Doctor Slammer, of the 97th Regiment into custody, I say, do not."

Mr Snodgrass seized his friend's hand warmly, as he enthusiastically replied, "Not for worlds!"

The state of the case having been formally explained to Mr Snodgrass, and a case of satisfactory pistols, with the satisfactory accompaniments of powder, ball, and caps, having been hired from a manufacturer in Rochester, the two friends returned to their inn; Mr Winkle to ruminate on the approaching struggle, and Mr Snodgrass to arrange the weapons of war, and put them into proper order for immediate use.

It was a dull and heavy evening when they sallied forth on their awkward errand. Mr Winkle was muffled up in a huge cloak to escape observation, and Mr Snodgrass bore under his the instruments of destruction.

14

"Have you got everything?" said Mr Winkle, in an agitated tone.

"Everything," replied Mr Snodgrass; "plenty of ammunition, in case the shots don't take effect. There's a quarter of a pound of powder in the case, and I have got two newspapers in my pocket for the loadings."

These were instances of friendship for which any man might reasonably feel most grateful. Mr Winkle said nothing, but continued to walk on – rather slowly.

"There's the officer," exclaimed Mr Winkle, after a few minutes walking.

The officer acknowledged their presence by slightly beckoning with his hand; and the two friends followed him at a little distance, as he walked away. The officer turned suddenly from the path, and after climbing a paling, and scaling a hedge, entered a secluded field. Two gentlemen were waiting in it; one was a little, fat man, with black hair; and the other – a portly personage – was sitting with perfect equanimity on a camp-stool.

"The other party, and a surgeon, I suppose," said Mr Snodgrass; "take a drop of brandy."

Mr Winkle seized the wicker bottle which his friend proffered, and took a lengthened pull at the exhilarating liquid.

"My friend, sir, Mr Snodgrass," said Mr Winkle, as the officer approached. Doctor Slammer's friend bowed, and produced a case similar to that which Mr Snodgrass carried.

"We have nothing further to say, sir, I think," he coldly remarked, as he opened the case; "an apology has been resolutely declined."

"Nothing, sir," said Mr Snodgrass, who began to feel rather uncomfortable himself.

"Will you step forward?" said the officer.

"Certainly," replied Mr Snodgrass.

The ground was measured, and preliminaries arranged.

"You will find these better than your own," said the opposite second, producing his pistols. "You saw me load them. Do you object to use them?"

"Certainly not," replied Mr Snodgrass. The offer relieved him from considerable embarrassment, for his previous notions of loading a pistol were rather vague and undefined.

"We may place our men, then, I think," observed the officer, with as much indifference as if the principals were chess-men.

"I think we may," replied Mr Snodgrass; who would have assented to any proposition, because he knew nothing about the matter.

The officer crossed to Doctor Slammer, and Mr Snodgrass went up to Mr Winkle.

"It's all ready," said he, offering the pistol. "Give me your cloak."

"You have got the packet, my dear fellow," said poor Winkle.

"All right," said Mr Snodgrass. "Be steady, and wing him."

Mr Winkle took off his cloak, – it always took a long time to undo that cloak – and accepted the pistol. The seconds retired, the gentleman on the camp-stool did the same, and the belligerents approached each other.

Mr Winkle was always remarkable for extreme humanity. His unwillingness to hurt a fellow-creature was the cause of his shutting his eyes when he arrived at the fatal spot; and his eyes being closed prevented his observing the very extraordinary demeanour of Doctor Slammer. That gentleman started, stared, retreated, rubbed his eyes, stared again, and, finally, shouted, "Stop, stop!"

"What's all this?" said Doctor Slammer, as his friend and Mr Snodgrass came running up; "that's not the man."

"Not the man!" said Doctor Slammer's second.

"Not the man!" said Mr Snodgrass.

"Not the man!" said the gentleman with the camp-stool in his hand.

"Certainly not," replied the little doctor. "That's not the person who insulted me last night."

"Very extraordinary!" exclaimed the officer.

"Very," said the gentleman with the camp-stool.

Now Mr Winkle had opened his eyes, and his ears too, when he heard that there was some mistake in the matter, he at once foresaw the reputation he should inevitably acquire by concealing the real motive of his coming out; he therefore stepped boldly forward, and said – "I am not the person. I know it."

Said the doctor's second. "Why did you not communicate this fact to me this morning, sir?"

"Because, sir," replied Mr Winkle, who had had time to deliberate upon his answer, "you described an intoxicated and ungentlemanly person as wearing a coat which I have the honour, not only to wear but to have invented – the proposed uniform, sir, of the Pickwick Club in London. The honour of that uniform I feel bound to maintain, and I therefore, accepted the challenge which you offered me."

"My dear sir," said the good-humoured little doctor advancing with extended hand, "I honour your gallantry. Permit me to say, sir, that I highly admire your conduct, and extremely regret having caused you the inconvenience of this meeting, to no purpose."

"I beg you won't mention it, sir," said Mr Winkle.

"I shall feel proud of your acquaintance, sir," said the little doctor.

"It will afford me the greatest pleasure to know you, sir," replied Mr Winkle. Thereupon the doctor and Mr Winkle shook hands, and then Mr Winkle and Lieutenant Tappleton (the doctor's second), and then Mr Winkle and the man with the camp-stool, and, finally, Mr Winkle and Mr Snodgrass – the last-named gentleman in an excess of admiration at the noble conduct of his heroic friend.

By this time they had reached the road. Cordial farewells were exchanged, and the party separated. Doctor Slammer and his friends repaired to the barracks, and Mr Winkle, accompanied by Mr Snodgrass, returned to their inn.

CHAPTER 2

A Field Day and Bivouac – More New Friends –
An Invitation to the Country

The whole population of Rochester and the adjoining towns rose from their beds at an early hour of the following morning, in a state of the utmost bustle and excitement. A grand review was to take place upon the lines; temporary fortifications had been erected, the citadel was to be attacked and taken, and a mine was to be sprung.

Mr Pickwick and his three companions stationed themselves in the front of the crowd, and patiently awaited the commencement of the proceedings. At length that low roar of many voices ran through the crowd which usually announces the arrival of whatever they have been waiting for. A few moments of eager expectation, and colours were seen fluttering gaily in the air, arms glistened brightly in the sun, column after column poured on to the plain. The military bands struck up; the horses stood upon two legs each, cantered backwards, and whisked their tails about; the dogs barked, the mob screamed, the troops recovered, and nothing was to be seen on either side, as far as the eye could reach, but a long perspective of red coats and white trousers, fixed and motionless.

Mr Pickwick had been so fully occupied in disentangling himself, miraculously, from between the legs of horses, that he had not observed the scene before him. When he was at last enabled to stand firmly on his legs, his gratification and delight were unbounded.

"Can anything be finer or more delightful?" he inquired of Mr Winkle.

"Nothing," replied that gentleman, who had had a short man standing on each of his feet for the quarter of an hour immediately preceding.

"It is indeed a noble and a brilliant sight," said Mr Snodgrass, in whose bosom a blaze of poetry was rapidly bursting forth.

"We are in a capital situation now," said Mr Pickwick, looking round him. The crowd had gradually dispersed and they were nearly alone.

"Capital!" echoed both Mr Snodgrass and Mr Winkle.

"What are they doing now?" inquired Mr Pickwick, adjusting his spectacles.

"I – I – rather think," said Mr Winkle, changing colour – "I rather think they're going to fire."

"Nonsense," said Mr Pickwick hastily.

"I – I – really think they are," urged Mr Snodgrass, somewhat alarmed.

"Impossible," replied Mr Pickwick. He had hardly uttered the word, when the whole half-dozen regiments levelled their muskets as if they had but one common object, and that object the Pickwickians, and burst forth with the most awful and tremendous discharge that ever shook the earth to its centres, or an elderly gentleman off his.

Mr Pickwick displayed that perfect coolness and self-possession, which are the accompaniments of a great mind. He seized Mr Winkle by the arm, and placing himself between that gentleman and Mr Snodgrass, earnestly besought them to remember that beyond the possibility of being rendered deaf by the noise, there was no immediate danger to be apprehended from the firing.

"But – but – suppose some of the men should happen to have ball cartridges by mistake," remonstrated Mr Winkle. "I heard something whistle through the air now – so sharp; close to my ear."

"We had better throw ourselves on our faces, hadn't we?" said Mr Snodgrass.

"No, no – it's over now," said Mr Pickwick. His lip might quiver, and his cheek might blanch, but no expression of fear or concern escaped the lips of that immortal man.

Mr Pickwick was right – the firing ceased; but he had scarcely time to congratulate himself on the accuracy of his opinion, when a quick movement was visible in the line; the hoarse shout of the word of command ran along it, and before either of the party could form a guess at the meaning of this new manoeuvre, the half-dozen regiments, with fixed bayonets, charged at double-quick time down upon the very spot on which Mr Pickwick and his friends were stationed.

Mr Pickwick gazed through his spectacles for an instant on the advancing mass, and then fairly turned his back and he trotted away, at as quick a rate as his legs would convey him; so quickly, indeed, that he did not perceive the awkwardness of his situation, to the full extent, until too late.

Mr Pickwick and his two companions found themselves suddenly enclosed between two lines of great length, the one advancing at a rapid pace, and the other firmly waiting the collision in hostile array.

"Where are we to go to?" screamed the agitated Pickwickians.

There was a moment of intense bewilderment, a heavy tramp of footsteps, a violent concussion, a smothered laugh; the half-dozen regiments were half a thousand yards off, and the soles of Mr Pickwick's boots were elevated in air. Mr Snodgrass and Mr Winkle had each performed a compulsory somersault with remarkable agility, when the first object that met their eyes was their venerated leader, running after his own hat, which was gambolling playfully away.

The hat was blown with some violence against the wheel of a carriage, which was drawn up in a line with half a dozen other vehicles. Mr Pickwick, perceiving his advantage, darted briskly forward, secured his property, planted it on his head, and paused to take breath. He had not been stationary half a minute, when he heard his own name eagerly pronounced by a voice, which he at once recognised as Mr Tupman's, and, looking upwards, he beheld a sight which filled him with surprise and pleasure. In an open barouche stood a stout old gentleman, in a blue coat and bright buttons, corduroy breeches and top-boots, two young ladies in scarfs and feathers, a young gentleman apparently enamoured of one of the young ladies, a lady of doubtful age and Mr Tupman, as easy and unconcerned as if he had belonged to the family from the first moments of his infancy.

Mr Pickwick had bestowed a hasty glance on these interesting objects, when he was again greeted by his faithful disciple.

"Pickwick – Pickwick," said Mr Tupman; "come up here. Make haste."

"Come along, sir. Pray, come up," said the stout gentleman. "Joe! – damn that boy, he's gone to sleep again. – Joe, let down the steps." The fat boy rolled slowly off the box, let down the steps, and held the carriage door invitingly open. Mr Snodgrass and Mr Winkle came up at the moment.

"Room for you all, gentlemen," said the stout man. "Two inside, and one out. Joe, make room for one of these gentlemen on the box. Now, sir, come along;" and the stout gentleman extended his arm, and pulled first Mr Pickwick, and then Mr Snodgrass, into the barouche by main force. Mr Winkle mounted to the box, the fat boy waddled to the same perch, and fell fast asleep instantly.

"Well, gentlemen," said the stout man, "very glad to see you. Picked up my friend Mr Tupman here this morning, and very glad I was to see him. Well, sir, and how are you? You do look uncommon well, to be sure."

Mr Pickwick acknowledged the compliment, and cordially shook hands with the stout gentleman in the top-boots.

"My daughters, gentlemen – my gals these are; and that's my sister, Miss Rachael Wardle. She's a Miss, she is; and yet she ain't amis – eh, sir, eh?" And the stout gentleman playfully inserted his elbow between the ribs of Mr Pickwick, and laughed very heartily.

"Lor, brother!" said Miss Wardle, with a deprecating smile.

"True, true," said the stout gentleman; "no one can deny it. Gentlemen, this is my friend Mr Trundle. And now you all know each other, let's be comfortable and happy, and see what's going forward; that's what I say."

So the stout gentleman put on his spectacles, and Mr Pickwick pulled out his glass, and everybody stood up in the carriage, and looked over somebody else's shoulder at the evolutions of the military.

"Joe, Joe!" said the stout gentleman, when the citadel was taken, and the besiegers and besieged sat down to dinner. "Damn that boy, he's gone to sleep again. Be good enough to pinch him, sir – in the leg, if you please; nothing else wakes him – thank you. Undo the hamper, Joe."

The fat boy rolled off the box once again, and proceeded to unpack the hamper with more expedition than could have been expected from his previous inactivity.

"Now we must sit close," said the stout gentleman. After a great many jokes about squeezing the ladies' sleeves, and sundry proposals, that the ladies should sit in the gentlemen's laps, the whole party were stowed down in the barouche; and the stout gentleman proceeded to hand the things from the fat boy into the carriage.

"Now, Joe, the fowls. Damn that boy; he's gone to sleep again. Joe! Joe!" (Sundry taps on the head with a stick, and the fat boy, with some difficulty, roused from his lethargy.) "Come, hand in the eatables."

There was something in the sound of the last word which roused the unctuous boy. He jumped up, and the leaden eyes which twinkled behind his mountainous cheeks leered horribly upon the food as he unpacked it from the basket.

"Now make haste," said Mr Wardle; for the fat boy was hanging fondly over a capon, which he seemed wholly unable to part with. The boy sighed deeply, and, bestowing an ardent gaze upon its plumpness, unwillingly consigned it to his master.

"That's right – look sharp. Now the tongue – now the pigeon pie. Take care of that veal and ham – mind the lobsters – take the salad out of the cloth – give me the dressing."

Such were the hurried orders which issued from the lips of Mr Wardle, as he handed in the different articles described, and placed dishes in everybody's hands, and on everybody's knees, in endless number.

"Now ain't this capital?" inquired that jolly personage, when the work of destruction had commenced.

"Capital!" said Mr Winkle, who was carving a fowl up on the box.

"Glass of wine?"

"With the greatest pleasure."

"You'd better have a bottle to yourself up there, hadn't you?"

"You're very good."

"Joe!"

"Yes, sir." (He wasn't asleep this time, having just succeeded in abstracting a veal patty.)

"Bottle of wine to the gentleman on the box. Glad to see you, sir."

"Thank'ee." Mr Winkle emptied his glass, and placed the bottle on the coach-box, by his side.

"Will you permit me to have the pleasure, sir?" said Mr Trundle to Mr Winkle.

"With great pleasure," replied Mr Winkle to Mr Trundle, and then the two gentlemen took wine, after which they took a glass of wine round, ladies and all.

"Aunt and the little old gentleman want to have it all to themselves, I think," whispered Miss Isabella Wardle to her sister Emily. The young ladies laughed very heartily, and the old one tried to look amiable, but couldn't manage it.

"Will you permit me?" said Mr Tupman, in his blandest manner, touching the enchanting Rachael's wrist with one hand, and gently elevating the bottle with the other.

"Oh, sir!"

Mr Tupman looked most impressive; and Rachael expressed her fear that more guns were going off, in which case, of course, she should require support again.

"Do you think my dear nieces pretty?" whispered their affectionate aunt to Mr Tupman.

"I should, if their aunt wasn't here," replied the ready Pickwickian, with a passionate glance.

"Well, you are a quiz!"

Mr Tupman had no objection to earning the reputation at so cheap a rate: so he looked very knowing, and smiled mysteriously.

"I'm sure aunt's talking about us," whispered Miss Emily Wardle to her sister – "I'm quite certain of it – she looks so malicious."

"Is she?" replied Isabella. – "Hem! aunt, dear!"

"Yes, my dear love!"

"I'm *so* afraid you'll catch cold, aunt – have a silk handkerchief to tie round your dear old head – you really should take care of yourself – consider your age!"

There is no guessing in what form of reply the aunt's indignation would have vented itself, had not Mr Wardle unconsciously changed the subject, by calling emphatically for Joe.

"Damn that boy," said the old gentleman, "he's gone to sleep again. Here, Joe – Joe – take these things away, and open another bottle – d'ye hear?"

The fat boy rose, opened his eyes, swallowed the huge piece of pie he had been in the act of masticating when he last fell asleep, and slowly obeyed his master's orders – gloating languidly over the remains of the feast, as he removed the plates, and deposited them in the hamper. The fresh bottle was produced, and speedily emptied: the hamper was made fast in its old place – the fat boy once more mounted the box – the spectacles and pocket-glass were again adjusted – and the evolutions of the military recommenced. There was a great fizzing and banging of guns, and starting of ladies – and a mine was sprung, to the gratification of everybody – and when the mine had gone off, the military and the company followed its example, and went off too.

"Now, mind," said the old gentleman, as he shook hands with Mr Pickwick, "we shall see you all to-morrow."

"Most certainly," replied Mr Pickwick.

"You have got the address?"

"Manor Farm, Dingley Dell," said Mr Pickwick, consulting his pocket-book.

"That's it," said the old gentleman. "I don't let you off, mind, under a week; and undertake that you shall see everything worth seeing. If you've come down for a country life, come to me, and I'll give you plenty of it. Joe – damn that boy, he's gone to sleep again – Joe, help Tom put in the horses." The horses were put in – the driver mounted – the fat boy clambered up by his side – farewells were exchanged – and the carriage rattled off. As the Pickwickians turned round to take a last glimpse of it, the setting sun cast a rich glow on the faces of their entertainers, and fell upon the form of the fat boy. His head was sunk upon his bosom; and he slumbered again.

CHAPTER 3

How Mr Winkle, Instead of Shooting at the Pigeon and Killing the Crow, Shot at the Crow and Wounded the Pigeon; How the Dingley Dell Cricket Club Played All-Muggleton, and How All-Muggleton Dined at the Dingley Dell Expense

The fatiguing adventures of the previous day operated so strongly on the drowsy tendencies of Mr Pickwick, that in less than five minutes after he had been shown to his comfortable bedroom at Dingley Dell he fell into a sound and dreamless sleep, from which he was only awakened by the morning sun darting his bright beams reproachfully into the apartment.

Mr Pickwick thrust his head out of the lattice and looked around him and fell into an enchanting and delicious reverie.

"Hallo!" was the sound that roused him.

He looked into the garden, and there saw Mr Wardle.

"How are you?" said the good-humoured individual, out of breath with his own anticipations of pleasure. "Beautiful morning, ain't it? Glad to see you up so early. Make haste down, and come out. I'll wait for you here."

Mr Pickwick needed no second invitation. Ten minutes sufficed for the completion of his toilet, and at the expiration of that time he was by the old gentleman's side.

"Hallo!" said Mr Pickwick in his turn, seeing that his companion was armed with a gun, and that another lay ready on the grass; "what's going forward?"

"Why, your friend and I," replied the host, "are going out rook-shooting before breakfast. He's a very good shot, ain't he?"

"I've heard him say he's a capital one," replied Mr Pickwick, "but I never saw him aim at anything."

"Well," said the host, "I wish he'd come. Joe – Joe!"

The fat boy, who under the exciting influence of the morning did not appear to be more than three parts and a fraction asleep, emerged from the house.

"Go up, and call the gentleman, and tell him he'll find me and Mr Pickwick in the rookery. Show the gentleman the way there; d'ye hear?"

The boy departed to execute his commission; and the host, carrying both guns like a second Robinson Crusoe, led the way from the garden.

"This is the place," said the old gentleman, pausing after a few minutes walking, in an avenue of trees. The information was unnecessary; for the incessant cawing of the unconscious rooks sufficiently indicated their whereabouts. The old gentleman laid one gun on the ground, and loaded the other.

"Here they are," said Mr Pickwick; and, as he spoke, the forms of Mr Tupman, Mr Snodgrass, and Mr Winkle appeared in the distance.

"Come along," shouted the old gentleman, addressing Mr Winkle; "a keen hand like you ought to have been up long ago, even to such poor work as this."

Mr Winkle responded with a forced smile, and took up the spare gun with an expression which might have been keenness, but it looked remarkably like misery.

The old gentleman nodded; and two ragged boys who had been marshalled to the spot commenced climbing up two of the trees.

"Very well. Shall I begin?"

"If you please," said Mr Winkle, glad of any respite.

"Stand aside, then. Now for it."

The boy shouted, and shook a branch with a nest on it. Half a dozen young rooks flew out to ask what the matter was. The old gentleman fired by way of reply. Down fell one bird, and off flew the others.

"Take him up, Joe," said the old gentleman.

There was a smile upon the youth's face as he advanced. Indistinct visions of rook-pie floated through his imagination.

"Now, Mr Winkle," said the host, reloading his own gun. "Fire away." Mr Winkle advanced, and levelled his gun. Mr Pickwick and his friends cowered involuntarily to escape damage from the heavy fall of rooks, which they felt quite certain would be occasioned by the devastating barrel of their friend. There was a solemn pause – a shout – a flapping of wings – a faint click.

"Won't it go?" inquired Mr Pickwick.

"Missed fire," said Mr Winkle, who was very pale – probably from disappointment.

"Odd," said the old gentleman, taking the gun. "Never knew one of them miss fire before. Why, I don't see anything of the cap."

"Bless my soul!" said Mr Winkle, "I declare I forgot the cap!"

The slight omission was rectified. Mr Pickwick crouched again. Mr Winkle stepped forward with an air of determination and resolution; and Mr Tupman looked out from behind a tree.

The boy shouted; four birds flew out. Mr Winkle fired. There was a scream of anguish. Mr Tupman had saved the lives of innumerable unoffending birds by receiving a portion of the charge in his left arm.

To describe the confusion that ensued would be as impossible as it would be to depict the gradual recovering of the unfortunate individual, the binding up of his arm with pocket-handkerchiefs, and the conveying him back by slow degrees supported by the arms of his anxious friends.

They drew near the house. The ladies were at the garden gate, waiting for their arrival and their breakfast. The spinster aunt appeared; she smiled, and beckoned them to walk quicker. 'Twas evident she knew not of the disaster. Poor thing! there are times when ignorance is bliss indeed. They approached nearer.

"Why, what is the matter with the little old gentleman?" said Isabella Wardle. The spinster aunt heeded not the remark; she thought it applied to Mr Pickwick. In her eyes Tracy Tupman was a youth; she viewed his years through a diminishing glass.

"Don't be frightened," said the host.

"What's the matter?" screamed the ladies.

"Mr Tupman has met with a little accident; that's all."

The spinster aunt uttered a piercing scream, burst into an hysteric laugh, and fell backwards in the arms of her nieces.

"Throw some cold water over her," said the old gentleman.

"No, no," murmured the spinster aunt; "I am better now. Bella, Emily – a surgeon! Is he wounded? – Is he dead? – Is he – Ha, ha, ha!" Here the spinster aunt burst into fit number two, of hysteric laughter interspersed with screams.

"Calm yourself," said Mr Tupman, affected almost to tears by this expression of sympathy with his sufferings. "Dear, dear madam, calm yourself."

"It is his voice!" exclaimed the spinster aunt; and strong symptoms of fit number three developed themselves.

"Do not agitate yourself, I entreat you, dearest madam," said Mr Tupman soothingly. "I am very little hurt, I assure you."

"Then you are not dead!" ejaculated the hysterical lady. "Oh, say you are not dead!"

"Don't be a fool, Rachael," interposed Mr Wardle, rather more roughly than was consistent with the poetic nature of the scene. "What the devil's the use of his saying he isn't dead?"

"No, no, I am not," said Mr Tupman. "I require no assistance but yours. Let me lean on your arm." He added, in a whisper, "Oh, Miss Rachael!"

The agitated female advanced, and offered her arm. They turned into the breakfast parlour. Mr Tracy Tupman gently pressed her hand to his lips, and sank upon the sofa.

"Are you faint?" inquired the anxious Rachael.

"No," said Mr Tupman. "It is nothing. I shall be better presently." He closed his eyes.

"He sleeps," murmured the spinster aunt. (His organs of vision had been closed nearly twenty seconds.) "Dear – dear – Mr Tupman!"

Mr Tupman jumped up – "Oh, say those words again!" he exclaimed.

The lady started. "Surely you did not hear them!" she said bashfully.

"Oh, yes, I did!" replied Mr Tupman; "repeat them. If you would have me recover, repeat them."

"Hush!" said the lady. "My brother."

Mr Tracy Tupman resumed his former position; and Mr Wardle, accompanied by a surgeon, entered the room.

The arm was examined, the wound dressed, and pronounced to be a very slight one; and the minds of the company having been thus satisfied, they proceeded to satisfy their appetites with countenances to which an expression of cheerfulness was again restored. Mr Pickwick alone was silent and reserved. Doubt and distrust were exhibited in his countenance. His confidence in Mr Winkle had been shaken – greatly shaken – by the proceedings of the morning.

"Are you a cricketer?" inquired Mr Wardle of the marksman.

At any other time, Mr Winkle would have replied in the affirmative. He felt the delicacy of his situation, and modestly replied, "No."

"Are you, sir?" inquired Mr Snodgrass.

"I was once upon a time," replied the host; "but I have given it up now. I subscribe to the club here, but I don't play."

"The grand match is played to-day, I believe," said Mr Pickwick.

"It is," replied the host. "Of course you would like to see it."

"I, sir," replied Mr Pickwick, "am delighted to view any sports which may be safely indulged in, and in which unskilful people do not endanger human life." Mr Pickwick paused, and looked steadily on Mr Winkle, who quailed beneath his leader's searching glance. The great man withdrew his eyes after a few minutes, and added: "Shall we be justified in leaving our wounded friend to the care of the ladies?"

"You cannot leave me in better hands," said Mr Tupman.

"Quite impossible," said Mr Snodgrass.

It was therefore settled that Mr Tupman should be left at home in charge of the females; and that the remainder of the guests, under the guidance of Mr Wardle, should proceed to the spot where was to be held that trial of skill, which had roused all Muggleton from its torpor, and inoculated Dingley Dell with a fever of excitement.

The wickets were pitched, and so were a couple of marquees for the rest and refreshment of the contending parties. Several dozen of "How-are-you's?" hailed the old gentleman's arrival; and a general raising of the straw hats, and bending forward of the flannel jackets, followed his introduction of his guests as gentlemen from London, who were extremely anxious to witness the proceedings of the day, with which, he had no doubt, they would be greatly delighted.

"You had better step into the marquee, I think, sir," said one very stout gentleman.

"Capital game – smart sport – fine exercise – very," were the words which fell upon Mr Pickwick's ear as he entered the tent; and the first object that met his eyes was his green-coated friend of the Rochester coach, holding forth, to the no small delight and edification of a select circle of the chosen of All-Muggleton. His dress was slightly improved, and he wore boots; but there was no mistaking him. The stranger recognised his friends immediately; and, darting forward and seizing Mr Pickwick by the hand, dragged him to a seat with his usual impetuosity, talking all the while as if the whole of the arrangements were under his especial patronage and direction.

"This way – this way – capital fun – lots of beer – hogsheads; rounds of beef – bullocks; mustard – cart-loads; glorious day – down with you – make yourself at home – glad to see you – very."

Mr Pickwick sat down as he was bid, and Mr Winkle and Mr Snodgrass also complied with the directions of their mysterious friend. Mr Wardle looked on in silent wonder.

"Mr Wardle – a friend of mine," said Mr Pickwick.

"Friend of yours! – My dear sir, how are you? – Friend of my friend's – give me your hand, sir," – and the stranger grasped Mr Wardle's hand with all the fervour of a close intimacy of many years.

All-Muggleton had the first innings; and the interest became intense when Mr Dumkins and Mr Podder, two of the most renowned members of that distinguished club, walked, bat in hand, to their respective wickets.

"Play!" suddenly cried the bowler. The ball flew from his hand straight and swift towards the centre stump of the wicket. The wary Dumkins was on the alert: it fell upon the tip of the bat, and bounded far away over the heads of the scouts, who had just stooped low enough to let it fly over them.

"Run – run – another. – Now, then throw her up – up with her – stop there – another – no – yes – no – throw her up, throw her up!" – Such were the shouts which followed the stroke; and at the conclusion of which All-Muggleton had scored two. Nor was Podder behindhand in earning laurels wherewith to garnish himself and Muggleton. He blocked the doubtful balls, missed the bad ones, took the good ones, and sent them flying to all parts of the field. The scouts were hot and tired; the bowlers were changed and bowled till their arms ached; but Dumkins and Podder remained unconquered. In short, when Dumkins was caught out, and Podder stumped out, All-Muggleton had notched some fifty-four, while the score of the Dingley Dellers was as blank as their faces. The advantage was too great to be recovered. In vain did the eager Luffey, and the enthusiastic Struggles, do all that skill and experience could suggest, to regain the ground Dingley Dell had lost in the contest – it was of no avail; and in an early period of the winning game Dingley Dell gave in, and allowed the superior prowess of All-Muggleton.

"Capital game – well played – some strokes admirable," said the stranger, as both sides crowded into the tent, at the conclusion of the game.

"You have played it, sir?" inquired Mr Wardle, who had been much amused by his loquacity.

"Played it! Think I have – thousands of times – not here – West Indies – exciting thing – hot work – very."

"It must be rather a warm pursuit in such a climate," observed Mr Pickwick.

"Warm! – red hot – scorching – glowing."

Here the stranger buried his countenance in a brown jug, but whether to hide his emotion or imbibe its contents, we cannot distinctly affirm. We only know that he paused suddenly, drew a long and deep breath, and looked anxiously on, as two of the principal members of the Dingley Dell club approached Mr Pickwick, and said –

"We are about to partake of a plain dinner at the Blue Lion, sir; we hope you and your friends will join us."

"Of course," said Mr Wardle, "among our friends we include Mr – ;" and he looked towards the stranger.

"Jingle," said that versatile gentleman, taking the hint at once. "Jingle – Alfred Jingle, Esq., of No Hall, Nowhere."

"I shall be very happy, I am sure," said Mr Pickwick.

"So shall I," said Mr Alfred Jingle, drawing one arm through Mr Pickwick's, and another through Mr Wardle's.

There being no further preliminaries to arrange, the company straggled into the town in little knots of twos and threes; and within a quarter of an hour were all seated in the great room of the Blue Lion Inn, Muggleton.

There was a vast deal of talking and rattling of knives and forks, and plates; a great running about of three waiters, and a rapid disappearance of the substantial viands on the table. When everybody had eaten as much as possible, the cloth was removed, bottles, glasses, and dessert were placed on the table; and the waiters withdrew to "clear away," or in other words, to appropriate to their own private use whatever remnants of the eatables and drinkables they could contrive to lay their hands on.

Here the company commenced a raising of voices, and thumping of tables, which lasted with little intermission during the remainder of the evening. Toasts were drunk. Mr Luffey and Mr Struggles, Mr Pickwick and Mr Jingle, were, each in his turn, the subject of unqualified eulogium; and each in due course returned thanks for the honour.

Some few minutes before twelve o'clock that night, the convocation of worthies of Dingley Dell and Muggleton were heard to sing, with great feeling and emphasis, the beautiful and pathetic national air of

"We won't go home till morning,
We won't go home till morning,
We won't go home till morning,
Till daylight doth appear."

CHAPTER 4

Strongly Illustrative of the Position, That the Course of True Love is Not a Railway

The quiet seclusion of Dingley Dell, the presence of so many of the gentler sex, and the solicitude and anxiety they evinced in his behalf, were all favourable to the growth and development of those softer feelings which nature had implanted deep in the bosom of Mr Tracy

Tupman, and which now appeared destined to centre in one lovely object. Her name was the first that rose to Mr Tupman's lips as he lay wounded on the grass; and her hysteric laughter was the first sound that fell upon his ear when he was supported to the house. But had her agitation arisen from an amiable and feminine sensibility; or had it been called forth by a more ardent and passionate feeling, which he, of all men living, could alone awaken? These were the doubts which racked his brain as he lay extended on the sofa; these were the doubts which he determined should be at once and for ever resolved.

"I have forgotten my flowers," said the spinster aunt.

"Water them now," said Mr Tupman, in accents of persuasion.

"You will take cold in the evening air," urged the spinster aunt affectionately.

"No, no," said Mr Tupman, rising; "it will do me good. Let me accompany you."

The lady paused to adjust the sling in which the left arm of the youth was placed, and taking his right arm led him to the garden.

There was a bower at the farther end, with honeysuckle, jessamine, and creeping plants – one of those sweet retreats which humane men erect for the accommodation of spiders. The spinster aunt took up a large watering-pot which lay in one corner, and was about to leave the arbour. Mr Tupman detained her, and drew her to a seat beside him.

"Miss Wardle!" said he.

The spinster aunt trembled, till some pebbles which had accidentally found their way into the large watering-pot shook like an infant's rattle.

"Miss Wardle," said Mr Tupman, "you are an angel."

"Mr Tupman!" exclaimed Rachael, blushing as red as the watering-pot itself. "All women are angels, they say," murmured the lady playfully.

"Where was the woman ever seen who resembled you? Where else could I hope to find so rare a combination of excellence and beauty? Where else could I seek to – Oh!" Here Mr Tupman paused, and pressed the hand which clasped the handle of the happy watering-pot.

The lady turned her head. "Men are such deceivers," she whispered.

"They are, they are," ejaculated Mr Tupman; "but not all men. There lives at least one being who would be content to devote his whole existence to your happiness – who lives but in your eyes – who breathes but in your smile."

"Could such an individual be found – " said the lady.

"But he *can* be found," said the ardent Mr Tupman, interposing. "He *is* found. He is here, Miss Wardle." And ere the lady was aware of his intention, Mr Tupman had sunk upon his knees at her feet.

"Mr Tupman, rise," said Rachael.

"Never!" was the valorous reply. "Oh, Rachael!" He seized her passive hand, and the watering-pot fell to the ground as he pressed it to his lips. – "Oh, Rachael! say you love me."

"Mr Tupman," said the spinster aunt, with averted head, "I can hardly speak the words; but – but – you are not wholly indifferent to me."

Mr Tupman no sooner heard this avowal, than he proceeded to do what his enthusiastic emotions prompted. He jumped up, and, throwing his arm round the neck of the spinster aunt, imprinted upon her lips numerous kisses, which after a due show of struggling and resistance, she received so passively, that there is no telling how many more Mr Tupman might have bestowed, if the lady had not given a very unaffected start, and exclaimed in an affrighted tone –

"Mr Tupman, we are observed! – we are discovered!"

Mr Tupman looked round. There was the fat boy, perfectly motionless, with his large circular eyes staring into the arbour. Mr Tupman gazed on the fat boy, and the fat boy stared at him; and the longer Mr Tupman observed the utter vacancy of the fat boy's countenance, the more convinced he became that he either did not know, or did not understand, anything that had been going forward. Under this impression, he said with great firmness –

"What do you want here, sir?"

"Supper's ready, sir," was the prompt reply.

"Have you just come here, sir?" inquired Mr Tupman, with a piercing look.

"Just," replied the fat boy.

Mr Tupman looked at him very hard again; but there was not a wink in his eye, or a curve in his face. Mr Tupman took the arm of the spinster aunt, and walked towards the house; the fat boy followed behind.

"He knows nothing of what has happened," he whispered.

"Nothing," said the spinster aunt.

There was a sound behind them, as of an imperfectly suppressed chuckle. Mr Tupman turned sharply round. No; it could not have been the fat boy; there was not a gleam of mirth, or anything but feeding in his whole visage.

"He must have been fast asleep," whispered Mr Tupman.

"I have not the least doubt of it," replied the spinster aunt.

They both laughed heartily.

Mr Tupman was wrong. The fat boy, for once, had not been fast asleep. He was awake – wide awake – to what had been going forward.

Old Mrs Wardle, that is, Mr Wardle's mother, was in the habit, on the fine summer mornings, of repairing to the arbour, having put on her bonnet and shawl, would lean one hand on the stick and the other on the fat boy's shoulder, and walk leisurely to the arbour, where the fat boy would leave her to enjoy the fresh air for the space of half an hour; after which time he would return and reconduct her to the house.

The old lady was a little surprised, on this particular morning, to see the fat boy, instead of leaving the arbour walk a few paces out of it, look carefully round him in every direction, and return towards her with great stealth.

"Missus!"

Now it so happened that Mr Jingle was walking in the garden close to the arbour at that moment. He too heard the shouts of "Missus," and stopped to hear more.

"Missus!" shouted the fat boy.

"Well, Joe," said the trembling old lady. "What can you want to do now?"

"What do you think I see in this very arbour last night?" inquired the boy.

"Bless us! What?" exclaimed the old lady, alarmed at the solemn manner of the corpulent youth.

"The strange gentleman – him as had his arm hurt – a-kissin' and huggin' – "

"Who, Joe? None of the servants, I hope."

"Worser than that," roared the fat boy, in the old lady's ear.

"Not one of my grandda'aters?"

"Worser than that."

"Worse than that, Joe!" said the old lady. "Who was it, Joe? I insist upon knowing."

The fat boy looked cautiously round, and having concluded his survey, shouted in the old lady's ear – "Miss Rachael."

"What!" said the old lady, in a shrill tone. "Speak louder."

"Miss Rachael," roared the fat boy.

"My da'ater!"

The train of nods which the fat boy gave by way of assent, communicated a blanc-mange like motion to his fat cheeks.

"And she let him!" exclaimed the old lady.

A grin stole over the fat boy's features as he said –

"I see her a-kissin' of him agin."

Mr Jingle, from his place of concealment, listened attentively. Fragments of angry sentences such as, "Without my permission!" – "At her time of life" – "Miserable old 'ooman like me" – "Might have waited till I was dead," and so forth, reached his ears; and then he heard the heels of the fat boy's boots crunching the gravel, as he retired and left the old lady alone.

Now Mr Jingle within five minutes of his arrival at Manor Farm, had inwardly resolved to lay siege to the heart of the spinster aunt without delay. He had observation enough to see, that his off-hand manner was by no means disagreeable to the fair object of his attack; and he had more than a strong suspicion that she possessed that most desirable of all requisites, a small independence. The necessity of ousting his rival by some means or other, flashed quickly upon him, and he immediately resolved to adopt certain proceedings tending to that end and object, without a moment's delay. The breakfast-parlour door was partially open. He peeped in.

The spinster aunt was knitting. He coughed; she looked up and smiled. Hesitation formed no part of Mr Alfred Jingle's character. He laid his finger on his lips mysteriously, walked in, and closed the door.

"Miss Wardle," said Mr Jingle, with affected earnestness, "forgive intrusion – short acquaintance – no time for ceremony – all discovered."

"Sir!" said the spinster aunt, rather astonished by the unexpected apparition and somewhat doubtful of Mr Jingle's sanity.

"Hush!" said Mr Jingle, in a stage-whisper – "Large boy – dumpling face – round eyes – rascal!" Here he shook his head expressively, and the spinster aunt trembled with agitation.

"I presume you allude to Joseph, sir?" said the lady, making an effort to appear composed.

"Yes, ma'am – damn that Joe! – treacherous dog, Joe – told the old lady

– old lady furious – wild – raving – arbour – Tupman – kissing and hugging – all that sort of thing – eh, ma'am – eh?"

"Mr Jingle," said the spinster aunt, "if you come here, sir, to insult me – "

"Not at all – by no means," replied the unabashed Mr Jingle – "overheard the tale – came to warn you of your danger – tender my services – prevent the hubbub. Never mind – think it an insult – leave the room" – and he turned, as if to carry the threat into execution.

"What *shall* I do!" said the poor spinster, bursting into tears. "My brother will be furious."

"Of course he will," said Mr Jingle pausing – "outrageous."

"Oh, Mr Jingle, what *can* I say!" exclaimed the spinster aunt, in another flood of despair.

"Say he dreamt it," replied Mr Jingle coolly.

A ray of comfort darted across the mind of the spinster aunt at this suggestion. Mr Jingle perceived it, and followed up his advantage.

"Pooh, pooh! – nothing more easy – blackguard boy – lovely woman – fat boy horsewhipped – you believed – end of the matter – all comfortable."

She blushed slightly, and cast a grateful look on Mr Jingle.

That insinuating gentleman sighed deeply, fixed his eyes on the spinster aunt's face for a couple of minutes, started melodramatically, and suddenly withdrew them.

"You seem unhappy, Mr Jingle," said the lady, in a plaintive voice. "May I show my gratitude for your kind interference, by inquiring into the cause?"

"Ha!" exclaimed Mr Jingle, with another start – "remove my unhappiness, and your love bestowed upon a man who is insensible to the blessing – who even now contemplates a design upon the affections of the niece – but no; he is my friend; I will not expose his vices. Miss Wardle – farewell!" At the conclusion of this address Mr Jingle applied to his eyes the remnant of a handkerchief before noticed, and turned towards the door.

"Stay, Mr Jingle!" said the spinster aunt emphatically. "You have made an allusion to Mr Tupman – explain it."

"Never!" exclaimed Jingle, with a professional (i.e. theatrical) air. "Never!" and, by way of showing that he had no desire to be questioned further, he drew a chair close to that of the spinster aunt and sat down.

"Mr Jingle," said the aunt, "I entreat – I implore you, if there is any dreadful mystery connected with Mr Tupman, reveal it."

Mr Jingle appeared to be struggling with various conflicting emotions for a few seconds, and then said in a low voice –

"Tupman only wants your money."

"The wretch!" exclaimed the spinster, with energetic indignation. (Mr Jingle's doubts were resolved. She *had* money.)

"More than that," said Jingle – "loves another."

"Another!" ejaculated the spinster. "Who?"

"Short girl – black eyes – niece Emily."

There was a pause.

Now, if there was one individual in the whole world, of whom the spinster aunt entertained a mortal and deep-rooted jealousy, it was this identical niece. The colour rushed over her face and neck, and she tossed her head in silence with an air of ineffable contempt. At last, biting her thin lips, and bridling up, she said –

"It can't be. I won't believe it."

"Watch 'em," said Jingle.

"I will," said the aunt.

"Watch his looks."

"I will."

"His whispers."

"I will."

"He'll sit next her at table."

"Let him."

"He'll flatter her."

"Let him."

"He'll pay her every possible attention."

"Let him."

"And he'll cut you."

"Cut *me*!" screamed the spinster aunt. "*He* cut *me*; will he!" and she trembled with rage and disappointment.

"You will convince yourself?" said Jingle.

"I will."

"You'll show your spirit?"

"I will."

"You'll not have him afterwards?"

"Never."

"You'll take somebody else?"

"Yes."

"You shall."

Mr Jingle fell on his knees, remained thereupon for five minutes thereafter; and rose the accepted lover of the spinster aunt – conditionally upon Mr Tupman's perjury being made clear and manifest.

The burden of proof lay with Mr Alfred Jingle; and he produced his evidence that very day at dinner. The spinster aunt could hardly believe her eyes. Mr Tracy Tupman was established at Emily's side, ogling, whispering, and smiling, in opposition to Mr Snodgrass. Not a word, not a look, not a glance, did he bestow upon his heart's pride of the evening before.

"Damn that boy!" thought old Mr Wardle to himself – he had heard the story from his mother. "Damn that boy! He must have been asleep. It's all imagination."

"Traitor!" thought the spinster aunt. "Dear Mr Jingle was not deceiving me. Ugh! how I hate the wretch!"

The following conversation may serve to explain this apparently unaccountable alteration of deportment on the part of Mr Tracy Tupman.

The time was evening; the scene the garden. There were two figures walking in a side path; one was rather short and stout; the other tall and slim. They were Mr Tupman and Mr Jingle.

The stout figure commenced the dialogue.

"How did I do it?" he inquired.

"Splendid – capital – couldn't act better myself – you must repeat the part to-morrow – every evening till further notice."

"Does Rachael still wish it?"

"Of course – she don't like it – but must be done – avert suspicion – afraid of her brother – says there's no help for it – only a few days more – when old folks blinded – crown your happiness."

"Any message?"

"Love – best love – kindest regards – unalterable affection. Can I say anything for you?"

"My dear fellow," replied the unsuspicious Mr Tupman, fervently grasping his "friend's" hand – "carry my best love – say anything that's kind: but add how sensible I am of the necessity of the suggestion she made to me, through you, this morning. Say I applaud her wisdom and admire her discretion."

"I will. Anything more?"

"Nothing, only add how ardently I long for the time when I may call her mine, and all dissimulation may be unnecessary."

"Certainly, certainly. Anything more?"

"Oh, my friend!" said poor Mr Tupman, again grasping the hand of his companion, "receive my warmest thanks for your disinterested kindness; and forgive me if I have ever, even in thought, done you the injustice of supposing that you could stand in my way. My dear friend, can I ever repay you?"

"Don't talk of it," replied Mr Jingle. He stopped short, as if suddenly recollecting something, and said – "By the bye – can't spare ten pounds, can you? – very particular purpose – pay you in three days."

"I dare say I can," replied Mr Tupman, in the fullness of his heart. "Three days, you say?"

"Only three days – all over then – no more difficulties."

Mr Tupman counted the money into his companion's hand, and he dropped it piece by piece into his pocket, as they walked towards the house.

"Be careful," said Mr Jingle – "not a look."

"Not a wink," said Mr Tupman.

"Not a syllable."

"Not a whisper."

"All your attentions to the niece – rather rude, than otherwise, to the aunt – only way of deceiving the old ones."

"I'll take care," said Mr Tupman aloud.

"And *I'll* take care," said Mr Jingle internally; and they entered the house.

The scene of that afternoon was repeated that evening, and on the three afternoons and evenings next ensuing. On the fourth, the host was in high spirits, for he had satisfied himself that there was no ground for the charge against Mr Tupman. So was Mr Tupman, for Mr Jingle had told him that his affair would soon be brought to a crisis. So was Mr Pickwick, for he was seldom otherwise. So was not Mr Snodgrass, for he had grown jealous of Mr Tupman. So was the old lady, for she had been winning at whist. So were Mr Jingle and Miss Wardle, for reasons of sufficient importance in this eventful history to be narrated in another chapter.

CHAPTER 5

A Discovery and a Chase

The supper was ready laid, the chairs were drawn round the table, bottles, jugs, and glasses were arranged upon the sideboard, and everything betokened the approach of the most convivial period in the whole four-and-twenty hours.

"Where's Rachael?" said Mr Wardle.

"Ay, and Jingle?" added Mr Pickwick.

"Dear me," said the host, "I wonder I haven't missed him before. Why, I don't think I've heard his voice for two hours at least. Emily, my dear, ring the bell."

The bell was rung, and the fat boy appeared.

"Where's Miss Rachael?" He couldn't say.

"Where's Mr Jingle, then?" He didn't know.

Everybody looked surprised. It was late – past eleven o'clock.

Mr Tupman laughed in his sleeve. They were loitering somewhere, talking about him. Ha, ha! capital notion that – funny.

"Never mind," said Wardle, after a short pause. "They'll turn up presently, I dare say. I never wait supper for anybody."

"Excellent rule, that," said Mr Pickwick – "admirable."

"Pray, sit down," said the host.

"Certainly," said Mr Pickwick; and down they sat.

There was a gigantic round of cold beef on the table, and Mr Pickwick was supplied with a plentiful portion of it. He had raised his fork to his lips, and was on the very point of opening his mouth for the reception of a piece of beef, when the hum of many voices suddenly arose in the kitchen. He paused, and laid down his fork. Mr Wardle paused too, and insensibly released his hold of the carving-knife, which remained inserted in the beef. He looked at Mr Pickwick. Mr Pickwick looked at him.

Heavy footsteps were heard in the passage; the parlour door was suddenly burst open; and the man who had cleaned Mr Pickwick's boots on his first arrival, rushed into the room, followed by the fat boy and all the domestics.

"What the devil's the meaning of this?" exclaimed the host.

"The kitchen chimney ain't a-fire, is it, Emma?" inquired the old lady.

"Lor, grandma! No," screamed both the young ladies.

"What's the matter?" roared the master of the house.

The man gasped for breath, and faintly ejaculated – "they ha' gone, mas'r! – gone right clean off, sir!" (At this juncture Mr Tupman was observed to lay down his knife and fork, and to turn very pale.)

"Who's gone?" said Mr Wardle fiercely.

"Mas'r Jingle and Miss Rachael, in a po'-chay, from Blue Lion, Muggleton. I was there; but I couldn't stop 'em; so I run off to tell 'ee."

"I paid his expenses!" said Mr Tupman, jumping up frantically. "He's got ten pounds of mine! – stop him! – he's swindled me! – I won't bear it! – I'll have justice, Pickwick! – I won't stand it!" and with sundry incoherent exclamations of the like nature, the unhappy gentleman spun round and round the apartment, in a transport of frenzy.

"Lord preserve us!" ejaculated Mr Pickwick, eyeing the extraordinary gestures of his friend with terrified surprise. "He's gone mad! What shall we do?"

"Do!" said the stout old host, who regarded only the last words of the sentence. "Put the horse in the gig! I'll get a chaise at the Lion, and follow 'em instantly. Where's that villain, Joe?"

"Here I am! but I hain't a willin," replied a voice. It was the fat boy's.

"Let me get at him, Pickwick," cried Wardle, as he rushed at the ill-starred youth. "He was bribed by that scoundrel, Jingle, to put me on a wrong scent, by telling a cock-and-bull story of my sister and your friend Tupman!" (Here Mr Tupman sank into a chair.) "Let me get at him!"

"Don't let him!" screamed all the women, above whose exclamations the blubbering of the fat boy was distinctly audible.

"I won't be held!" cried the old man. "Mr Winkle, take your hands off. Mr Pickwick, let me go, sir!" It was a beautiful sight, in that moment of turmoil and confusion, to behold the placid and philosophical expression of Mr Pickwick's face, somewhat flushed with exertion, as he stood with his arms firmly clasped round the extensive waist of their corpulent host, thus restraining his passion, while the fat boy was scratched, and pulled, and pushed from the room by all the females congregated therein. He had no sooner released his hold, than the man entered to announce that the gig was ready.

"Don't let him go alone!" screamed the females. "He'll kill somebody!"

"I'll go with him," said Mr Pickwick.

"You're a good fellow, Pickwick," said the host, grasping his hand. "Emma, give Mr Pickwick a shawl to tie round his neck – make haste. Look after your grandmother, girls; she has fainted away. Now then, are you ready?"

Mr Pickwick's mouth and chin having been hastily enveloped in a large shawl, his hat having been put on his head, and his great-coat thrown over his arm, he replied in the affirmative. They jumped into the gig.

"Give her her head, Tom," cried the host; and away they went, down the narrow lanes; jolting in and out of the cart-ruts, and bumping up against the hedges on either side, as if they would go to pieces every moment.

"How much are they ahead?" shouted Wardle, as they drove up to the door of the Blue Lion, round which a little crowd had collected, late as it was.

"Not above three-quarters of an hour," was everybody's reply.

"Chaise-and-four directly! – out with 'em! Put up the gig afterwards."

"Now, boys!" cried the landlord – "chaise-and-four out – make haste – look alive there!"

Away ran the hostlers and the boys. The lanterns glimmered, as the men ran to and fro; the horses' hoofs clattered on the uneven paving of the yard; the chaise rumbled as it was drawn out of the coach-house; and all was noise and bustle.

"Now then! – is that chaise coming out to-night?" cried Wardle.

"Coming down the yard now, sir," replied the hostler.

Out came the chaise – in went the horses – on sprang the boys – in got the travellers.

"Mind – the seven-mile stage in less than half an hour!" shouted Wardle. "Off with you!"

The boys applied whip and spur, the waiters shouted, the hostlers cheered, and away they went, fast and furiously. For the first three or four miles, not a word was spoken by either of the gentlemen, each being too much immersed in his own reflections to address any observations to his companion. When they had gone over that much ground, however, and the horses getting thoroughly warmed began to do their work in really good style, Mr Pickwick became too much exhilarated with the rapidity of the motion, to remain any longer perfectly mute.

"We're sure to catch them, I think," said he.

"Hope so," replied his companion.

"Fine night," said Mr Pickwick, looking up at the moon, which was shining brightly.

"So much the worse," returned Wardle; "for they'll have had all the advantage of the moonlight to get the start of us, and we shall lose it. It will have gone down in another hour."

"It will be rather unpleasant going at this rate in the dark, won't it?" inquired Mr Pickwick.

"I dare say it will," replied his friend dryly.

Mr Pickwick's temporary excitement began to sober down a little, as he reflected upon the inconveniences and dangers of the expedition in which he had so thoughtlessly embarked. He was roused by a loud shouting of the post-boy on the leader.

"What's the matter?" inquired Mr Pickwick.

"There's a gate here," replied old Wardle. "We shall hear something of the fugitives."

After a lapse of five minutes, consumed in incessant knocking and shouting, an old man in his shirt and trousers emerged from the turnpike-house, and opened the gate.

"How long is it since a post-chaise went through here?" inquired Mr Wardle.

"How long? Why, I don't rightly know. It worn't a long time ago, nor it worn't a short time ago – just between the two, perhaps."

"Has any chaise been by at all?"

"Oh, yes, there's been a shay by."

"How long ago, my friend," interposed Mr Pickwick; "an hour?"

"Ah, I dare say it might be," replied the man.

"Or two hours?" inquired the post-boy on the wheeler.

"Well, I shouldn't wonder if it was," returned the old man doubtfully.

"Drive on, boys," cried the testy old gentleman; "don't waste any more time with that old idiot!"

"Idiot!" exclaimed the old man with a grin, watching the chaise which rapidly diminished in the increasing distance. "No – not much o' that either; you've lost ten minutes here, and gone away as wise as you came, arter all. If every man on the line as has a guinea give him, earns it half as well, you won't catch t'other shay this side Mich'lmas, old short-and-fat." And with another prolonged grin, the old man closed the gate, re-entered his house, and bolted the door after him.

Meanwhile the chaise proceeded, without any slackening of pace, towards the conclusion of the stage. The moon, as Wardle had foretold, was rapidly on the wane; large tiers of dark, heavy clouds, which had been gradually overspreading the sky for some time past, now formed one black mass overhead; and large drops of rain pattered every now and then against the windows of the chaise. Mr Pickwick drew his coat closer about him, coiled himself more snugly up into the corner of the chaise, and fell into a sound sleep, from which he was only awakened by the stopping of the vehicle, the sound of the hostler's bell, and a loud cry of "Horses on directly!"

But here another delay occurred. The boys were sleeping with such mysterious soundness, that it took five minutes a-piece to wake them. The hostler had somehow or other mislaid the key of the stable, and even when that was found, two sleepy helpers put the wrong harness on the wrong horses, and the whole process of harnessing had to be gone through afresh. Had Mr Pickwick been alone, these multiplied obstacles would have completely put an end to the pursuit at once, but old Wardle was not to be so easily daunted.

They resumed their journey; and certainly the prospect before them was by no means encouraging. The stage was fifteen miles long, the night was dark, the wind high, and the rain pouring in torrents. It was hard upon one o'clock already; and nearly two hours were consumed in getting to the end of the stage. Here, however, an object presented itself, which rekindled their hopes, and reanimated their drooping spirits.

"When did this chaise come in?" cried old Wardle, leaping out of his own vehicle, and pointing to one covered with wet mud, which was standing in the yard.

"Not a quarter of an hour ago, sir," replied the hostler, to whom the question was addressed.

"Lady and gentleman?" inquired Wardle, almost breathless with impatience.

"Yes, sir."

"Tall gentleman – dress-coat – long legs – thin body?"

"Yes, sir."

"Elderly lady – thin face – rather skinny – eh?"

"Yes, sir."

"By heavens, it's the couple, Pickwick," exclaimed the old gentleman.

43

"Would have been here before," said the hostler, "but they broke a trace."

"'Tis them!" said Wardle, "it is, by Jove! Chaise-and-four instantly! We shall catch them yet before they reach the next stage. A guinea a-piece, boys – be alive there – bustle about – there's good fellows."

And with such admonitions as these, the old gentleman ran up and down the yard, and bustled to and fro, in a state of excitement which communicated itself to Mr Pickwick also.

"Jump in – jump in!" cried old Wardle, climbing into the chaise, pulling up the steps, and slamming the door after him. "Come along! Make haste!"

And before Mr Pickwick knew precisely what he was about, he felt himself forced in at the other door, by one pull from the old gentleman and one push from the hostler; and off they were again.

"Ah! we are moving now," said the old gentleman exultingly.

They had travelled in this way about three miles, when Mr Wardle, who had been looking out of the window for two or three minutes, suddenly drew in his face, covered with splashes, and exclaimed in breathless eagerness –

"Here they are!"

Mr Pickwick thrust his head out of his window. Yes: there was a chaise-and-four, a short distance before them, dashing along at full gallop.

"Go on, go on," almost shrieked the old gentleman. "Two guineas a-piece, boys – don't let 'em gain on us – keep it up – keep it up."

The horses in the first chaise started on at their utmost speed; and those in Mr Wardle's galloped furiously behind them.

"I see his head," exclaimed the choleric old man; "damme, I see his head."

"So do I," said Mr Pickwick; "that's he." Mr Pickwick was not mistaken. The countenance of Mr Jingle, completely coated with mud thrown up by the wheels, was plainly discernible at the window of his chaise and Jingle's voice could be plainly heard, even above the din of the wheels, urging on the boys.

Old Mr Wardle foamed with rage and excitement. He roared out scoundrels and villains by the dozen, clenched his fist and shook it expressively at the object of his indignation; but Mr Jingle only answered with a contemptuous smile, and replied to his menaces by a shout of triumph, as his horses, answering the increased application of whip and spur, broke into a faster gallop, and left the pursuers behind.

Mr Pickwick had just drawn in his head, and Mr Wardle, exhausted with shouting, had done the same, when a tremendous jolt threw them forward against the front of the vehicle. There was a sudden bump – a loud crash – away rolled a wheel, and over went the chaise. After a very few seconds of bewilderment and confusion, in which nothing but the plunging of horses, and breaking of glass could be made out, Mr Pickwick felt himself violently pulled out from among the ruins of the chaise; and as soon as he had gained his feet, the full disaster of the case met his view.

Old Mr Wardle without a hat, and his clothes torn in several places, stood by his side, and the fragments of the chaise lay scattered at their feet. The post-boys, who had succeeded in cutting the traces, were standing, disfigured with mud and disordered by hard riding, by the horses' heads. About a hundred yards in advance was the other chaise, which had pulled up on hearing the crash and Mr Jingle was contemplating the wreck from the coach window, with evident satisfaction. The day was just breaking, and the whole scene was rendered perfectly visible by the grey light of the morning.

"Hallo!" shouted the shameless Jingle, "anybody damaged? – elderly gentlemen – no light weights – dangerous work – very."

"You're a rascal," roared Wardle.

"Ha! ha!" replied Jingle; and then he added, with a knowing wink, and a jerk of the thumb towards the interior of the chaise – "I say – she's very well – desires her compliments – begs you won't trouble yourself – love to *tuppy* – won't you get up behind? – drive on, boys."

And away rattled the chaise, Mr Jingle fluttering in derision a white handkerchief from the coach window.

Nothing in the whole adventure, not even the upset, had disturbed the calm and equable current of Mr Pickwick's temper. The villainy, however, which could first borrow money of his faithful follower, and then abbreviate his name to "Tuppy," was more than he could patiently bear. He drew his breath hard, and coloured up to the very tips of his spectacles, as he said, slowly and emphatically –

"If ever I meet that man again, I'll – "

"Yes, yes," interrupted Wardle, "that's all very well; but while we stand talking here, they'll get their licence, and be married in London."

Mr Pickwick paused, bottled up his vengeance, and corked it down.

"How far is it to the next stage?" inquired Mr Wardle, of one of the boys.

"Six mile, ain't it, Tom?"

"Rayther better."

"Rayther better nor six mile, sir."

"Can't be helped," said Wardle, "we must walk it, Pickwick."

"No help for it," replied that truly great man.

So sending forward one of the boys on horseback, to procure a fresh chaise and horses, and leaving the other behind to take care of the broken one, Mr Pickwick and Mr Wardle set manfully forward on the walk, first tying their shawls round their necks, and slouching down their hats to escape as much as possible from the deluge of rain, which after a slight cessation had again begun to pour heavily down.

CHAPTER 6

Clearing up all Doubts (if any Existed) of the Disinterestedness of Mr A. Jingle's Character

There are in London several old inns, once the headquarters of celebrated coaches in the days when coaches performed their journeys in a graver and more solemn manner than they do in these times; but which have now degenerated into little more than the abiding and booking-places of country wagons.

It was in the yard of one of these inns – of no less celebrated a one than the White Hart – that a man was busily employed in brushing the dirt off a pair of boots, early on the morning succeeding the events narrated in the last chapter. There were two rows of boots before him, one cleaned and the other dirty, and at every addition he made to the clean row, he paused from his work, and contemplated its results with evident satisfaction.

There was a loud ring; and the bustling old landlady of the White Hart made her appearance in the opposite gallery.

"Sam," cried the landlady, "where's that lazy, idle – why, Sam – oh, there you are; why don't you answer?"

"Wouldn't be gen-teel to answer, till you'd done talking," replied Sam gruffly.

"Here, clean these shoes for number seventeen directly, and take 'em to private sitting-room, number five, first floor."

The landlady flung a pair of lady's shoes into the yard, and bustled away.

"Number five," said Sam, as he picked up the shoes, and taking a piece of chalk from his pocket, made a memorandum of their destination on the soles – "Lady's shoes and private sittin'-room! I suppose she didn't come in the vaggin."

"She came in early this morning," cried a girl, who was leaning over the railing of the gallery, "with a gentleman in a hackney-coach, and it's him as wants his boots, and you'd better do 'em, that's all about it."

"Vy didn't you say so before," said Sam, with great indignation, singling out the boots in question from the heap before him. "For all I know'd he was one o' the regular three-pennies. Private room! and a lady too! If he's anything of a gen'l'm'n, he's vurth a shillin' a day, let alone the arrands."

Stimulated by this inspiring reflection, Mr Samuel brushed away with such hearty good-will and soon arrived at the door of number five.

"Come in," said a man's voice, in reply to Sam's rap at the door.

Sam made his best bow, and stepped into the presence of a lady and gentleman seated at breakfast. Having officiously deposited the gentleman's boots right and left at his feet, and the lady's shoes right and left at hers, he backed towards the door.

"Boots," said the gentleman.

"Sir," said Sam, closing the door, and keeping his hand on the knob of the lock.

"Do you know – what's a-name – Doctors' Commons?"

"Yes, sir."

"Where is it?"

"Paul's Churchyard, sir; low archway on the carriage side, bookseller's at one corner, hot-el on the other."

Having said which, and having paused for an instant to see whether he was wanted for anything more, Sam left the room.

"Half-past nine – just the time – off at once;" said the gentleman, whom we need hardly introduce as Mr Jingle.

"Time – for what?" said the spinster aunt coquettishly.

"Licence, dearest of angels – give notice at the church – call you mine, to-morrow" – said Mr Jingle, and he squeezed the spinster aunt's hand.

"The licence!" said Rachael, blushing.

"The licence," repeated Mr Jingle – "In hurry, post-haste for a licence. In hurry, ding dong I come back."

"How you run on," said Rachael.

"Run on – nothing to the hours, days, weeks, months, years, when we're united – run on – they'll fly on – bolt – mizzle – steam-engine – thousand-horse power – nothing to it."

"Can't – can't we be married before to-morrow morning?" inquired Rachael.

"Impossible – can't be – notice at the church – leave the licence to-day – ceremony come off to-morrow."

"I am so terrified, lest my brother should discover us!" said Rachael.

"Discover – nonsense – too much shaken by the break-down – besides – extreme caution – gave up the post-chaise – walked on – came to the Borough – last place in the world that he'd look in – ha! ha! – capital notion that – very."

"Don't be long," said the spinster affectionately, as Mr Jingle stuck the pinched-up hat on his head.

"Long away from you? – Cruel charmer;" and Mr Jingle skipped playfully up to the spinster aunt, imprinted a chaste kiss upon her lips, and danced out of the room.

"Dear man!" said the spinster, as the door closed after him.

"Rum old girl," said Mr Jingle, as he walked down the passage.

Having procured a highly flattering address on parchment, from the Archbishop of Canterbury, to his "trusty and well-beloved Alfred Jingle and Rachael Wardle, greeting," he carefully deposited the mystic document in his pocket, and retraced his steps in triumph to the Borough.

He was yet on his way to the White Hart, when two plump gentleman and one thin one entered the yard, and looked round in search of some authorised person of whom they could make a few inquiries. Mr Samuel Weller happened to be at that moment engaged in burnishing a pair of painted tops and to him the thin gentleman straightway advanced.

"This is a curious old house of yours," said the little man, looking round him.

"If you'd sent word you was a-coming, we'd ha' had it repaired;" replied the imperturbable Sam.

The little man seemed rather baffled and a short consultation took place between him and the two plump gentlemen. At its conclusion one of the plump gentlemen, who in addition to a benevolent countenance, possessed a pair of spectacles, and a pair of black gaiters, interfered –

"The fact of the matter is," said the benevolent gentleman, "that my friend here (pointing to the other plump gentleman) will give you half a guinea, if you'll answer one or two – "

"Really, Mr – " the small man turned to the other plump gentleman, and said, "I forget your friend's name."

"Pickwick," said Mr Wardle, for it was no other than that jolly personage.

"Ah, Pickwick – really Mr Pickwick, my dear sir, excuse me – and the little man took an argumentative pinch of snuff, and looked very profound.

"My only wish, sir," said Mr Pickwick, "was to bring this very unpleasant matter to as speedy a close as possible."

"Quite right – quite right," said the little man.

"With which view," continued Mr Pickwick, "I made use of the argument which my experience of men has taught me is the most likely to succeed in any case."

"Never mind," interrupted Sam, who had remained a wondering listener during this short colloquy. "That's neither here nor there. You want me to accept of half a guinea wery well, I'm agreeable: I can't say no fairer than that, can I, sir?" (Mr Pickwick smiled.) "Then the next question is, what the devil do you want with me, as the man said, wen he see the ghost?"

"We want to know – " said Mr Wardle.

"Now, my dear sir – my dear sir," interposed the busy little man. Mr Wardle shrugged his shoulders, and was silent.

"We want to know," said the little man solemnly, who you've got in this house at present?"

"Who there is in the house!" said Sam, in whose mind the inmates were always represented by that particular article of their costume, which came under his immediate superintendence.

"There's a vooden leg in number six; there's a pair of Hessians in thirteen; there's two pair of halves in the commercial; there's these here painted tops in the snuggery inside the bar; and five more tops in the coffee-room."

"Nothing more?" said the little man.

"Stop a bit," replied Sam, suddenly recollecting himself. "Yes; there's a pair of Vellingtons a good deal worn, and a pair o' lady's shoes, in number five."

"What sort of shoes?" hastily inquired Wardle, who, together with Mr Pickwick, had been lost in bewilderment at the singular catalogue of visitors.

"Country make," replied Sam.

"Any maker's name?"

"Brown."

"Where of?"

"Muggleton."

"It is them," exclaimed Wardle. "By heavens, we've found them."

"Hush!" said Sam. "The Vellingtons has gone to Doctors' Commons."

"No," said the little man.

"Yes, for a licence."

"We're in time," exclaimed Wardle. "Show us the room; not a moment is to be lost."

"Pray, my dear sir – pray," said the little man; "caution, caution." He drew from his pocket a red silk purse, and looked very hard at Sam as he drew out a sovereign.

Sam grinned expressively.

"Show us into the room at once, without announcing us," said the little man, "and it's yours."

Sam led the way through a dark passage, and up a wide staircase. He paused at the end of a second passage, and held out his hand.

"Here it is," whispered the attorney, as he deposited the money on the hand of their guide. The man stepped forward for a few paces, followed by the two friends and their legal adviser. He stopped at a door.

"Is this the room?" murmured the little gentleman.

Sam nodded assent.

Old Wardle opened the door; and the whole three walked into the room just as Mr Jingle, who had that moment returned, had produced the licence to the spinster aunt. The spinster uttered a loud shriek, and throwing herself into a chair, covered her face with her hands. Mr Jingle crumpled up the licence, and thrust it into his coat pocket. The unwelcome visitors advanced into the middle of the room.

"You – you are a nice rascal, arn't you?" exclaimed Wardle, breathless with passion.

"My dear sir, my dear sir," said the little man, laying his hat on the table, "pray, consider – pray. Defamation of character: action for damages. Calm yourself, my dear sir, pray – "

"How dare you drag my sister from my house?" said the old man.

"Ay – ay – very good," said the little gentleman, "you may ask that. How dare you, sir? – eh, sir?"

"Who the devil are you?" inquired Mr Jingle, in so fierce a tone, that the little gentleman involuntarily fell back a step or two.

"Who is he, you scoundrel," interposed Wardle. "He's my lawyer, Mr Perker, of Gray's Inn. Perker, I'll have this fellow prosecuted – indicted – I'll – I'll – I'll ruin him. And you," continued Mr Wardle, turning abruptly round to his sister – "you, Rachael, at a time of life when you ought to know better, what do you mean by running away with a vagabond, disgracing your family, and making yourself miserable? Get on your bonnet and come back. Call a hackney-coach there, directly, and bring this lady's bill, d'ye hear – d'ye hear?"

"Cert'nly, sir," replied Sam, who had answered Wardle's violent ringing of the bell with a degree of celerity which must have appeared marvellous to anybody who didn't know that his eye had been applied to the outside of the keyhole during the whole interview.

"Get on your bonnet," repeated Wardle.

"Do nothing of the kind," said Jingle. "Leave the room, sir – no business here – lady's free to act as she pleases – more than one-and-twenty."

"More than one-and-twenty!" ejaculated Wardle contemptuously. "More than one-and-forty!"

"I ain't," said the spinster aunt, her indignation getting the better of her determination to faint.

"You are," replied Wardle; "you're fifty if you're an hour."

Here the spinster aunt uttered a loud shriek, and became senseless.

"A glass of water," said the humane Mr Pickwick, summoning the landlady.

"A glass of water!" said the passionate Wardle. "Bring a bucket, and throw it all over her; it'll do her good, and she richly deserves it."

"Ugh, you brute!" ejaculated the kind-hearted landlady. "Poor dear." And the landlady, assisted by a chambermaid, proceeded to vinegar the forehead, beat the hands, titillate the nose, and unlace the stays of the spinster aunt, and to administer such other restoratives as are usually applied by compassionate females to ladies who are endeavouring to ferment themselves into hysterics.

"Coach is ready, sir," said Sam, appearing at the door.

"Come along," cried Wardle. "I'll carry her downstairs."

At this proposition, the hysterics came on with redoubled violence.

The landlady was about to enter a very violent protest against this proceeding, and had already given vent to an indignant inquiry whether Mr Wardle considered himself a lord of the creation, when Mr Jingle interposed –

"Boots," said he, "get me an officer."

"Stay, stay," said little Mr Perker. "Consider, sir, consider."

"I'll not consider," replied Jingle. "She's her own mistress – see who dares to take her away – unless she wishes it."

"I *won't* be taken away," murmured the spinster aunt. "I *don't* wish it." (Here there was a frightful relapse.)

"My dear sir," said the little man, in a low tone, taking Mr Wardle and Mr Pickwick apart -- "my dear sir, we're in a very awkward situation. It's a distressing case – very; I never knew one more so; but really, my dear sir, really we have no power to control this lady's actions. I warned you before we came, my dear sir, that there was nothing to look to but a compromise."

There was a short pause.

"What kind of compromise would you recommend?" inquired Mr Pickwick.

"Why, my dear sir, our friend's in an unpleasant position – very much so. We must be content to suffer some pecuniary loss."

"I'll suffer any, rather than submit to this disgrace, and let her, fool as she is, be made miserable for life," said Wardle.

"I rather think it can be done," said the bustling little man. "Mr Jingle, will you step with us into the next room for a moment?"

Mr Jingle assented, and the quartette walked into an empty apartment.

"Now, sir," said the little man, as he carefully closed the door, "is there no way of accommodating this matter? Now, my dear sir, between you and I, we know very well, my dear sir, that you have run off with this lady for the sake of her money. Don't frown, sir, don't frown; I say, between you and I, *we* know it. We are both men of the world, and *we* know very well that our friends here, are not – eh?"

Mr Jingle's face gradually relaxed; and something distantly resembling a wink quivered for an instant in his left eye.

"Very good, very good," said the little man, observing the impression he had made. "Now, the fact is, that beyond a few hundreds, the lady has little or nothing till the death of her mother – fine old lady, my dear sir."

"*Old*," said Mr Jingle briefly but emphatically.

"Why, yes," said the attorney, with a slight cough. "You are right, my dear sir, she is rather old. She comes of an old family though, my dear sir; old in every sense of the word. The founder of that family came into Kent when Julius Caesar invaded Britain; – only one member of it since who hasn't lived to eighty-five, and he was beheaded by one of the Henrys. The old lady is not seventy-three now, my dear sir." The little man paused, and took a pinch of snuff. Don't you think – now, my dear sir, I put it to you don't you think – that fifty pounds and liberty would be better than Miss Wardle and expectation?"

"More to be done with a hundred and fifty," replied Mr Jingle coolly. "Expensive affair. Money out of pocket – posting, nine pounds; licence, three – that's twelve – compensation, a hundred – hundred and twelve – breach of honour – and loss of the lady – "

"Yes, my dear sir, yes," said the little man, with a knowing look, "never mind the last two items. That's a hundred and twelve – say a hundred – come."

"And twenty," said Mr Jingle.

"Come, come, I'll write you a cheque," said the little man; and down he sat at the table for that purpose.

"I'll make it payable the day after to-morrow," said the little man, with a look towards Mr Wardle; "and we can get the lady away, meanwhile." Mr Wardle sullenly nodded assent.

"A hundred," said the little man.

"And twenty," said Mr Jingle.

"My dear sir," remonstrated the little man.

"Give it him," interposed Mr Wardle, "and let him go."

The cheque was written by the little gentleman, and pocketed by Mr Jingle.

"Now, leave this house instantly!" said Wardle, starting up.

"Off directly," said the unabashed Jingle. "Bye bye, Pickwick. Here," continued the hardened traitor, tossing the licence at Mr Pickwick's feet; "get the name altered – take home the lady – do for Tuppy."

Mr Pickwick, in the frenzy of his rage, hurled the inkstand madly forward, and followed it up himself. But Mr Jingle had disappeared, and he found himself caught in the arms of Sam.

"Hallo," said that eccentric functionary, "Hold still, sir; wot's the use o' runnin' arter a man as has made his lucky, and got to t'other end of the Borough by this time?"

Mr Pickwick's mind, like those of all truly great men, was open to conviction. He was a quick and powerful reasoner; and a moment's reflection sufficed to remind him of the impotency of his rage. It subsided as quickly as it had been roused. He panted for breath, and looked benignantly round upon his friends.

Slowly and sadly did the two friends and the deserted lady return next day in the Muggleton heavy coach. Dimly and darkly had the sombre shadows of a summer's night fallen upon all around, when they again reached Dingley Dell, and stood within the entrance to Manor Farm.

CHAPTER 7

Descriptive of a Very Important Proceeding on the Part of Mr Pickwick; No Less an Epoch in his Life, than in this History

Mr Pickwick's apartments in Goswell Street, although on a limited scale, were not only of a very neat and comfortable description, but peculiarly adapted for the residence of a man of his genius and observation. His landlady, Mrs Bardell was a comely woman of bustling manners and agreeable appearance, with a natural genius for cooking, improved by study and long practice, into an exquisite talent. Cleanliness and quiet reigned throughout the house; and in it Mr Pickwick's will was law.

To any one acquainted with the admirable regulation of Mr Pickwick's mind, his appearance and behaviour on that morning would have been most mysterious and unaccountable. He paced the room to and fro with hurried steps, popped his head out of the window at intervals of about three minutes each, constantly referred to his watch, and exhibited many other manifestations of impatience very unusual with him. It was evident that something of great importance was in contemplation, but what that something was, not even Mrs Bardell had been enabled to discover.

"Mrs Bardell," said Mr Pickwick, at last, as that amiable female approached the termination of a prolonged dusting of the apartment.

"Sir," said Mrs Bardell.

"Your little boy is a very long time gone."

"Why, it's a good long way to the Borough, sir," remonstrated Mrs Bardell.

"Ah," said Mr Pickwick, "very true; so it is."

Mr Pickwick relapsed into silence, and Mrs Bardell resumed her dusting.

"Mrs Bardell," said Mr Pickwick, at the expiration of a few minutes.

"Sir," said Mrs Bardell again.

"Do you think it a much greater expense to keep two people, than to keep one?"

"La, Mr Pickwick," said Mrs Bardell, colouring up to the very border of her cap, as she fancied she observed a species of matrimonial twinkle in the eyes of her lodger; "La, Mr Pickwick, what a question!"

"Well, but do you?" inquired Mr Pickwick.

"That depends," said Mrs Bardell, approaching the duster very near to Mr Pickwick's elbow which was planted on the table, "that depends a good deal upon the person, you know, Mr Pickwick; and whether it's a saving and careful person, sir."

"That's very true," said Mr Pickwick, "but the person I have in my eye (here he looked very hard at Mrs Bardell) I think possesses these qualities; and has, moreover, a considerable knowledge of the world, and a great deal of sharpness, Mrs Bardell, which may be of material use to me."

"La, Mr Pickwick," said Mrs Bardell, the crimson rising to her cap-border again.

"I do," said Mr Pickwick, growing energetic, as was his wont in speaking of a subject which interested him – "and to tell you the truth, Mrs Bardell, I have made up my mind."

"Dear me, sir," exclaimed Mrs Bardell.

"You'll think it very strange now," said the amiable Mr Pickwick, with a good-humoured glance at his companion, "that I never consulted you about this matter, and never even mentioned it, till I sent your little boy out this morning – eh?"

Mrs Bardell could only reply by a look. She had long worshipped Mr Pickwick at a distance, but here she was, all at once, raised to a pinnacle to which her wildest and most extravagant hopes had never dared to aspire. Mr Pickwick was going to propose – a deliberate plan, too – sent her little boy to the Borough, to get him out of the way – how thoughtful – how considerate!

"Well," said Mr Pickwick, "what do you think?"

"Oh, Mr Pickwick," said Mrs Bardell, trembling with agitation, "you're very kind, sir."

"It'll save you a good deal of trouble, won't it?" said Mr Pickwick.

"Oh, I never thought anything of the trouble, sir," replied Mrs Bardell; "and, of course, I should take more trouble to please you then, than ever; but it is so kind of you, Mr Pickwick, to have so much consideration for my loneliness."

"Ah, to be sure," said Mr Pickwick; "I never thought of that. When I am in town, you'll always have somebody to sit with you. To be sure, so you will."

"I am sure I ought to be a very happy woman," said Mrs Bardell.

"And your little boy – " said Mr Pickwick.

"Bless his heart!" interposed Mrs Bardell, with a maternal sob.

"He, too, will have a companion," resumed Mr Pickwick, "a lively one, who'll teach him, I'll be bound, more tricks in a week than he would ever learn in a year." And Mr Pickwick smiled placidly.

"Oh, you dear – " said Mrs Bardell.

Mr Pickwick started.

"Oh, you kind, good, playful dear," said Mrs Bardell; and without more ado, she rose from her chair, and flung her arms round Mr Pickwick's neck, with a cataract of tears and a chorus of sobs.

"Bless my soul," cried the astonished Mr Pickwick; "Mrs Bardell, my good woman – dear me, what a situation – pray consider. – Mrs Bardell, don't – if anybody should come – "

"Oh, let them come," exclaimed Mrs Bardell frantically; "I'll never leave you – dear, kind, good soul;" and, with these words, Mrs Bardell clung the tighter.

"Mercy upon me," said Mr Pickwick, struggling violently, "I hear somebody coming up the stairs. Don't, don't, there's a good creature, don't." But entreaty and remonstrance were alike unavailing; for Mrs Bardell had fainted in Mr Pickwick's arms; and before he could gain time to deposit her on a chair, Master Bardell entered the room, ushering in Mr Tupman, Mr Winkle, and Mr Snodgrass.

Mr Pickwick was struck motionless and speechless. He stood with his lovely burden in his arms, gazing vacantly on the countenances of his friends, without the slightest attempt at recognition or explanation. They, in their turn, stared at him; and Master Bardell, in his turn, stared at everybody. He at first stood at the door astounded and uncertain; but by degrees, the impression that his mother must have suffered some personal damage pervaded his partially developed mind, and considering Mr Pickwick as the aggressor, he set up an appalling and semi-earthly kind of howling, and butting forward with his head, commenced assailing that immortal gentleman about the back and legs.

"Take this little villain away," said the agonised Mr Pickwick, "he's mad."

"What is the matter?" said the three tongue-tied Pickwickians.

"I don't know," replied Mr Pickwick pettishly. "Take away the boy." (Here Mr Winkle carried the interesting boy, screaming and struggling, to the farther end of the apartment.) "Now help me, lead this woman downstairs."

"Oh, I am better now," said Mrs Bardell faintly.

"Let me lead you downstairs," said the ever-gallant Mr Tupman.

"Thank you, sir – thank you;" exclaimed Mrs Bardell hysterically.

And downstairs she was led accordingly, accompanied by her affectionate son.

"I cannot conceive," said Mr Pickwick when his friend returned – "I cannot conceive what has been the matter with that woman. I had merely announced to her my intention of keeping a man-servant, when she fell into the extraordinary paroxysm in which you found her. Very extraordinary thing."

"Very," said his three friends.

"Placed me in such an extremely awkward situation," continued Mr Pickwick.

"Very," was the reply of his followers, as they coughed slightly, and looked dubiously at each other.

This behaviour was not lost upon Mr Pickwick. He remarked their incredulity. They evidently suspected him.

"There is a man in the passage now," said Mr Tupman.

"It's the man I spoke to you about," said Mr Pickwick; "I sent for him to the Borough this morning. Have the goodness to call him up, Snodgrass."

Mr Snodgrass did as he was desired; and Mr Samuel Weller forthwith presented himself.

"Oh – you remember me, I suppose?" said Mr Pickwick. "Sit down."

"Thank'ee, sir," said Sam. And down he sat without further bidding.

Mr Weller smiled agreeably upon the assembled Pickwickians.

"Now with regard to the matter on which I sent for you," said Mr Pickwick.

"That's the pint, sir," interposed Sam; "out vith it, as the father said to his child, when he swallowed a farden."

A sunbeam of placid benevolence played on Mr Pickwick's features as he said, "I have half made up my mind to engage you myself."

"Have you, though?" said Sam.

Mr Pickwick nodded in the affirmative.

"Wages?" inquired Sam.

"Twelve pounds a year," replied Mr Pickwick.

"Clothes?"

"Two suits."

"Work?"

"To attend upon me; and travel about with me and these gentlemen here."

"Take the bill down," said Sam emphatically. "I'm let to a single gentleman, and the terms is agreed upon."

"You accept the situation?" inquired Mr Pickwick.

"Cert'nly," replied Sam. "If the clothes fits me half as well as the place, they'll do."

"Can you come this evening?"

"I'll get into the clothes this minute, if they're here," said Sam, with great alacrity.

With the promptness and energy which characterised all the actions of this extraordinary man, he at once led his new attendant to one of those convenient emporiums where gentlemen's new and second-hand clothes are provided, and before night had closed in, Mr Weller was furnished with a grey coat with the P.C. button, a black hat with a cockade to it, a pink striped waistcoat, light breeches and gaiters, and a variety of other necessaries, too numerous to recapitulate.

"Well," said that suddenly-transformed individual, as he took his seat on the outside of the Eatanswill coach next morning; "I wonder whether I'm meant to be a footman, or a groom, or a gamekeeper, or a seedsman. I looks like a sort of compo of every one on 'em. Never mind; there's a change of air, plenty to see, and little to do; and all this suits my complaint uncommon; so long life to the Pickvicks, says I!"

CHAPTER 8

In Which is Given a Faithful Portraiture of Two Distinguished Persons; and an Accurate Description of a Public Breakfast in their House and Grounds

Mr Pickwick was just on the point of walking forth when his faithful valet put into his hand a card, on which was engraved the following inscription: –

Mrs Leo Hunter
The Den, Eatanswill.

"Person's a-waitin'," said Sam, epigrammatically. "and he's a-waitin' in the drawing-room – said he'd rather wait all day, than not see you."

Mr Pickwick, on hearing this determination, descended to the drawing-room, where sat a grave man, who started up on his entrance, and said, with an air of profound respect:

"Mr Pickwick, I presume?"

"The same."

"Allow me, sir, the honour of grasping your hand. Permit me, sir, to shake it," said the grave man.

"Certainly," said Mr Pickwick.

"My wife, sir – Mrs Leo Hunter – is proud to number among her acquaintance all those who have rendered themselves celebrated by their works and talents."

"I shall be extremely happy to make the acquaintance of such a lady, sir," replied Mr Pickwick.

"You *shall* make it, sir," said the grave man. "To-morrow morning, sir, we give a public breakfast to a great number of those who have rendered themselves celebrated by their works and talents. Permit Mrs Leo Hunter, sir, to have the gratification of seeing you at the Den."

"With great pleasure," replied Mr Pickwick.

"You have a gentleman in your train, who has produced some beautiful little poems, I think, sir."

"My friend Mr Snodgrass has a great taste for poetry," replied Mr Pickwick.

"So has Mrs Leo Hunter, sir. She has produced some delightful pieces, herself, sir. You may have met with her "Ode to an Expiring Frog."

"I don't think I have," said Mr Pickwick.

"You astonish me, sir," said Mr Leo Hunter. "It created an immense sensation. It commenced –

> ""Can I view thee panting, lying
>   On thy stomach, without sighing;
>   Can I unmoved see thee dying
>   On a log
>   Expiring frog!""

"Beautiful!" said Mr Pickwick.

"Fine," said Mr Leo Hunter; "so simple."

"Very," said Mr Pickwick.

"The next verse is still more touching. Shall I repeat it?"

"If you please," said Mr Pickwick.

"It runs thus," said the grave man, still more gravely.

> ""Say, have fiends in shape of boys,
>   With wild halloo, and brutal noise,
>   Hunted thee from marshy joys,
>   With a dog,
>   Expiring frog!""

"Finely expressed," said Mr Pickwick.

"You shall hear Mrs Leo Hunter repeat it. She will repeat it, in character, sir, to-morrow morning."

"In character!"

"As Minerva. But I forgot – it's fancy-dress."

"Dear me," said Mr Pickwick, glancing at his own figure – "I can't possibly – "

The grave man considered deeply, for a few seconds, and then said – "On reflection, sir, I don't know whether it would not afford Mrs Leo Hunter greater pleasure, if her guests saw a gentleman of your celebrity in his own costume, rather than in an assumed one."

"In that case," said Mr Pickwick, "I shall have great pleasure in coming."

Mr Pickwick took up his hat, and repaired to the Peacock, but Mr Winkle had conveyed the intelligence of the fancy-ball there, before him. It was accordingly settled that Mr Tupman, Mr Winkle, and Mr Snodgrass, should all wear fancy-dresses and a carriage was hired from the Town Arms, for the accommodation of the Pickwickians.

The morning came: it was a pleasant sight to behold Mr Tupman in full Brigand's costume, with a very tight jacket, sitting like a pincushion over his back and shoulders, his legs incased in the velvet shorts, the lower part swathed in the complicated bandages to which all Brigands are peculiarly attached, his countenance, well mustachioed and corked, looking out from an open shirt collar at the sugar-loaf hat, decorated with ribbons of all colours. Equally humorous and agreeable was the appearance of Mr Snodgrass in blue satin trunks and cloak, white silk tights and shoes, and Grecian helmet, which everybody knows to have been the regular, authentic, everyday costume of a Troubadour, from the earliest ages down to the time of their final disappearance from the face of the earth.

Then there emerged from the house, Mrs Pott, who would have looked very like Apollo if she hadn't had a gown on, conducted by Mr Winkle, who, in his light-red coat could not possibly have been mistaken for anything but a sportsman, if he had not borne an equal resemblance to a general postman. Last of all came Mr Pickwick, whom the boys applauded as loud as anybody, probably under the impression that his tights and gaiters were some remnants of the dark ages.

The grounds were more than an acre and a quarter in extent, and they were filled with people! Never was such a blaze of beauty, and fashion, and literature. There were hosts of these geniuses, and any reasonable person would have thought it honour enough to meet them. But more than these, there were real authors, who had written whole books, and printed them afterwards – and here you might see 'em, walking about, like ordinary men, smiling, and talking – aye, and talking pretty considerable nonsense too.

And above all, there was Mrs Leo Hunter in the character of Minerva, receiving the company, and overflowing with pride and gratification at the notion of having called such distinguished individuals together.

"Mr Pickwick, ma'am," said a servant, as that gentleman approached the presiding goddess, with his hat in his hand, and the Brigand and Troubadour on either arm.

"Is it possible that I have really the gratification of beholding Mr Pickwick himself!" ejaculated Mrs Leo Hunter.

"No other, ma'am," replied Mr Pickwick, bowing very low. "Permit me to introduce my friends -- Mr Tupman – Mr Winkle – Mr Snodgrass – to the authoress of 'The Expiring Frog.'"

"Mr Pickwick," said Mrs Leo Hunter, "I must make you promise not to stir from my side the whole day. There are hundreds of people here, that I must positively introduce you to."

"You are very kind, ma'am," said Mr Pickwick.

Four singers had ranged themselves in front of a small apple-tree and commenced singing their national songs, which appeared by no means difficult, as the grand secret seemed to be that three of them should grunt, while the fourth howled.

This was succeeded by Mrs Leo Hunter's recitation of her far-famed "Ode to an Expiring Frog," which was encored once, and would have been encored twice, if the major part of the guests, who thought it was high time to get something to eat, had not said that it was perfectly shameful to take advantage of Mrs Hunter's good nature. So although Mrs Leo Hunter professed her perfect willingness to recite the ode again, her kind and considerate friends wouldn't hear of it on any account; and the refreshment room being thrown open, all the people who had ever been there before, scrambled in with all possible despatch –

Mrs Leo Hunter looked round her in triumph. Count Smorltork was busily engaged in taking notes of the contents of the dishes; Mr Tupman was doing the honours of the lobster salad to several ladies, with a degree of grace which no brigand ever exhibited before; Mr Snodgrass, having cut out the young gentleman who cut up the books for the *Eatanswill Gazette*, was engaged in an impassioned argument with the young lady who did the poetry; and Mr Pickwick was making himself universally agreeable. Nothing seemed wanting to render the select circle complete, when Mr Leo Hunter – whose department on these occasions, was to stand about in doorways, and talk to the less important people – suddenly called out –

"My dear; here's Mr Charles Fitz-Marshall."

"Oh dear," said Mrs Leo Hunter, "how anxiously I have been expecting him. Tell Mr Fitz-Marshall, my dear, to come up to me directly, to be scolded for coming so late."

"Coming, my dear ma'am," cried a voice, "as quick as I can – crowds of people – full room – hard work – very."

Mr Pickwick's knife and fork fell from his hand. He stared across the table at Mr Tupman, who had dropped his knife and fork, and was looking as if he were about to sink into the ground without further notice.

"Ah!" cried the voice, as its owner pushed his way among the last five-and-twenty Turks, officers, cavaliers, and Charles the Seconds, that remained between him and the table, "regular mangle – not a crease in my coat, after all this squeezing as I came along – queer thing to have it mangled when it's upon one, though – trying process – very."

With these broken words, a young man dressed as a naval officer made his way up to the table, and presented to the astonished Pickwickians the identical form and features of Mr Alfred Jingle. The offender had barely time to take Mrs Leo Hunter's proffered hand, when his eyes encountered the indignant orbs of Mr Pickwick.

"Hallo!" said Jingle. "Quite forgot – no directions to postillion – give 'em at once – back in a minute."

With these words he disappeared among the crowd.

"Will you allow me to ask you, ma'am," said the excited Mr Pickwick, rising from his seat, "who that young man is, and where he resides?"

"He is a gentleman of fortune, Mr Pickwick," said Mrs Leo Hunter, "to whom I very much want to introduce you."

"Yes, yes," said Mr Pickwick hastily. "His residence – "

"Is at present at the Angel at Bury."

"At Bury?"

"At Bury St Edmunds, not many miles from here. But dear me, Mr Pickwick, you are not going to leave us; surely, Mr Pickwick, you cannot think of going so soon?"

But long before Mrs Leo Hunter had finished speaking, Mr Pickwick had plunged through the throng, and reached the garden, whither he was shortly afterwards joined by Mr Tupman, who had followed his friend closely.

"It's of no use," said Mr Tupman. "He has gone."

"I know it," said Mr Pickwick, "and I will follow him."

"Follow him! Where?" inquired Mr Tupman.

"To the Angel at Bury," replied Mr Pickwick, speaking very quickly. "How do we know whom he is deceiving there? He deceived a worthy man once, and we were the innocent cause. He shall not do it again, if I can help it; I'll expose him! Sam! Where's my servant?"

"Here you are, sir," said Mr Weller, emerging from a sequestered spot, where he had been engaged in discussing a bottle of Madeira, which he had abstracted from the breakfast-table an hour or two before.

"Follow me instantly," said Mr Pickwick. "Tupman, if I stay at Bury, you can join me there, when I write. Till then, good-bye!"

Remonstrances were useless. Mr Pickwick was roused, and his mind was made up. Mr Tupman returned to his companions; and in another hour had drowned all present recollection of Mr Alfred Jingle, or Mr Charles Fitz-Marshall, in an exhilarating quadrille and a bottle of champagne. By that time, Mr Pickwick and Sam Weller, perched on the outside of a stage-coach, were every succeeding minute placing a less and less distance between themselves and the good old town of Bury St Edmunds.

CHAPTER 9

Too Full of Adventure to be Briefly Described

Intent upon the resolution he had formed, of exposing the real character of the nefarious Jingle, in any quarter in which he might be pursuing his fraudulent designs, Mr Pickwick sat at first taciturn and contemplative, brooding over the means by which his purpose could be best attained. By degrees his attention grew more and more attracted by the objects around him; and at last he derived as much enjoyment from the ride, as if it had been undertaken for the pleasantest reason in the world. The coach rattled through the well-paved streets of a handsome little town, of thriving and cleanly appearance, and stopped before a large inn situated in a wide open street, nearly facing the old abbey.

"And this," said Mr Pickwick, looking up. "Is the Angel! We alight here, Sam. But some caution is necessary. Order a private room, and do not mention my name. You understand."

"Right as a trivet, sir," replied Mr Weller, with a wink of intelligence; and having dragged Mr Pickwick's portmanteau from the hind boot, Mr Weller disappeared on his errand. A private room was speedily engaged; and into it Mr Pickwick was ushered without delay.

"Now, Sam," said Mr Pickwick, "the first thing to be done is to – "

"Order dinner, sir," interposed Mr Weller. "It's wery late, sir."

"Ah, so it is," said Mr Pickwick, looking at his watch. "You are right, Sam."

"And if I might adwise, sir," added Mr Weller, "I'd just have a good night's rest arterwards, and not begin inquiring arter this here deep 'un till the mornin'. There's nothin' so refreshen' as sleep, sir, as the servant girl said afore she drank the egg-cupful of laudanum."

"I think you are right, Sam," said Mr Pickwick. "But I must first ascertain that he is in the house, and not likely to go away."

"Leave that to me, sir," said Sam. "Let me order you a snug little dinner, and make my inquiries below while it's a-getting ready; I could worm ev'ry secret out o' the boots's heart, in five minutes, sir."

"Do so," said Mr Pickwick; and Mr Weller at once retired.

In half an hour, Mr Pickwick was seated at a very satisfactory dinner; and in three-quarters Mr Weller returned with the intelligence that Mr Charles Fitz-Marshall had ordered his private room to be retained for him, until further notice. He was going to spend the evening at some private house in the neighbourhood, had ordered the boots to sit up until his return, and had taken his servant with him.

"Now, sir," argued Mr Weller, when he had concluded his report, "if I can get a talk with this here servant in the mornin', he'll tell me all his master's concerns."

"How do you know that?" interposed Mr Pickwick.

"Bless your heart, sir, servants always do," replied Mr Weller.

65

"Oh, ah, I forgot that," said Mr Pickwick. "Well."

"Then, you can arrange what's best to be done, sir, and we can act accordingly."

Early on the ensuing morning, Mr Weller was dispelling all the feverish remains of the previous evening's conviviality with a halfpenny shower-bath (having induced a young gentleman attached to the stable department, by the offer of that coin, to pump over his head and face, until he was perfectly restored), when he was attracted by the appearance of a young fellow in mulberry-coloured livery, who was sitting on a bench in the yard, reading what appeared to be a hymn-book, with an air of deep abstraction, but who occasionally stole a glance at the individual under the pump, as if he took some interest in his proceedings, nevertheless.

So at last, Sam said with a familiar nod – "How are you, governor?"

"I am happy to say, I am pretty well, sir," said the man, speaking with great deliberation, and closing the book. "I hope you are the same, sir?"

"Why, if I felt less like a walking brandy-bottle I shouldn't be so staggery this mornin'," replied Sam. "Are you stoppin' in this house, old 'un?"

The mulberry man replied in the affirmative.

"How was it you worn't one of us in the tap, last night?" inquired Sam, scrubbing his face with the towel.

"I was out last night with my master," replied the stranger.

"What's his name?" inquired Mr Weller, colouring up very red with sudden excitement, and the friction of the towel combined.

"Fitz-Marshall," said the mulberry man.

"Give us your hand," said Mr Weller, advancing; "I should like to know you. I like your appearance, old fellow."

"Well, that is very strange," said the mulberry man, with great simplicity of manner. "I like yours so much, that I wanted to speak to you, from the very first moment I saw you under the pump."

"Did you though?"

"Upon my word. Now, isn't that curious?"

"Wery sing'ler," said Sam, inwardly congratulating himself upon the softness of the stranger. "What's your name, my patriarch?"

"Job."

"And a wery good name it is; only one I know that ain't got a nickname to it. What's the other name?"

"Trotter," said the stranger. "What is yours?"

Sam bore in mind his master's caution, and replied – "My name's Walker; my master's name's Wilkins. Will you take a drop o' somethin' this mornin', Mr Trotter?"

Mr Trotter acquiesced in this agreeable proposal and accompanied Mr Weller to the tap, where they were soon occupied in discussing an exhilarating compound, formed by mixing together, in a pewter vessel, certain quantities of British Hollands and the fragrant essence of the clove.

"And what sort of a place have you got?" inquired Sam, as he filled his companion's glass, for the second time.

"Bad," said Job, smacking his lips, "very bad."

"You don't mean that?" said Sam.

"I do, indeed. Worse than that, my master's going to be married."

"No."

"Yes; and worse than that, too, he's going to run away with an immense rich heiress, from boarding-school."

"What a dragon!" said Sam, refilling his companion's glass. "It's some boarding-school in this town, I suppose, ain't it?"

"No, no," said Mr Trotter, in conclusion, "that's not to be told to everybody. That is a secret – a great secret, Mr Walker."

As the mulberry man said this, he turned his glass upside down, by way of reminding his companion that he had nothing left wherewith to slake his thirst. Sam observed the hint; and feeling the delicate manner in which it was conveyed, ordered the pewter vessel to be refilled, whereat the small eyes of the mulberry man glistened.

"And so it's a secret?" said Sam.

"I should rather suspect it was," said the mulberry man, sipping his liquor, with a complacent face.

"I suppose your mas'r's wery rich?" said Sam.

Mr Trotter smiled, and gave four distinct slaps on the pockets of his mulberry indescribables as if to intimate that his master might have done the same without alarming anybody much by the chinking of coin.

"Ah," said Sam, "that's the game, is it?"

The mulberry man nodded significantly.

"Well, and don't you think, old feller," remonstrated Mr Weller, "that if you let your master take in this here young lady, you're a precious rascal?"

"I know that," said Job Trotter, turning upon his companion a countenance of deep contrition, and groaning slightly, "I know that, and that's what it is that preys upon my mind. But what am I to do?"

"Do!" said Sam; "di-wulge to the missis, and give up your master."

"Who'd believe me?" replied Job Trotter. "The young lady's considered the very picture of innocence and discretion. She'd deny it, and so would my master. Who'd believe me?"

"There's somethin' in that," said Sam, ruminating; "there's somethin' in that."

"If I knew any respectable gentleman who would take the matter up," continued Mr Trotter. "I might have some hope of preventing the elopement; but I know no gentleman in this strange place; and ten to one if I did, whether he would believe my story."

"Come this way," said Sam, suddenly jumping up, and grasping the mulberry man by the arm. "My mas'r's the man you want, I see."

And after a slight resistance on the part of Job Trotter, Sam led his newly-found friend to the apartment of Mr Pickwick, to whom he presented him, together with a brief summary of the dialogue we have just repeated.

"I am very sorry to betray my master, sir," said Job Trotter, applying to his eyes a pink checked pocket-handkerchief about six inches square.

"The feeling does you a great deal of honour," replied Mr Pickwick; "but it is your duty, nevertheless. You are a very good fellow," said Mr Pickwick, much affected; "an honest fellow."

"Come, come," interposed Sam, who had witnessed Mr Trotter's tears with considerable impatience, "blow this 'ere water-cart bis'ness. It won't do no good, this won't."

"Sam," said Mr Pickwick reproachfully. "I am sorry to find that you have so little respect for this young man's feelings."

"Tears never yet wound up a clock, or worked a steam ingin'."

"My man is in the right," said Mr Pickwick, accosting Job, "although his mode of expressing his opinion is somewhat homely, and occasionally incomprehensible."

"He is, sir, very right," said Mr Trotter, "and I will give way no longer."

"Very well," said Mr Pickwick. "Now, where is this boarding-school?"

"It is a large, old, red brick house, just outside the town, sir," replied Job Trotter.

"And when," said Mr Pickwick, "is this elopement to take place?"

"To-night, sir," replied Job.

"To-night!" exclaimed Mr Pickwick.

"This very night, sir," replied Job Trotter. "That is what alarms me so much."

"Instant measures must be taken," said Mr Pickwick. "I will see the lady who keeps the establishment immediately."

"I beg your pardon, sir," said Job, "but that course of proceeding will never do."

"Why not?" inquired Mr Pickwick.

"My master, sir, is a very artful man."

"I know he is," said Mr Pickwick.

"And he has so wound himself round the old lady's heart, sir," resumed Job, "that she would believe nothing to his prejudice, if you went down on your bare knees, and swore it; especially as you have no proof but the word of a servant, who, for anything she knows (and my master would be sure to say so), was discharged for some fault, and does this in revenge."

"What had better be done, then?" said Mr Pickwick.

"Nothing but taking him in the very act of eloping, will convince the old lady, sir," replied Job.

"But this taking him in the very act of elopement, would be a very difficult thing to accomplish, I fear," said Mr Pickwick.

"I don't know, sir," said Mr Trotter, after a few moments' reflection. "I think it might be very easily done."

"How?" was Mr Pickwick's inquiry.

"Why," replied Mr Trotter, "my master and I, being in the confidence of the two servants, will be secreted in the kitchen at ten o'clock. When the family have retired to rest, we shall come out of the kitchen, and the young lady out of her bedroom. A post-chaise will be waiting, and away we go."

"Well?" said Mr Pickwick.

"Well, sir, I have been thinking that if you were in waiting in the garden behind, alone – "

"Alone," said Mr Pickwick. "Why alone?"

"I thought it very natural," replied Job, "that the old lady wouldn't like such an unpleasant discovery to be made before more persons than can possibly be helped. The young lady, too, sir – consider her feelings."

"You are very right," said Mr Pickwick. "The consideration evinces your delicacy of feeling. Go on; you are very right."

"Well, sir, I have been thinking that if you were waiting in the back garden alone, and I was to let you in, at the door which opens into it, from the end of the passage, at exactly half-past eleven o'clock, you would be just in the very moment of time to assist me in frustrating the designs of this bad man, by whom I have been unfortunately ensnared." Here Mr Trotter sighed deeply.

"Don't distress yourself on that account," said Mr Pickwick; "if he had one grain of the delicacy of feeling which distinguishes you, humble as your station is, I should have some hopes of him."

Job Trotter bowed low; and in spite of Mr Weller's previous remonstrance, the tears again rose to his eyes.

"I never see such a feller," said Sam, "Blessed if I don't think he's got a water main in his head as is always turned on."

"Sam," said Mr Pickwick, with great severity, "hold your tongue."

"Wery well, sir," replied Mr Weller.

"I don't like this plan," said Mr Pickwick, after deep meditation. "Why cannot I communicate with the young lady's friends?"

"Because they live one hundred miles from here, sir," responded Job Trotter.

"That's a clincher," said Mr Weller, aside.

"Then this garden," resumed Mr Pickwick. "How am I to get into it?"

"The wall is very low, sir, and your servant will give you a leg up."

"My servant will give me a leg up," repeated Mr Pickwick mechanically. "You will be sure to be near this door that you speak of?"

"You cannot mistake it, sir; it's the only one that opens into the garden. Tap at it when you hear the clock strike, and I will open it instantly."

"I don't like the plan," said Mr Pickwick; "but as I see no other, and as the happiness of this young lady's whole life is at stake, I adopt it. I shall be sure to be there."

Thus, for the second time, did Mr Pickwick's innate good-feeling involve him in an enterprise from which he would most willingly have stood aloof.

Mr Trotter made another bow, and turned to depart, when Mr Pickwick thrust a guinea into his hand.

"You're a fine fellow," said Mr Pickwick, "and I admire your goodness of heart. No thanks. Remember – eleven o'clock."

"There is no fear of my forgetting it, sir," replied Job Trotter.

With these words he left the room, followed by Sam.

"I say," said the latter, "not a bad notion that 'er crying. I'd cry like a rain-water spout in a shower on such good terms. How do you do it?"

"It comes from the heart, Mr Walker," replied Job solemnly. "Good-morning, sir."

"You're a soft customer, you are; we've got it all out o' you, anyhow," thought Mr Weller, as Job walked away.

The day wore on, evening came, and at a little before ten o'clock Sam Weller reported that Mr Jingle and Job had gone out together, that their luggage was packed up, and that they had ordered a chaise. The plot was evidently in execution, as Mr Trotter had foretold.

Half-past ten o'clock arrived, and it was time for Mr Pickwick to issue forth on his delicate errand. Resisting Sam's offer of his great-coat, in order that he might have no encumbrance in scaling the wall, he set forth, followed by his attendant.

It was a fine dry night, but it was most uncommonly dark. The atmosphere was hot and sultry, the summer lightning quivered faintly on the verge of the horizon, and was the only sight that varied the dull gloom in which everything was wrapped.

They found the house, read the brass-plate, walked round the wall, and stopped at that portion of it which divided them from the bottom of the garden.

"You will return to the inn, Sam, when you have assisted me over," said Mr Pickwick.

"Wery well, sir."

"And you will sit up, till I return."

"Cert'nly, sir."

"Take hold of my leg; and, when I say 'Over,' raise me gently."

"All right, sir."

Having settled these preliminaries, Mr Pickwick grasped the top of the wall, and gave the word 'Over,' which was literally obeyed. Whether his body partook in some degree of the elasticity of his mind, or whether Mr Weller's notions of a gentle push were of a somewhat rougher description than Mr Pickwick's, the immediate effect of his assistance was to jerk that immortal gentleman completely over the wall on to the bed beneath, where, after crushing three gooseberry-bushes and a rose-tree, he finally alighted at full length.

"You ha'n't hurt yourself, I hope, sir?" said Sam, in a loud whisper, as soon as he had recovered from the surprise upon the mysterious disappearance of his master.

"I have not hurt *myself*, Sam, certainly," replied Mr Pickwick, from the other side of the wall, "but I rather think that *you* have hurt me."

"I hope not, sir," said Sam.

"Never mind," said Mr Pickwick, rising, "it's nothing but a few scratches. Go away, or we shall be overheard."

"Good-bye, sir."

"Good-bye."

With stealthy steps Sam Weller departed, leaving Mr Pickwick alone in the garden.

Lights occasionally appeared in the different windows of the house, or glanced from the staircases, as if the inmates were retiring to rest. Not caring to go too near the door, until the appointed time, Mr Pickwick crouched into an angle of the wall, and awaited its arrival. Mr Pickwick had meditated himself into a doze, when he was roused by the chimes of the neighbouring church ringing out the hour – half-past eleven.

"That's the time," thought Mr Pickwick, getting cautiously on his feet.

He looked up at the house. The lights had disappeared, and the shutters were closed – all in bed, no doubt. He walked on tiptoe to the door, and gave a gentle tap. Two or three minutes passing without any reply, he gave another tap rather louder, and then another rather louder than that. At length the sound of feet was audible upon the stairs, and then the light of a candle shone through the keyhole of the door.

There was a good deal of unchaining and unbolting, and the door was slowly opened. Now the door opened outwards; and as the door opened wider and wider, Mr Pickwick receded behind it, more and more. What was his astonishment when he just peeped out, by way of caution, to see that the person who had opened it was – not Job Trotter, but a servant-girl with a candle in her hand! Mr Pickwick drew in his head again, with the swiftness displayed by that admirable melodramatic performer, Mr Punch.

"It must have been the cat, Sarah," said the girl, addressing herself to some one in the house. "Puss, puss, puss, – tit, tit, tit."

But no animal being decoyed by these blandishments, the girl slowly closed the door, and re-fastened it; leaving Mr Pickwick drawn up straight against the wall.

He had not been here five minutes, when a vivid flash of lightning was followed by a loud peal of thunder that crashed and rolled away in the distance with a terrific noise – and then down came the rain, with a force and fury that swept everything before it.

Mr Pickwick was perfectly aware that a tree is a very dangerous neighbour in a thunderstorm. He had a tree on his right, a tree on his left, a third before him, and a fourth behind. If he remained where he was, he might fall the victim of an accident; if he showed himself in the centre of the garden, he might be consigned to a constable. Once or twice he tried to scale the wall, but having no other legs this time, than those with which Nature had furnished him, the only effect of his struggles was to inflict a variety of very unpleasant gratings on his knees and shins, and to throw him into a state of the most profuse perspiration.

"What a dreadful situation," said Mr Pickwick, pausing to wipe his brow after this exercise. He looked up at the house – all was dark. They must be gone to bed now. He would try the signal again.

He walked on tiptoe across the moist gravel, and tapped at the door. He held his breath, and listened at the key-hole. No reply: very odd. Another knock. He listened again. There was a low whispering inside, and then a voice cried –

"Who's there?"

"That's not Job," thought Mr Pickwick, hastily drawing himself straight up against the wall again. "It's a woman."

He had scarcely had time to form this conclusion, when a window above stairs was thrown up, and three or four female voices repeated the query – "Who's there?"

Mr Pickwick dared not move hand or foot. It was clear that the whole establishment was roused. He made up his mind to remain where he was, until the alarm had subsided; and then by a supernatural effort, to get over the wall, or perish in the attempt. What was his discomfiture, when he heard the chain and bolts withdrawn, and saw the door slowly opening, wider and wider! He retreated into the corner, step by step; but that merely prevented the door's being opened to its utmost width.

"Who's there?" screamed a numerous chorus of treble voices from the staircase inside, consisting of the spinster lady of the establishment, three teachers, five female servants, and thirty boarders, all half-dressed and in a forest of curl-papers.

Of course Mr Pickwick didn't say who was there: and then the burden of the chorus changed into – "Lor! I am so frightened."

"Cook," said the lady abbess, who took care to be on the top stair, the very last of the group – "cook, I insist upon your looking into the garden immediately."

The unfortunate cook, thus strongly urged, advanced a step or two, and holding her candle just where it prevented her from seeing at all, declared there was nothing there, and it must have been the wind. The door was just going to be closed when an inquisitive boarder, who had been peeping between the hinges, set up a fearful screaming, which called back the cook and housemaid, and all the more adventurous, in no time.

"What is the matter with Miss Smithers?" said the lady abbess, as Miss Smithers proceeded to go into hysterics of four young lady power.

"Oh, the man – the man – behind the door!" screamed Miss Smithers.

The lady abbess no sooner heard this appalling cry, than she retreated to her own bedroom, double-locked the door, and fainted away comfortably. The boarders, and the teachers, and the servants, fell back upon the stairs, and upon each other; and never was such a screaming, and fainting, and struggling beheld.

In the midst of the tumult, Mr Pickwick emerged from his concealment, and presented himself amongst them.

"Ladies – dear ladies," said Mr Pickwick.

"Oh! he says we're dear," cried the oldest and ugliest teacher.

"Oh, the wretch!"

"Ladies," roared Mr Pickwick, rendered desperate by the danger of his situation. "Hear me. I am no robber. I want the lady of the house."

"Oh, what a ferocious monster!" screamed another teacher. "He wants Miss Tomkins."

Here there was a general scream.

"Ring the alarm bell, somebody!" cried a dozen voices.

"Don't – don't," shouted Mr Pickwick. "Look at me. Do I look like a robber! My dear ladies – you may bind me hand and leg, or lock me up in a closet, if you like. Only hear what I have got to say – only hear me."

"How did you come in our garden?" faltered the housemaid.

"Call the lady of the house, and I'll tell her everything," said Mr Pickwick, exerting his lungs to the utmost pitch. "Call her – only be quiet, and call her, and you shall hear everything ."

It might have been Mr Pickwick's appearance, or it might have been his manner, or it might have been the temptation – irresistible to a female mind – of hearing something enveloped in mystery, that reduced the more reasonable portion of the establishment (some four individuals) to a state of comparative quiet. By them it was proposed, as a test of Mr Pickwick's sincerity, that he should immediately submit to personal restraint; and that gentleman, having consented to hold a conference with Miss Tomkins, from the interior of a closet in which the day boarders hung their bonnets and sandwich-bags, he at once stepped into it, of his own accord, and was securely locked in. This revived the others; and Miss Tomkins having been brought to, and brought down, the conference began.

"What did you do in my garden, man?" said Miss Tomkins, in a faint voice.

"I came to warn you that one of your young ladies was going to elope to-night," replied Mr Pickwick, from the interior of the closet.

"Elope!" exclaimed Miss Tomkins, the three teachers, the thirty boarders, and the five servants. "Who with?"

"Your friend, Mr Charles Fitz-Marshall."

"My friend! I don't know any such person."

"Well, Mr Jingle, then."

"I never heard the name in my life."

"Then, I have been deceived, and deluded," said Mr Pickwick. "I have been the victim of a conspiracy – a foul and base conspiracy. Send to the Angel, my dear ma'am, if you don't believe me. Send to the Angel for Mr Pickwick's manservant, I implore you, ma'am."

"He must be respectable – he keeps a manservant," said Miss Tomkins to the governess.

"It's my opinion, Miss Tomkins," said the governess, "that his manservant keeps him. I think he's a madman, Miss Tomkins, and the other's his keeper."

"I think you are very right, Miss Gwynn," responded Miss Tomkins. "Let two of the servants repair to the Angel, and let the others remain here, to protect us."

So two of the servants were despatched to the Angel in search of Mr Samuel Weller; and the remaining three stopped behind to protect Miss Tomkins, and the three teachers, and the thirty boarders. And Mr Pickwick sat down in the closet, beneath a grove of sandwich-bags, and awaited the return of the messengers, with all the philosophy and fortitude he could summon to his aid.

An hour and a half elapsed before they came back, and when they did come, Mr Pickwick recognised, in addition to the voice of Mr Samuel Weller, two other voices, the tones of which struck familiarly on his ear; but whose they were, he could not for the life of him call to mind. A very brief conversation ensued. The door was unlocked.

Mr Pickwick stepped out of the closet, and found himself in the presence of the whole establishment of Westgate House, Mr Samuel Weller, and – old Wardle, and his destined son-in-law, Mr Trundle!

"My dear friend," said Mr Pickwick, running forward and grasping Wardle's hand, "my dear friend, pray, for Heaven's sake, explain to this lady the unfortunate and dreadful situation in which I am placed. You must have heard it from my servant; say, at all events, my dear fellow, that I am neither a robber nor a madman."

"I have said so, my dear friend. I have said so already," replied Mr Wardle, shaking the right hand of his friend, while Mr Trundle shook the left.

Mr Pickwick's explanation having already been partially made, was soon concluded. But neither in the course of his walk home with his friends, nor afterwards when seated before a blazing fire at the supper he so much needed, could a single observation be drawn from him. He seemed bewildered and amazed. Once, and only once, he turned round to Mr Wardle, and said –

"How did you come here?"

"Trundle and I came down here, for some good shooting on the first," replied Wardle. "We arrived to-night, and were astonished to hear from your servant that you were here too. But I am glad you are," said the old fellow, slapping him on the back – "I am glad you are. We shall have a jovial party on the first, and we'll give Winkle another chance – eh, old boy?"

Mr Pickwick made no reply, he did not even ask after his friends at Dingley Dell, and shortly afterwards retired for the night, desiring Sam to fetch his candle when he rung. The bell did ring in due course, and Mr Weller presented himself.

"Sam," said Mr Pickwick, looking out from under the bed-clothes.

"Sir," said Mr Weller.

Mr Pickwick paused, and Mr Weller snuffed the candle.

"Sam," said Mr Pickwick again, as if with a desperate effort.

"Sir," said Mr Weller, once more.

"Where is that Trotter?"

"Job, sir?"

"Yes.

"Gone, sir."

"With his master, I suppose?"

"Friend or master, or whatever he is, he's gone with him," replied Mr Weller. "There's a pair on 'em, sir."

"Jingle suspected my design, and set that fellow on you, with this story, I suppose?" said Mr Pickwick, half choking.

"Just that, sir," replied Mr Weller.

"It was all false, of course?"

"All, sir," replied Mr Weller. "Reg'lar do, sir; artful dodge."

"I don't think he'll escape us quite so easily the next time, Sam!" said Mr Pickwick.

"I don't think he will, sir."

"Whenever I meet that Jingle again, wherever it is," said Mr Pickwick, raising himself in bed, and indenting his pillow with a tremendous blow, "I'll inflict personal chastisement on him, in addition to the exposure he so richly merits. I will, or my name is not Pickwick."

"And venever I catches hold o' that there melan-cholly chap with the black hair," said Sam, "if I don't bring some real water into his eyes, for once in a way, my name ain't Weller. Good-night, sir!"

CHAPTER 10

Briefly Illustrative of the Force of Circumstances

His friends were ready, the coach was nearly so, and in half an hour they were proceeding on their journey, along the road over which Mr Pickwick and Sam had so recently travelled. Mr Weller was standing at the door of the Angel, ready to receive them, and by that gentleman they were ushered to the apartment of Mr Pickwick, where, to the no small surprise of Mr Winkle and Mr Snodgrass, and the no small embarrassment of Mr Tupman, they found old Wardle and Trundle.

"How are you?" said the old man, grasping Mr Tupman's hand. "Don't hang back, or look sentimental about it; it can't be helped, old fellow. For her sake, I wish you'd had her; for your own, I'm very glad you have not. A young fellow like you will do better one of these days, eh?" With this conclusion, Wardle slapped Mr Tupman on the back, and laughed heartily. "Well, and how are you, my fine fellows?" said the old gentleman, shaking hands with Mr Winkle and Mr Snodgrass at the same time. "I have just been telling Pickwick that we must have you all down at Christmas. We're going to have a wedding – a real wedding this time."

"A wedding!" exclaimed Mr Snodgrass, turning very pale.

"Yes, a wedding. But don't be frightened," said the good-humoured old man; "it's only Trundle there, and Bella."

"Oh, is that all?" said Mr Snodgrass, relieved from a painful doubt which had fallen heavily on his breast. "Give you joy, sir. How is Joe?"

"Very well," replied the old gentleman. "Sleepy as ever."

"Where," said Mr Tupman, with an effort – "where is – *she*, sir?" and he turned away his head, and covered his eyes with his hand.

"*She*!" said the old gentleman, with a knowing shake of the head. "Do you mean my single relative – eh?"

Mr Tupman, by a nod, intimated that his question applied to the disappointed Rachael.

"Oh, she's gone away," said the old gentleman. "She's living at a relation's, far enough off. She couldn't bear to see the girls, so I let her go. But come! Here's the dinner. You must be hungry after your ride. I am, without any ride at all; so let us fall to."

Ample justice was done to the meal; and when they were seated round the table, after it had been disposed of, Mr Pickwick, to the intense horror and indignation of his followers, related the adventure he had undergone, and the success which had attended the base artifices of the diabolical Jingle.

"And the attack of rheumatism which I caught in that garden," said Mr Pickwick, in conclusion, "renders me lame at this moment."

Mr Pickwick would in all probability have gone on for some time, had not the entrance of Sam, with a letter, caused him to break off in his eloquent discourse. He passed his handkerchief across his forehead, took off his spectacles, wiped them, and put them on again; and his voice had recovered its wonted softness of tone when he said –

"What have you there, Sam?"

"Called at the post-office just now, and found this here letter, as has laid there for two days," replied Mr Weller. "It's sealed vith a vafer, and directed in round hand."

"I don't know this hand," said Mr Pickwick, opening the letter. "Mercy on us! what's this? It must be a jest; it – it – can't be true."

"What's the matter?" was the general inquiry.

"Nobody dead, is there?" said Wardle, alarmed at the horror in Mr Pickwick's countenance.

Mr Pickwick made no reply, but, pushing the letter across the table, and desiring Mr Tupman to read it aloud, fell back in his chair with a look of vacant astonishment quite alarming to behold.

Mr Tupman, with a trembling voice, read the letter, of which the following is a copy: –

Freeman's Court, Cornhill,
August 28th, 1827.
Bardell against Pickwick.
Sir,

Having been instructed by Mrs Martha Bardell to commence an action against you for a breach of promise of marriage, for which the plaintiff lays her damages at fifteen hundred pounds, we beg to inform you that a writ has been issued against you in this suit in the Court of Common Pleas; and request to know, by return of post, the name of your attorney in London, who will accept service thereof.

We are, sir,
Your obedient servants,
Dodson & Fogg.
Mr Samuel Pickwick.

There was something so impressive in the mute astonishment with which each man regarded his neighbour, and every man regarded Mr Pickwick, that all seemed afraid to speak. The silence was at length broken by Mr Tupman.

"Dodson and Fogg," he repeated mechanically.

"Bardell and Pickwick," said Mr Snodgrass, musing.

"It's a conspiracy," said Mr Pickwick, at length recovering the power of speech; "a base conspiracy between these two grasping attorneys, Dodson and Fogg. Mrs Bardell would never do it; – she hasn't the heart to do it; – she hasn't the case to do it. Ridiculous – ridiculous."

"Of her heart," said Wardle, with a smile, "you should certainly be the best judge. I don't wish to discourage you, but I should certainly say that, of her case, Dodson and Fogg are far better judges than any of us can be."

"It's a vile attempt to extort money," said Mr Pickwick.

"I hope it is," said Wardle, with a short, dry cough.

"Who ever heard me address her in any way but that in which a lodger would address his landlady?" continued Mr Pickwick, with great vehemence. "Who ever saw me with her? Not even my friends here – "

"Except on one occasion," said Mr Tupman.

Mr Pickwick changed colour.

"Ah," said Mr Wardle. "Well, that's important. There was nothing suspicious then, I suppose?"

Mr Tupman glanced timidly at his leader. "Why," said he, "there was nothing suspicious; but – I don't know how it happened, mind – she certainly was reclining in his arms."

"Gracious powers!" ejaculated Mr Pickwick, as the recollection of the scene in question struck forcibly upon him; "what a dreadful instance of the force of circumstances! So she was – so she was."

"And our friend was soothing her anguish," said Mr Winkle, rather maliciously.

"So I was," said Mr Pickwick. "I don't deny it. So I was."

"Hallo!" said Wardle; "for a case in which there's nothing suspicious, this looks rather queer – eh, Pickwick? Ah, sly dog – sly dog!" and he laughed till the glasses on the sideboard rang again.

"What a dreadful conjunction of appearances!" exclaimed Mr Pickwick, resting his chin upon his hands. "Winkle – Tupman – we are all the victims of circumstances, and I the greatest." With this Mr Pickwick buried his head in his hands, and ruminated; while Wardle measured out a regular circle of nods and winks, addressed to the other members of the company.

"I'll have it explained, though," said Mr Pickwick, raising his head and hammering the table. "I'll see this Dodson and Fogg! I'll go to London to-morrow."

"Not to-morrow," said Wardle; "you're too lame."

"Well, then, next day."

"Next day is the first of September, and you're pledged to ride out with us, as far as Sir Geoffrey Manning's grounds at all events, and to meet us at lunch, if you don't take the field."

"Well, then, the day after," said Mr Pickwick; "Thursday. – Sam!"

"Sir," replied Mr Weller.

"Take two places outside to London, on Thursday morning, for yourself and me."

"Wery well, sir."

Mr Weller left the room, and departed slowly on his errand, with his hands in his pocket and his eyes fixed on the ground.

"Rum feller, the hemperor," said Mr Weller, as he walked slowly up the street. "Think o' his makin' up to that 'ere Mrs Bardell – vith a little boy, too! Always the vay vith these here old 'uns howsoever, as is such steady goers to look at. I didn't think he'd ha' done it, though – I didn't think he'd ha' done it!"

Moralising in this strain, Mr Samuel Weller bent his steps towards the booking-office.

CHAPTER 11

A Pleasant Day with an Unpleasant Termination

It was a fine morning – so fine that you would scarcely believe that the few months of an English summer had yet flown by. Everything bore the stamp of summer, and none of its beautiful colour had yet faded from the dye. Such was the morning, when an open carriage, in which were three Pickwickians (Mr Snodgrass having preferred to remain at home), Mr Wardle, and Mr Trundle, with Sam Weller on the box beside the driver, pulled up by a gate at the roadside, before which stood a tall, raw-boned gamekeeper, and a half-booted, leather-legginged boy, each bearing a bag of capacious dimensions, and accompanied by a brace of pointers.

"I say," whispered Mr Winkle to Wardle, as the man let down the steps, "they don't suppose we're going to kill game enough to fill those bags, do they?"

"Fill them!" exclaimed old Wardle. "Bless you, yes! You shall fill one, and I the other; and when we've done with them, the pockets of our shooting-jackets will hold as much more."

Mr Winkle dismounted without saying anything in reply to this observation; but he thought within himself, that if the party remained in the open air, till he had filled one of the bags, they stood a considerable chance of catching colds in their heads.

The tall gamekeeper replied in the affirmative, and looked with some surprise from Mr Winkle, who was holding his gun as if he wished his coat pocket to save him the trouble of pulling the trigger, to Mr Tupman, who was holding his as if he was afraid of it.

"My friends are not much in the way of this sort of thing yet, Martin," said Wardle, noticing the look. "Live and learn, you know. They'll be good shots one of these days. I beg my friend Winkle's pardon, though; he has had some practice."

Mr Winkle smiled feebly over his blue neckerchief in acknowledgement of the compliment, and got himself so mysteriously entangled with his gun, in his modest confusion, that if the piece had been loaded, he must inevitably have shot himself dead upon the spot.

"You mustn't handle your piece in that 'ere way, when you come to have the charge in it, sir," said the tall gamekeeper gruffly; "or I'm damned if you won't make cold meat of some on us."

Mr Winkle, thus admonished, abruptly altered his position, and in so doing, contrived to bring the barrel into pretty smart contact with Mr Weller's head.

"Hallo!" said Sam, picking up his hat, which had been knocked off, and rubbing his temple. "Hallo, sir! if you comes it this vay, you'll fill one o' them bags, and something to spare, at one fire." Here the leather-legginged boy laughed very heartily, and then tried to look as if it was somebody else, whereat Mr Winkle frowned majestically.

"Where did you tell the boy to meet us with the snack, Martin?" inquired Wardle.

"Side of One-tree Hill, at twelve o'clock, sir. It's Captain Boldwig's land; but there'll be nobody to interrupt us, and there's a fine bit of turf there."

"Very well," said old Wardle. "Now the sooner we're off the better. Will you join us at twelve, then, Pickwick?"

Mr Pickwick was particularly desirous to view the sport, the more especially as he was rather anxious in respect of Mr Winkle's life and limbs. On so inviting a morning, too, it was very tantalising to turn back, and leave his friends to enjoy themselves. It was, therefore, with a very rueful air that he replied –

"Why, I suppose I must."

"Ain't the gentleman a shot, sir?" inquired the long gamekeeper.

"No," replied Wardle; "and he's lame besides."

"I should very much like to go," said Mr Pickwick – "very much."

There was a short pause of commiseration.

"There's a barrow t'other side the hedge," said the boy. "If the gentleman's servant would wheel along the paths, he could keep nigh us, and we could lift it over the stiles, and that."

"The wery thing," said Mr Weller, who was a party interested, as he ardently longed to see the sport. "The wery thing. Well said, Smallcheek; I'll have it out in a minute."

Mr Pickwick was placed in it, and off the party set; Wardle and the long gamekeeper leading the way, and Mr Pickwick in the barrow, propelled by Sam, bringing up the rear.

"Stop, Sam," said Mr Pickwick, when they had got half across the first field.

"What's the matter now?" said Wardle.

"I won't suffer this barrow to be moved another step," said Mr Pickwick, resolutely, "unless Winkle carries that gun of his in a different manner."

"How am I to carry it?" said the wretched Winkle.

"Carry it with the muzzle to the ground," replied Mr Pickwick.

"It's so unsportsmanlike," reasoned Winkle.

"I don't care whether it's unsportsmanlike or not," replied Mr Pickwick; "I am not going to be shot in a wheel-barrow, for the sake of appearances, to please anybody."

"I know the gentleman'll put that 'ere charge into somebody afore he's done," growled the long man.

"Well, well – I don't mind," said poor Winkle, turning his gun-stock uppermost – "there."

"Anythin' for a quiet life," said Mr Weller; and on they went again.

"Stop!" said Mr Pickwick, after they had gone a few yards farther.

"What now?" said Wardle.

"That gun of Tupman's is not safe: I know it isn't," said Mr Pickwick.

"Eh? What! not safe?" said Mr Tupman, in a tone of great alarm.

"Not as you are carrying it," said Mr Pickwick. "I am very sorry to make any further objection, but I cannot consent to go on, unless you carry it as Winkle does his."

"I think you had better, sir," said the long gamekeeper, "or you're quite as likely to lodge the charge in yourself as in anything else."

Mr Tupman, with the most obliging haste, placed his piece in the position required, and the party moved on again; the two amateurs marching with reversed arms, like a couple of privates at a royal funeral.

There was a sharp whirring noise, that made Mr Winkle start back as if he had been shot himself. Bang, bang, went a couple of guns – the smoke swept quickly away over the field, and curled into the air.

"Where are they?" said Mr Winkle, in a state of the highest excitement, turning round and round in all directions. "Where are they? Tell me when to fire. Where are they – where are they?"

"Where are they!" said Wardle, taking up a brace of birds which the dogs had deposited at his feet. "Why, here they are."

"No, no; I mean the others," said the bewildered Winkle.

"Far enough off, by this time," replied Wardle, coolly reloading his gun.

"We shall very likely be up with another covey in five minutes," said the long gamekeeper. "If the gentleman begins to fire now, perhaps he'll just get the shot out of the barrel by the time they rise."

"Ha! ha! ha!" roared Mr Weller.

"Brave old fellow!" said Wardle to Mr Tupman; "you fired that time, at all events."

"Oh, yes," replied Mr Tupman, with conscious pride. "I let it off."

"Well done. You'll hit something next time, if you look sharp. Very easy, ain't it?"

"Yes, it's very easy," said Mr Tupman. "How it hurts one's shoulder, though. It nearly knocked me backwards. I had no idea these small firearms kicked so."

"Ah," said the old gentleman, smiling, "you'll get used to it in time. Now then – all ready – all right with the barrow there?"

"All right, sir," replied Mr Weller.

"Come along, then."

"Hold hard, sir," said Sam, raising the barrow.

"Aye, aye," replied Mr Pickwick; and on they went, as briskly as need be.

"Keep that barrow back now," cried Wardle, when it had been hoisted over a stile into another field, and Mr Pickwick had been deposited in it once more.

"All right, sir," replied Mr Weller, pausing.

"Now, Winkle," said the old gentleman, "follow me softly, and don't be too late this time."

"Never fear," said Mr Winkle. "Are they pointing?"

"Quietly now, quietly." On they crept, and very quietly they would have advanced, if Mr Winkle, in the performance of some very intricate evolutions with his gun, had not accidentally fired, at the most critical moment.

"Why, what on earth did you do that for?" said old Wardle, as the birds flew unharmed away.

"I never saw such a gun in my life," replied poor Mr Winkle, looking at the lock, as if that would do any good. "It goes off of its own accord. It *will* do it."

"Will do it!" echoed Wardle, with something of irritation in his manner. "I wish it would kill something of its own accord."

"It'll do that afore long, sir," observed the tall man, in a low, prophetic voice. "Load again, sir, load again."

"Take away his gun," cried Mr Pickwick from the barrow, horror-stricken at the long man's dark insinuations. "Take away his gun, do you hear, somebody?"

Nobody, however, volunteered to obey the command; and Mr Winkle, after darting a rebellious glance at Mr Pickwick, reloaded his gun, and proceeded onwards with the rest.

Mr Tupman's process, like many of our most sublime discoveries, was extremely simple. With the quickness and penetration of a man of genius, he had at once observed that the two great points to be attained were – first, to discharge his piece without injury to himself, and, secondly, to do so, without danger to the bystanders – obviously, the best thing to do, after surmounting the difficulty of firing at all, was to shut his eyes firmly, and fire into the air.

On one occasion, after performing this feat, Mr Tupman, on opening his eyes, beheld a plump partridge in the act of falling, wounded, to the ground. He was on the point of congratulating Mr Wardle on his invariable success, when that gentleman advanced towards him, and grasped him warmly by the hand.

"Tupman," said the old gentleman, "you singled out that particular bird?"

"No," said Mr Tupman – "no."

"You did," said Wardle. "I saw you do it – I observed you pick him out – I noticed you, as you raised your piece to take aim; and I will say this, that the best shot in existence could not have done it more beautifully. You are an older hand at this than I thought you, Tupman; you have been out before."

It was in vain for Mr Tupman to protest, with a smile of self-denial, that he never had. The very smile was taken as evidence to the contrary; and from that time forth his reputation was established.

Meanwhile, Mr Winkle flashed, and blazed, and smoked away, without producing any material results worthy of being noted down. As a display of fancy-shooting, it was extremely varied and curious; as an exhibition of firing with any precise object, it was, upon the whole, perhaps a failure.

"Well," said Wardle, walking up to the side of the barrow, and wiping the streams of perspiration from his jolly red face; "smoking day, isn't it?"

"It is, indeed," replied Mr Pickwick. The sun is tremendously hot, even to me. I don't know how you must feel it."

"Why," said the old gentleman, "pretty hot. It's past twelve, though. You see that green hill there?"

"Certainly."

"That's the place where we are to lunch; and, by Jove, there's the boy with the basket, punctual as clockwork!"

"So he is," said Mr Pickwick, brightening up. "Good boy, that. I'll give him a shilling, presently. Now, then, Sam, wheel away."

"Hold on, sir," said Mr Weller, invigorated with the prospect of refreshments. "Out of the vay, young leathers." And quickening his pace to a sharp run, Mr Weller wheeled his master nimbly to the green hill, shot him dexterously out by the very side of the basket, and proceeded to unpack it with the utmost despatch.

"Weal pie," said Mr Weller, soliloquising, as he arranged the eatables

86

on the grass. "Wery good thing is weal pie, when you know the lady as made it, and is quite sure it ain't kittens."

Mr Weller continued his occupation of emptying the basket. "Tongue – well that's a wery good thing when it ain't a woman's. Bread – knuckle o' ham, reg'lar picter – cold beef in slices, wery good. What's in them stone jars, young touch-and-go?"

"Beer in this one," replied the boy, taking from his shoulder a couple of large stone bottles, fastened together by a leathern strap – "cold punch in t'other."

"And a wery good notion of a lunch it is, take it altogether," said Mr Weller, surveying his arrangement of the repast with great satisfaction. "Now, gen'l'm'n, 'fall on,' as the English said to the French when they fixed bagginets."

It needed no second invitation to induce the party to yield full justice to the meal.

"This is delightful – thoroughly delightful!" said Mr Pickwick; the skin of whose expressive countenance was rapidly peeling off, with exposure to the sun.

"So it is – so it is, old fellow," replied Wardle. "Come; a glass of punch!"

"Good," said Mr Pickwick, smacking his lips. "Very good. I'll take another. Cool; very cool. Come, gentlemen," continued Mr Pickwick, still retaining his hold upon the jar, "a toast. Our friends at Dingley Dell."

The toast was drunk with loud acclamations.

"Well, that certainly is most capital cold punch," said Mr Pickwick, looking earnestly at the stone bottle; "and the day is extremely warm, and – Tupman, my dear friend, a glass of punch?"

"With the greatest delight," replied Mr Tupman; and having drank that glass, Mr Pickwick took another. This constant succession of glasses produced considerable effect upon Mr Pickwick; his countenance beamed with the most sunny smiles, laughter played around his lips, and good-humoured merriment twinkled in his eye. Yielding by degrees to the influence of the exciting liquid, rendered more so by the heat, Mr Pickwick, after rising to his legs to address the company in an eloquent speech, he fell into the barrow, and fast asleep.

The basket having been repacked, and it being found perfectly impossible to awaken Mr Pickwick from his torpor, it was determined to leave Mr Pickwick asleep in the barrow, and to call for him on their return. So away they went, leaving Mr Pickwick snoring most comfortably in the shade.

Mr Pickwick had not been asleep half an hour when little Captain Boldwig, followed by the two gardeners, came striding along as fast as his size and importance would let him; and when he came near the oak tree, Captain Boldwig paused and drew a long breath.

"Well, Wilkins, what's the matter with you?" said Captain Boldwig.

"I beg your pardon, sir – but I think there have been trespassers here to-day."

"Ha!" said the captain, scowling around him.

"Yes, sir – they have been dining here, I think, sir."

"Why, damn their audacity, so they have," said Captain Boldwig, as the crumbs and fragments that were strewn upon the grass met his eye. "They have actually been devouring their food here. I wish I had the vagabonds here!" said the captain, clenching the thick stick.

"Beg your pardon, sir," said Wilkins, "but – "

"But what? Eh?" roared the captain; and following the timid glance of Wilkins, his eyes encountered the wheel-barrow and Mr Pickwick.

"Who are you, you rascal?" said the captain, administering several pokes to Mr Pickwick's body with the thick stick. "What's your name?"

"Cold punch," murmured Mr Pickwick, as he sank to sleep again.

"What?" demanded Captain Boldwig.

No reply.

"What did he say his name was?" asked the captain.

"Punch, I think, sir," replied Wilkins.

"That's his impudence – that's his confounded impudence," said Captain Boldwig. "He's drunk. Wheel him away, Wilkins, wheel him away directly."

"Where shall I wheel him to, sir?" inquired Wilkins, with great timidity.

"Wheel him," said the captain – "wheel him to the pound; and let us see whether he calls himself Punch when he comes to himself. He shall not bully me – he shall not bully me. Wheel him away."

Away Mr Pickwick was wheeled in compliance with this imperious mandate; and the great Captain Boldwig, swelling with indignation, proceeded on his walk.

Inexpressible was the astonishment of the little party when they returned, to find that Mr Pickwick had disappeared, and taken the wheel-barrow with him. They searched every nook and corner round, together and separately; they shouted, whistled, called – and all with the same result. Mr Pickwick was not to be found. After some hours of fruitless search, they arrived at the unwelcome conclusion that they must go home without him.

Meanwhile Mr Pickwick had been wheeled to the pound, and safely deposited therein, fast asleep in the wheel-barrow, to the immeasurable delight and satisfaction not only of all the boys in the village, but three-fourths of the whole population, who had gathered round, in expectation of his waking. If their most intense gratification had been awakened by seeing him wheeled in, how many hundredfold was their joy increased when, after a few indistinct cries of "Sam!" he sat up in the barrow, and gazed with indescribable astonishment on the faces before him.

A general shout was of course the signal of his having woke up; and his involuntary inquiry of "What's the matter?" occasioned another, louder than the first, if possible.

"Here's a game!" roared the populace.

"Where am I?" exclaimed Mr Pickwick.

"In the pound," replied the mob.

"How came I here? What was I doing? Where was I brought from?"

"Boldwig! Captain Boldwig!" was the only reply.

"Let me out," cried Mr Pickwick. "Where's my servant? Where are my friends?"

"You ain't got no friends. Hurrah!" Then there came a turnip, then a potato, and then an egg; with a few other little tokens of the playful disposition of the many-headed.

How long this scene might have lasted, or how much Mr Pickwick might have suffered, no one can tell, had not a carriage, which was driving swiftly by, suddenly pulled up, from whence there descended old Wardle and Sam Weller, the former of whom, in far less time than it takes to read it, had made his way to Mr Pickwick's side, and placed him in the vehicle, just as the latter had concluded the third and last round of a single combat with the town-beadle.

"I'll give directions for the commencement of an action for false imprisonment against this Captain Boldwig, directly I get to London," said Mr Pickwick, as soon as the carriage turned out of the town.

"We were trespassing, it seems," said Wardle.

"I don't care," said Mr Pickwick, "I'll bring the action."

"No, you won't," said Wardle.

"I will, by – " But as there was a humorous expression in Wardle's face, Mr Pickwick checked himself, and said, "Why not?"

"Because," said old Wardle, half-bursting with laughter, "because they might turn on some of us, and say we had taken too much cold punch."

Do what he would, a smile would come into Mr Pickwick's face; the smile extended into a laugh; the laugh into a roar; the roar became general. So, to keep up their good-humour, they stopped at the first roadside tavern they came to, and ordered a glass of brandy-and-water all round, with a magnum of extra strength for Mr Samuel Weller.

CHAPTER 12

Showing How Dodson and Fogg were Men of Business, and How an Affecting Interview Took Place Between Mr Weller and his Long-Lost Parent

The clerks' office of Messrs Dodson & Fogg was a dark, mouldy, earthy-smelling room, with a high partition to screen the clerks from the vulgar gaze, a couple of old wooden chairs, a very loud-ticking clock, an almanac, an umbrella-stand, a row of hat-pegs, and a few shelves, on which were deposited several ticketed bundles of dirty papers. There was a glass door leading into the passage which formed the entrance to the court, and on the outer side of this glass door, Mr Pickwick, closely followed by Sam Weller, presented himself on the Friday morning succeeding the occurrence given in the last chapter.

"Come in, can't you!" cried a voice from behind the partition, in reply to Mr Pickwick's gentle tap at the door. And Mr Pickwick and Sam entered accordingly.

"Mr Dodson or Mr Fogg at home, sir?" inquired Mr Pickwick, gently, advancing, hat in hand, towards the partition and at the same time a head, with a pen behind its ear, looked over the partition, and at Mr Pickwick.

"Mr Dodson ain't at home, and Mr Fogg's particularly engaged," said the man to whom the head belonged.

"When will Mr Dodson be back, sir?" inquired Mr Pickwick.

"Can't say."

"Will it be long before Mr Fogg is disengaged, sir?"

"Don't know."

Here the man proceeded to mend his pen with great deliberation.

"I think I'll wait," said Mr Pickwick.

There was no reply; so Mr Pickwick sat down unbidden, and listened to the loud ticking of the clock and the murmured conversation of the clerks.

Mr Pickwick coughed to attract the attention of the young gentlemen behind the partition, who, having now relaxed their minds by a little conversation among themselves, condescended to take some notice of the stranger.

"I wonder whether Fogg's disengaged now?" said Jackson.

"I'll see," said Wicks, dismounting leisurely from his stool.

"What name shall I tell Mr Fogg?"

"Pickwick," replied the illustrious subject of these memoirs.

Mr Jackson departed upstairs on his errand, and immediately returned with a message that Mr Fogg would see Mr Pickwick in five minutes; and having delivered it, returned again to his desk.

"What did he say his name was?" whispered Wicks.

"Pickwick," replied Jackson; "it's the defendant in Bardell and Pickwick."

A sudden scraping of feet, mingled with the sound of suppressed laughter, was heard from behind the partition.

"They're a-twiggin' of you, sir," whispered Mr Weller.

"Twigging of me, Sam!" replied Mr Pickwick; "what do you mean by twigging me?"

Mr Weller replied by pointing with his thumb over his shoulder, and Mr Pickwick, on looking up, became sensible of the pleasing fact, that all the four clerks, with countenances expressive of the utmost amusement, and with their heads thrust over the wooden screen, were minutely inspecting the figure and general appearance of the supposed trifler with female hearts, and disturber of female happiness.

A sudden ring at the bell which hung in the office, summoned Mr Jackson to the apartment of Fogg, from whence he came back to say that Fogg was ready to see Mr Pickwick if he would step upstairs. Upstairs Mr

Pickwick did step accordingly, leaving Sam Weller below. Jackson ushered Mr Pickwick into the presence.

"Is Mr Dodson in?" inquired Mr Fogg.

"Just come in, sir," replied Jackson.

"Ask him to step here."

"Yes, sir." Exit Jackson.

After a few minutes' silence, Mr Dodson, a plump, portly, stern-looking man, with a loud voice, appeared; and the conversation commenced.

"This is Mr Pickwick," said Fogg.

"Ah! You are the defendant, sir, in Bardell and Pickwick?" said Dodson.

"I am, sir," replied Mr Pickwick.

"Well, sir," said Dodson, "and what do you propose?"

"Ah!" said Fogg, thrusting his hands into his trousers' pockets, and throwing himself back in his chair, "what do you propose, Mr Pickwick?"

"Hush, Fogg," said Dodson, "let me hear what Mr Pickwick has to say."

"I came, gentlemen," said Mr Pickwick, gazing placidly on the two partners, "I came here, gentlemen, to express the surprise with which I received your letter of the other day, and to inquire what grounds of action you can have against me."

"Grounds of – " Fogg had ejaculated this much, when he was stopped by Dodson.

"Mr Fogg," said Dodson, "I am going to speak."

"I beg your pardon, Mr Dodson," said Fogg.

"For the grounds of action, sir," continued Dodson, with moral elevation in his air, "you will consult your own conscience and your own feelings. We, sir, we, are guided entirely by the statement of our client."

"Well, sir," said Mr Pickwick, with considerable pain depicted in his countenance, "you will permit me to assure you that I am a most unfortunate man, so far as this case is concerned."

"I hope you are, sir," replied Dodson; "I trust you may be, sir. If you are really innocent of what is laid to your charge, you are more unfortunate than I had believed any man could possibly be. What do you say, Mr Fogg?"

"I say precisely what you say," replied Fogg, with a smile of incredulity.

"The writ, sir, which commences the action," continued Dodson, "was issued regularly. Mr Fogg, where is the book?"

"Here it is," said Fogg, handing over a square book, with a parchment cover.

"Here is the entry," resumed Dodson. "'Middlesex, Capias *Martha Bardell, Widow, v. Samuel Pickwick*. Damages £1500. Dodson & Fogg for the plaintiff, Aug. 28, 1827.' All regular, sir; perfectly." Dodson coughed and looked at Fogg, who said "Perfectly," also. And then they both looked at Mr Pickwick.

"I am to understand, then," said Mr Pickwick, "that it really is your intention to proceed with this action?"

"Understand, sir! – that you certainly may," replied Dodson, with something as near a smile as his importance would allow.

"And that the damages are actually laid at fifteen hundred pounds?" said Mr Pickwick.

"I believe Mrs Bardell specially said," observed Fogg, glancing at Dodson, "that she would not compromise for a farthing less."

"As you offer no terms, sir," said Dodson, displaying a slip of parchment in his right hand, and affectionately pressing a paper copy of it, on Mr Pickwick with his left, "I had better serve you with a copy of this writ, sir. Here is the original, sir."

"Very well, gentlemen, very well," said Mr Pickwick, rising in person and wrath at the same time; "you shall hear from my solicitor, gentlemen."

"We shall be very happy to do so," said Fogg, rubbing his hands.

"Very," said Dodson, opening the door.

"And before I go, gentlemen," said the excited Mr Pickwick, turning round on the landing, "permit me to say, that of all the disgraceful and rascally proceedings – "

"Stay, sir, stay," interposed Dodson, with great politeness. "Mr Jackson! Mr Wicks!"

"Sir," said the two clerks, appearing at the bottom of the stairs.

"I merely want you to hear what this gentleman says," replied Dodson. "Pray, go on, sir – disgraceful and rascally proceedings, I think you said?"

"I did," said Mr Pickwick, thoroughly roused. "I said, sir, that of all the disgraceful and rascally proceedings that ever were attempted, this is the most so. I repeat it, sir."

"You hear that, Mr Wicks," said Dodson.

"You won't forget these expressions, Mr Jackson?" said Fogg.

"Perhaps you would like to call us swindlers, sir," said Dodson.

"Pray do, sir, if you feel disposed; now pray do, sir."

"I do," said Mr Pickwick. "You *are* swindlers."

"Very good," said Dodson. "You can hear down there, I hope, Mr Wicks?"

"Oh, yes, sir," said Wicks.

"You had better come up a step or two higher, if you can't," added Mr Fogg. "Go on, sir; do go on. You had better call us thieves, sir; or perhaps You would like to assault one *of us*. Pray do it, sir, if you would; we will not make the smallest resistance. Pray do it, sir."

As Fogg put himself very temptingly within the reach of Mr Pickwick's clenched fist, there is little doubt that that gentleman would have complied with his earnest entreaty, but for the interposition of Sam, who, hearing the dispute, emerged from the office, mounted the stairs, and seized his master by the arm.

"You just come away," said Mr Weller. "Battledore and shuttlecock's a wery good game, vhen you ain't the shuttlecock and two lawyers the battledores, in which case it gets too excitin' to be pleasant. Come avay, sir. If you want to ease your mind by blowing up somebody, come out into the court and blow up me; but it's rayther too expensive work to be carried on here."

And without the slightest ceremony, Mr Weller hauled his master down the stairs, and down the court, and having safely deposited him in Cornhill, fell behind, prepared to follow whithersoever he should lead.

His master turned round, and said –

"Sam, I will go immediately to Mr Perker's."

"That's just exactly the wery place vere you ought to have gone last night, sir," replied Mr Weller.

"I think it is, Sam," said Mr Pickwick.

"I *know* it is," said Mr Weller.

"Well, well, Sam," replied Mr Pickwick, "we will go there at once; but first, as I have been rather ruffled, I should like a glass of brandy-and-water warm, Sam. Where can I have it, Sam?"

Mr Weller replied, without the slightest consideration – "Second court on the right hand side – last house but vun on the same side."

Mr Pickwick observed his valet's directions implicitly, and bidding Sam follow him, entered the tavern he had pointed out, where the hot brandy-and-water was speedily placed before him; while Mr Weller, seated at a respectful distance, though at the same table with his master, was accommodated with a pint of porter.

The room was one of a very homely description, and was apparently under the especial patronage of stage-coachmen; for several gentleman, who had all the appearance of belonging to that learned profession, were drinking and smoking in the different boxes. Among the number was one stout, red-faced, elderly man, in particular, seated in an opposite box, who attracted Mr Pickwick's attention. The stout man was smoking with great vehemence, but between every half-dozen puffs, he took his pipe from his mouth, and looked first at Mr Weller and then at Mr Pickwick. The stout man having blown a thick cloud from his pipe, a hoarse voice, like some strange effort of ventriloquism, emerged from beneath the capacious shawls which muffled his throat and chest, and slowly uttered these sounds –

"Wy, Sammy!"

"Who's that, Sam?" inquired Mr Pickwick.

"Why, I wouldn't ha' believed it, sir," replied Mr Weller, with astonished eyes. "It's the old 'un."

"Old one," said Mr Pickwick. "What old one?"

"My father, sir," replied Mr Weller. "How are you, my ancient?"

Mr Weller made room on the seat beside him, for the stout man, who advanced pipe in mouth and pot in hand, to greet him.

"Wy, Sammy," said the father, "I ha'n't seen you, for two year and better."

"Nor more you have, old codger," replied the son. "How's mother-in-law?"

The elder Mr Weller shook his head, as he replied with a sigh, "Take example by your father, my boy, and be wery careful o' widders all your life, 'specially if they've kept a public-house, Sammy." Having delivered this parental advice with great pathos, Mr Weller, senior, refilled his pipe from a tin box he carried in his pocket; and, lighting his fresh pipe from the ashes of the old one, commenced smoking at a great rate.

"Beg your pardon, sir," he said, renewing the subject, and

addressing Mr Pickwick, after a considerable pause, "nothin' personal, I hope, sir; I hope you ha'n't got a widder, sir."

"Not I," replied Mr Pickwick, laughing; and while Mr Pickwick laughed, Sam Weller informed his parent in a whisper, of the relation in which he stood towards that gentleman.

"Beg your pardon, sir," said Mr Weller, senior, taking off his hat, "I hope you've no fault to find with Sammy, sir?"

"None whatever," said Mr Pickwick.

"Wery glad to hear it, sir," replied the old man; "I took a good deal o' pains with his eddication, sir; let him run in the streets when he was wery young, and shift for hisself. It's the only way to make a boy sharp, sir."

"Rather a dangerous process, I should imagine," said Mr Pickwick, with a smile.

"And not a wery sure one, neither," added Mr Weller; "I got reg'larly done the other day."

"No!" said his father.

"I did," said the son; and he proceeded to relate, in as few words as possible, how he had fallen a ready dupe to the stratagems of Job Trotter.

Mr Weller, senior, listened to the tale with the most profound attention, and, at its termination, said –

"Worn't one o' these chaps slim and tall, with long hair, and the gift o' the gab wery gallopin'?"

Mr Pickwick did not quite understand the last item of description, but, comprehending the first, said "Yes," at a venture.

"T'other's a black-haired chap in mulberry livery, with a wery large head?"

"Yes, yes, he is," said Mr Pickwick and Sam, with great earnestness.

"Then I know where they are, and that's all about it," said Mr Weller; "they're at Ipswich, safe enough, them two."

"No!" said Mr Pickwick.

"Fact," said Mr Weller, "and I'll tell you how I know it. I work an Ipswich coach now and then for a friend o' mine. I worked own the wery day arter the night as you caught the rheumatic, and I took 'em up, right through to Ipswich, where the man-servant – him in the mulberries – told me they was a-goin' to put up for a long time."

"I'll follow him," said Mr Pickwick; "we may as well see Ipswich as any other place. I'll follow him."

"You're quite certain it was them, governor?" inquired Mr Weller, junior.

"Quite, Sammy, quite," replied his father, "for their appearance is wery sing'ler; besides that 'ere, I wondered to see the gen'l'm'n so formiliar with his servant; and, more than that, as they sat in the front, right behind the box, I heerd 'em laughing and saying how they'd done old Fireworks."

"Old who?" said Mr Pickwick.

"Old Fireworks, sir; by which, I've no doubt, they meant you, sir."

There is nothing positively vile or atrocious in the appellation of "old Fireworks," but still it is by no means a respectful or flattering designation. The recollection of all the wrongs he had sustained at Jingle's hands, had crowded on Mr Pickwick's mind, the moment Mr Weller began to speak; it wanted but a feather to turn the scale, and "old Fireworks" did it.

"I'll follow him," said Mr Pickwick, with an emphatic blow on the table.

"I shall work down to Ipswich the day arter to-morrow, sir," said Mr Weller the elder, "from the Bull in Whitechapel; and if you really mean to go, you'd better go with me."

"So we had," said Mr Pickwick; "very true; I can write to Bury, and tell them to meet me at Ipswich. We will go with you. But don't hurry away, Mr Weller; won't you take anything?"

"You're wery good, sir," replied Mr W., stopping short; – "perhaps a small glass of brandy to drink your health, and success to Sammy, sir, wouldn't be amiss."

"Certainly not," replied Mr Pickwick. "A glass of brandy here!" The brandy was brought; and Mr Weller, after pulling his hair to Mr Pickwick, and nodding to Sam, jerked it down his capacious throat as if it had been a small thimbleful.

Mr Pickwick, after settling the reckoning, resumed his walk to Gray's Inn. By the time he reached its secluded groves, however, eight o'clock had struck, and the unbroken stream of gentlemen in muddy high-lows, soiled white hats, and rusty apparel, who were pouring towards the different avenues of egress, warned him that the majority of the offices had closed for that day.

"This is pleasant, Sam," said Mr Pickwick; "I shouldn't lose an hour in seeing Mr Perker; I shall not be able to get one wink of sleep to-night, I know, unless I have the satisfaction of reflecting that I have confided this matter to a professional man."

"Here's an old 'ooman comin' upstairs, sir," replied Mr Weller; "p'raps she knows where we can find somebody. Hallo, old lady, vere's Mr Perker's people?"

"Mr Perker's people," said a thin, miserable-looking old woman, stopping to recover breath after the ascent of the staircase – "Mr Perker's people's gone, and I'm a-goin' to do the office out."

"Are you Mr Perker's servant?" inquired Mr Pickwick.

"I am Mr Perker's laundress," replied the woman.

"Do you know where I can find Mr Perker, my good woman?"

"No, I don't," replied the old woman gruffly; "he's out o' town now."

"That's unfortunate," said Mr Pickwick; "where's his clerk? Do you know?"

"Yes, I know where he is, but he won't thank me for telling you," replied the laundress.

"I have very particular business with him," said Mr Pickwick.

"Won't it do in the morning?" said the woman.

"Not so well," replied Mr Pickwick.

"Well," said the old woman, "if it was anything very particular, I was to say where he was, so I suppose there's no harm in telling. If you just go to the Magpie and Stump, and ask at the bar for Mr Lowten, they'll show you in to him, and he's Mr Perker's clerk."

Mr Pickwick and Sam descended the rickety staircase in safety, and issued forth in quest of the Magpie and Stump.

On Mr Pickwick's presenting himself at the bar, an elderly female emerged from behind the screen therein, and presented herself before him.

"Is Mr Lowten here, ma'am?" inquired Mr Pickwick.

"Yes, he is, sir," replied the landlady. "Here, Charley, show the gentleman in to Mr Lowten."

Mr Pickwick, after desiring Sam to solace himself in the tap-room, suffered himself to be conducted into the presence of Mr Lowten.

At the announcement of "A gentleman to speak to you, sir," a puffy-faced young man, who filled the chair at the head of the table, looked with some surprise when his eyes rested on an individual whom he had never seen before.

"I beg your pardon, sir," said Mr Pickwick, "and I am very sorry to disturb the other gentlemen, too, but I come on very particular business; and if you will suffer me to detain you at this end of the room for five minutes, I shall be very much obliged to you."

The puffy-faced young man rose, and drawing a chair close to Mr Pickwick in an obscure corner of the room, listened attentively to his tale of woe.

"Ah," he said, when Mr Pickwick had concluded, "Dodson and Fogg – sharp practice theirs – capital men of business, Dodson and Fogg, sir."

Mr Pickwick admitted the sharp practice of Dodson and Fogg, and Lowten resumed.

"Perker ain't in town, and he won't be, neither, before the end of next week; but if you want the action defended, and will leave the copy with me, I can do all that's needful till he comes back."

"That's exactly what I came here for," said Mr Pickwick, handing over the document. "If anything particular occurs, you can write to me at the post-office, Ipswich."

"That's all right," replied Mr Perker's clerk; and then seeing Mr Pickwick's eye wandering curiously towards the table, he added, "will you join us, for half an hour or so? We are capital company here to-night."

Mr Pickwick could not resist so tempting an opportunity of studying human nature. He suffered himself to be led to the table, where, after having been introduced to the company in due form, he was accommodated with a seat near the chairman and called for a glass of his favourite beverage.

CHAPTER 13

Mr Pickwick Journeys to Ipswich and Meets with a Romantic Adventure with a Middle-aged Lady in Yellow Curl-papers

"That 'ere your governor's luggage, Sammy?" inquired Mr Weller of his affectionate son, as he entered the yard of the Bull Inn, Whitechapel, with a travelling-bag and a small portmanteau.

"You might ha' made a worser guess than that, old feller," replied Mr

Weller the younger, setting down his burden in the yard, and sitting himself down upon it afterwards. "The governor hisself'll be down here presently."

As Mr Weller spoke, Mr Pickwick dismounted from a cab, and entered the yard.

"Fine mornin', sir," said Mr Weller, senior.

"Beautiful indeed," replied Mr Pickwick.

"Beautiful indeed," echoed a red-haired man with an inquisitive nose and green spectacles, who had unpacked himself from a cab at the same moment as Mr Pickwick. "Going to Ipswich, sir?"

"I am," replied Mr Pickwick.

"Extraordinary coincidence. So am I."

Mr Pickwick bowed.

"Going outside?" said the red-haired man.

Mr Pickwick bowed again.

"Bless my soul, how remarkable – I am going outside, too," said the red-haired man; "we are positively going together." And the red-haired man, who was an important-looking, sharp-nosed, personage, with a bird-like habit of giving his head a jerk every time he said anything, smiled as if he had made one of the strangest discoveries that ever fell to the lot of human wisdom.

"I am happy in the prospect of your company, sir," said Mr Pickwick.

"Ah," said the new-comer, "it's a good thing for both of us, isn't it? Company, you see – company – is – is – it's a very different thing from solitude – ain't it? What's your name, sir?"

"Here is my card, sir," replied Mr Pickwick, much amused by the abruptness of the question, and the singular manner of the stranger.

"Ah," said the red-haired man, placing the card in his pocket-book, "Pickwick; very good. I like to know a man's name, it saves so much trouble. That's my card, sir. Magnus, you will perceive, sir – Magnus is my name. It's rather a good name, I think, sir."

"A very good name, indeed," said Mr Pickwick, wholly unable to repress a smile.

"Yes, I think it is," resumed Mr Magnus. "There's a good name before it, too, you will observe. Permit me, sir – if you hold the card a little slanting, this way, you catch the light upon the up-stroke. There – Peter Magnus – sounds well, I think, sir."

"Very," said Mr Pickwick.

"Curious circumstance about those initials, sir," said Mr Magnus. "You will observe – P.M. – post meridian. In hasty notes to intimate acquaintance, I sometimes sign myself 'Afternoon.' It amuses my friends very much, Mr Pickwick."

"It is calculated to afford them the highest gratification, I should conceive," said Mr Pickwick, rather envying the ease with which Mr Magnus's friends were entertained.

"Now, gen'l'm'n," said the hostler, "coach is ready, if you please."

"Is all my luggage in?" inquired Mr Magnus.

"All right, sir."

"Is the red bag in?"

"All right, sir."

"And the striped bag?"

"Fore boot, sir."

"And the brown-paper parcel?"

"Under the seat, sir."

"And the leather hat-box?"

"They're all in, sir."

"Now, will you get up?" said Mr Pickwick.

"Excuse me," replied Magnus, standing on the wheel. "Excuse me, Mr Pickwick. I cannot consent to get up, in this state of uncertainty. I am quite satisfied from that man's manner, that the leather hat-box is not in."

The solemn protestations of the hostler being wholly unavailing, the leather hat-box was obliged to be raked up from the lowest depth of the boot, to satisfy him that it had been safely packed; and after he had been assured on this head, he felt a solemn presentiment, first, that the red bag was mislaid, and next that the striped bag had been stolen, and then that the brown-paper parcel "had come untied." At length when he had received ocular demonstration of the groundless nature of each and every of these suspicions, he consented to climb up to the roof of the coach, observing that now he had taken everything off his mind, he felt quite comfortable and happy. And away went the coach up Whitechapel, to the admiration of the whole population of that pretty densely populated quarter.

Topics of conversation were never wanting, for even when any pause occurred in Mr Weller's loquacity, it was abundantly supplied by the desire of Mr Magnus to make himself acquainted with the whole of the personal history of his fellow-travellers, and his loudly-expressed anxiety at every stage, respecting the safety and well-being of the two bags, the leather hat-box, and the brown-paper parcel.

In the main street of Ipswich, on the left-hand side of the way, stands an inn known far and wide by the appellation of the Great White Horse, rendered the more conspicuous by a stone statue of some rampacious animal with flowing mane and tail, distantly resembling an insane cart-horse, which is elevated above the principal door.

It was at the door of this overgrown tavern that the London coach stopped, at the same hour every evening; and it was from this same London coach that Mr Pickwick, Sam Weller, and Mr Peter Magnus dismounted.

"Do you stop here, sir?" inquired Mr Peter Magnus, when the striped bag, and the red bag, and the brown-paper parcel, and the leather hat-box, had all been deposited in the passage.

"I do," said Mr Pickwick.

"Dear me," said Mr Magnus, "I never knew anything like these extraordinary coincidences. Why, I stop here too. I hope we dine together?"

"With pleasure," replied Mr Pickwick. "I am not quite certain whether I have any friends here or not, though. Is there any gentleman of the name of Tupman here, waiter?"

A corpulent man, after minutely inspecting that gentleman's appearance, from the crown of his hat to the lowest button of his gaiters, replied emphatically –

"No!"

"Nor any gentleman of the name of Snodgrass?" inquired Mr Pickwick.

"No!"

"Nor Winkle?"

"No!"

"My friends have not arrived to-day, sir," said Mr Pickwick. "We will dine alone, then. Show us a private room, waiter."

On this request being preferred, the corpulent man condescended to order the boots to bring in the gentlemen's luggage; and preceding them down a long, dark passage, ushered them into a large, badly-furnished apartment, with a dirty grate, in which a small fire was making a wretched attempt to be cheerful.

After the lapse of an hour, a bit of fish and a steak was served up to the travellers, and when the dinner was cleared away, Mr Pickwick and Mr Peter Magnus drew their chairs up to the fire, and having ordered a bottle of the worst possible port wine, at the highest possible price, for the good of the house, drank brandy-and-water for their own.

Mr Peter Magnus took a view of Mr Pickwick through his coloured spectacles for several minutes, and then said, with an air of modesty –

"And what do you think – what *do* you think, Mr Pickwick – I have come down here for?"

"Upon my word," said Mr Pickwick, "it is wholly impossible for me to guess; on business, perhaps."

"Partly right, sir," replied Mr Peter Magnus, "but partly wrong at the same time; try again, Mr Pickwick."

"Really," said Mr Pickwick, "I must throw myself on your mercy, to tell me or not, as you may think best; for I should never guess, if I were to try all night."

"Why, then, he-he-he!" said Mr Peter Magnus, with a bashful titter, "what should you think, Mr Pickwick, if I had come down here to make a proposal, sir, eh? He, he, he!"

"Think! That you are very likely to succeed," replied Mr Pickwick, with one of his beaming smiles.

"Ah!" said Mr Magnus. "But do you really think so, Mr Pickwick? Do you, though?"

"Certainly," said Mr Pickwick.

"No; but you're joking, though."

"I am not, indeed."

"Why, then," said Mr Magnus, "to let you into a little secret, I think so too. I don't mind telling you, Mr Pickwick, although I'm dreadful jealous by nature – horrid – that the lady is in this house." Here Mr Magnus took off his spectacles, on purpose to wink, and then put them on again.

"That's what you were running out of the room for, before dinner, then, so often," said Mr Pickwick archly.

"Hush! Yes, you're right, that was it; not such a fool as to see her, though."

"No!"

"No; wouldn't do, you know, after having just come off a journey. Wait till to-morrow, sir; double the chance then. Mr Pickwick, sir, there is a suit of clothes in that bag, and a hat in that box, which, I expect, in the effect they will produce, will be invaluable to me, sir."

"Indeed!" said Mr Pickwick.

"She's a fine creature," said Mr Magnus.

"Is she?" said Mr Pickwick.

"Very," said Mr Magnus. "very. She lives about twenty miles from here, Mr Pickwick. I heard she would be here to-night and all to-morrow forenoon, and came down to seize the opportunity. I think an inn is a good sort of a place to propose to a single woman in, Mr Pickwick. She is more likely to feel the loneliness of her situation in travelling, perhaps, than she would be at home. What do you think, Mr Pickwick?"

"I think it is very probable," replied that gentleman.

"I beg your pardon, Mr Pickwick," said Mr Peter Magnus, "but I am naturally rather curious; what may you have come down here for?"

"On a far less pleasant errand, sir," replied Mr Pickwick, the colour mounting to his face at the recollection. "I have come down here, sir, to expose the treachery and falsehood of an individual, upon whose truth and honour I placed implicit reliance."

"Dear me," said Mr Peter Magnus, "that's very unpleasant. It is a lady, I presume? Well, Mr Pickwick, sir, I wouldn't probe your feelings for the world. Don't mind me, Mr Pickwick, if you wish to give vent to your feelings. I know what it is to be jilted, sir; I have endured that sort of thing three or four times."

"I am much obliged to you, for your condolence on what you presume to be my melancholy case," said Mr Pickwick, winding up his watch, and laying it on the table, "but – "

"No, no," said Mr Peter Magnus, "not a word more; it's a painful subject. I see, I see. What's the time, Mr Pickwick?"

"Past twelve."

"Dear me, it's time to go to bed. It will never do, sitting here. I shall be pale to-morrow, Mr Pickwick."

At the bare notion of such a calamity, Mr Peter Magnus rang the bell for the chambermaid; and the striped bag, the red bag, the leathern hat-box, and the brown-paper parcel, having been conveyed to his bedroom, he retired in company with a japanned candlestick, to one side of the house, while Mr Pickwick, and another japanned candlestick, were conducted through a multitude of tortuous windings, to another.

"This is your room, sir," said the chambermaid.

"Very well," replied Mr Pickwick, looking round him.

It was a tolerably large double-bedded room, with a fire; upon the whole, a more comfortable-looking apartment than Mr Pickwick's short experience of the accommodations of the Great White Horse had led him to expect.

"Nobody sleeps in the other bed, of course," said Mr Pickwick.

"Oh, no, sir."

"Very good. Tell my servant to bring me up some hot water at half-past eight in the morning, and that I shall not want him any more to-night."

"Yes, sir," and bidding Mr Pickwick good-night, the chambermaid retired, and left him alone.

Mr Pickwick sat himself down in a chair before the fire, and fell into a train of rambling meditations. First he thought of his friends, and wondered when they would join him; then his mind reverted to Mrs Martha Bardell; and from that lady it wandered, by a natural process, to the dingy counting-house of Dodson and Fogg. From Dodson and Fogg's it flew off at a tangent, and then it came back to the Great White Horse at Ipswich, with sufficient clearness to convince Mr Pickwick that he was falling asleep. So he roused himself, and began to undress, when he recollected he had left his watch on the table downstairs.

Now this watch was a special favourite with Mr Pickwick. The possibility of going to sleep, unless it were ticking gently beneath his pillow, or in the watch-pocket over his head, had never entered Mr Pickwick's brain. So as it was pretty late now, and he was unwilling to ring his bell at that hour of the night, he slipped on his coat, and taking the japanned candlestick in his hand, walked quietly downstairs.

The more stairs Mr Pickwick went down, the more stairs there seemed to be to descend, and again and again, when Mr Pickwick got into some narrow passage, and began to congratulate himself on having gained the ground-floor, did another flight of stairs appear before his astonished eyes. At last he reached a stone hall, which he remembered to have seen when he entered the house and he opened the door of the identical room in which he had spent the evening, and beheld his missing property on the table.

Mr Pickwick seized the watch in triumph, and proceeded to retrace his steps to his bedchamber. If his progress downward had been attended with difficulties and uncertainty, his journey back was infinitely more perplexing. Rows of doors, garnished with boots of every shape, make, and size, branched off in every possible direction. A dozen times did he softly turn the handle of some bedroom door which resembled his own, when a gruff cry from within of "Who the devil's that?" or "What do you want here?" caused him to steal away, on tiptoe, with a perfectly marvellous celerity. He was reduced to the verge of despair, when an open door attracted his attention. He peeped in. Right at last!

There were the two beds, whose situation he perfectly remembered, and the fire still burning. His candle, not a long one when he first received it, had flickered away in the drafts of air through which he had passed and sank into the socket as he closed the door after him.

"No matter," said Mr Pickwick, "I can undress myself just as well by the light of the fire."

Having carefully drawn the curtains of his bed on the outside, Mr Pickwick sat down on the rush-bottomed chair, and leisurely divested himself of his shoes and gaiters. He then took off and folded up his coat, waistcoat, and neckcloth, and slowly drawing on his tasselled nightcap, secured it firmly on his head, by tying beneath his chin the strings which he always had attached to that article of dress. It was at this moment that the absurdity of his recent bewilderment struck upon his mind.

"It is the best idea," said Mr Pickwick to himself, smiling till he almost cracked the nightcap strings – "it is the best idea, my losing myself in this place, and wandering about these staircases, that I ever heard of. Droll, droll, very droll." Here Mr Pickwick smiled again, a broader smile than before, and was about to continue the process of undressing, in the best possible humour, when he was suddenly stopped by a most unexpected interruption: to wit, the entrance into the room of some person with a candle, who, after locking the door, advanced to the dressing-table, and set down the light upon it.

The smile that played on Mr Pickwick's features was instantaneously lost in a look of the most unbounded and wonder-stricken surprise. The person, whoever it was, had come in so suddenly and with so little noise, that Mr Pickwick had had no time to call out, or oppose their entrance. Who could it be? A robber? Some evil-minded person who had seen him come upstairs with a handsome watch in his hand, perhaps. What was he to do? The only way in which Mr Pickwick could catch a glimpse of his mysterious visitor with the least danger of being seen himself, was by creeping on to the bed, and peeping out from between the curtains on the opposite side. To this manoeuvre he accordingly resorted. Keeping the curtains carefully closed with his hand, so that nothing more of him could be seen than his face and nightcap and putting on his spectacles, he mustered up courage and looked out.

Mr Pickwick almost fainted with horror and dismay. Standing before the dressing-glass was a middle-aged lady, in yellow curl-papers, busily engaged in brushing what ladies call their "back-hair." However, the unconscious middle-aged lady came into that room, it was quite clear that she contemplated remaining there for the night.

"Hem!" said the lady; and in went Mr Pickwick's head with automaton-like rapidity.

"I never met with anything so awful as this," thought poor Mr Pickwick, the cold perspiration starting in drops upon his nightcap. "Never. This is fearful."

It was quite impossible to resist the urgent desire to see what was going forward. So out went Mr Pickwick's head again. The prospect was worse than before. The middle-aged lady had finished arranging her hair; had carefully enveloped it in a muslin nightcap with a small plaited border; and was gazing pensively on the fire.

"This matter is growing alarming," reasoned Mr Pickwick with himself. "I can't allow things to go on in this way. By the self-possession of that lady, it is clear to me that I must have come into the wrong room. If I call out she'll alarm the house; but if I remain here the consequences will be still more frightful."

Mr Pickwick, it is quite unnecessary to say, was one of the most modest and delicate-minded of mortals. The very idea of exhibiting his nightcap to a lady overpowered him, but he had tied those confounded strings in a knot, and, do what he would, he couldn't get it off. The disclosure must be made. There was only one other way of doing it. He shrunk behind the curtains, and called out very loudly –

"Ha-hum!"

"Gracious Heaven!" said the middle-aged lady, "what's that?"

"It's – it's – only a gentleman, ma'am," said Mr Pickwick, from behind the curtains.

"A gentleman!" said the lady, with a terrific scream.

"It's all over!" thought Mr Pickwick.

"A strange man!" shrieked the lady. Another instant and the house would be alarmed. Her garments rustled as she rushed towards the door.

"Ma'am," said Mr Pickwick, thrusting out his head in the extremity of his desperation, "ma'am!"

Now, although Mr Pickwick was not actuated by any definite object in putting out his head, it was instantaneously productive of a good effect. The lady, as we have already stated, was near the door. She must pass it, to reach the staircase, and she would most undoubtedly have done so by this time, had not the sudden apparition of Mr Pickwick's nightcap driven her back into the remotest corner of the apartment, where she stood staring wildly at Mr Pickwick, while Mr Pickwick in his turn stared wildly at her.

"Wretch," said the lady, covering her eyes with her hands, "what do you want here?"

"Nothing, ma'am; nothing whatever, ma'am," said Mr Pickwick earnestly.

"Nothing!" said the lady, looking up.

"Nothing, ma'am, upon my honour," said Mr Pickwick, nodding his head so energetically, that the tassel of his nightcap danced again. "I am almost ready to sink, ma'am, beneath the confusion of addressing a lady in my nightcap (here the lady hastily snatched off hers), but I can't get it off, ma'am (here Mr Pickwick gave it a tremendous tug, in proof of the statement). It is evident to me, ma'am, now, that I have mistaken this bedroom for my own. I had not been here five minutes, ma'am, when you suddenly entered it."

"If this improbable story be really true, sir," said the lady, sobbing violently, "you will leave it instantly."

"I will, ma'am, with the greatest pleasure," replied Mr Pickwick. "Instantly, sir," said the lady.

"Certainly, ma'am," interposed Mr Pickwick, very quickly. "Certainly, ma'am. I – I – am very sorry, ma'am," said Mr Pickwick, making his appearance at the bottom of the bed, "to have been the innocent occasion of this alarm and emotion; deeply sorry, ma'am."

The lady pointed to the door. One excellent quality of Mr Pickwick's character was beautifully displayed at this moment, under the most trying circumstances. Although he had hastily put on his hat over his nightcap;

although he carried his shoes and gaiters in his hand, and his coat and waistcoat over his arm; nothing could subdue his native politeness.

"I am exceedingly sorry, ma'am," said Mr Pickwick, bowing very low.

"If you are, sir, you will at once leave the room," said the lady.

"Immediately, ma'am; this instant, ma'am," said Mr Pickwick, opening the door, and dropping both his shoes with a crash in so doing. "I trust, ma'am," resumed Mr Pickwick, gathering up his shoes, and turning round to bow again – "I trust, ma'am, that my unblemished character, and the devoted respect I entertain for your sex, will plead as some slight excuse for this – " But before Mr Pickwick could conclude the sentence, the lady had thrust him into the passage, and locked and bolted the door behind him. Whatever grounds of self-congratulation Mr Pickwick might have for having escaped so quietly from his late awkward situation, his present position was by no means enviable. He was alone, in an open passage, in a strange house in the middle of the night, half dressed; it was not to be supposed that he could find his way in perfect darkness to a room which he had been wholly unable to discover with a light, and if he made the slightest noise in his fruitless attempts to do so, he stood every chance of being shot at, and perhaps killed, by some wakeful traveller. He had no resource but to remain where he was until daylight appeared. So after groping his way a few paces down the passage, and, to his infinite alarm, stumbling over several pairs of boots in so doing, Mr Pickwick crouched into a little recess in the wall, to wait for morning, as philosophically as he might.

He was not destined, however, to undergo this additional trial of patience; for he had not been long ensconced in his present concealment when, to his unspeakable horror, a man, bearing a light, appeared at the end of the passage. His horror was suddenly converted into joy, however, when he recognised the form of his faithful attendant. It was indeed Mr Samuel Weller, who after sitting up thus late, in conversation with the boots, who was sitting up for the mail, was now about to retire to rest.

"Sam," said Mr Pickwick, suddenly appearing before him, "where's my bedroom?"

Mr Weller stared at his master with the most emphatic surprise; and it was not until the question had been repeated three several times, that he turned round, and led the way to the long-sought apartment.

"Sam," said Mr Pickwick, as he got into bed, "I have made one of the most extraordinary mistakes to-night, that ever were heard of."

"Wery likely, sir," replied Mr Weller drily.

"But of this I am determined, Sam," said Mr Pickwick; "that if I were to stop in this house for six months, I would never trust myself about it, alone, again."

"That's the wery prudentest resolution as you could come to, sir," replied Mr Weller. "You rayther want somebody to look arter you, sir, when your judgment goes out a wisitin'."

"What do you mean by that, Sam?" said Mr Pickwick. He raised himself in bed, and extended his hand, as if he were about to say something more; but suddenly checking himself, turned round, and bade his valet "Good-night."

"Good-night, sir," replied Mr Weller. He paused when he got outside the door – shook his head – walked on – stopped – snuffed the candle – shook his head again – and finally proceeded slowly to his chamber, apparently buried in the profoundest meditation.

CHAPTER 14

Wherein Mr Peter Magnus Grows Jealous, and the Middle-aged Lady Apprehensive, Which Brings the Pickwickians Within the Grasp of the Law

When Mr Pickwick descended to the room in which he and Mr Peter Magnus had spent the preceding evening, he found that gentleman with the major part of the contents of the two bags, the leathern hat-box, and the brown-paper parcel, displaying to all possible advantage on his person, while he himself was pacing up and down the room in a state of the utmost excitement and agitation.

"Good-morning, sir," said Mr Peter Magnus. "What do you think of this, sir?"

"Very effective indeed," replied Mr Pickwick, surveying the garments of Mr Peter Magnus with a good-natured smile.

"Yes, I think it'll do," said Mr Magnus. "Mr Pickwick, sir, I have sent up my card."

"Have you?" said Mr Pickwick.

"And the waiter brought back word, that she would see me at eleven – at eleven, sir; it only wants a quarter now."

"Very near the time," said Mr Pickwick.

"Yes, it is rather near," replied Mr Magnus, "rather too near to be pleasant – eh! Mr Pickwick, sir?"

"Confidence is a great thing in these cases," observed Mr Pickwick.

"I believe it is, sir," said Mr Peter Magnus. "I am very confident, sir. Really, Mr Pickwick, I do not see why a man should feel any fear in such a case as this, sir. That's my view of the matter, Mr Pickwick."

"It is a very philosophical one," replied Mr Pickwick. "But breakfast is waiting, Mr Magnus. Come."

Down they sat to breakfast, but it was evident, notwithstanding the boasting of Mr Peter Magnus, that he laboured under a very considerable degree of nervousness, of which loss of appetite, a propensity to upset the tea-things, a spectral attempt at drollery, and an irresistible inclination to look at the clock, every other second, were among the principal symptoms.

"He-he-he," tittered Mr Magnus, affecting cheerfulness, and gasping with agitation. "It only wants two minutes, Mr Pickwick. Am I pale, sir?"

"Not very," replied Mr Pickwick.

There was a brief pause.

"I beg your pardon, Mr Pickwick; but have you ever done this sort of thing in your time?" said Mr Magnus.

"You mean proposing?" said Mr Pickwick.

"Yes."

"Never," said Mr Pickwick, with great energy, "never."

"You have no idea, then, how it's best to begin?" said Mr Magnus.

"Well, sir," said Mr Pickwick, "I should commence, sir, with a tribute to the lady's beauty and excellent qualities; from then, sir, I should diverge to my own unworthiness."

"Very good," said Mr Magnus.

"Unworthiness for *her* only, mind, sir," resumed Mr Pickwick; "I should then expatiate on the warmth of my love, and the depth of my devotion. Perhaps I might then be tempted to seize her hand."

"Yes, I see," said Mr Magnus; "that would be a very great point."

"I should then, sir," continued Mr Pickwick, growing warmer as the subject presented itself in more glowing colours before him – "I should then, sir, come to the plain and simple question, 'Will you have me?' I think I am justified in assuming that upon this, she would turn away her head."

"You think that may be taken for granted?" said Mr Magnus; "because, if she did not do that at the right place, it would be embarrassing."

"I think she would," said Mr Pickwick. "Upon this, sir, I should squeeze her hand, and I think – I think, Mr Magnus – that after I had done that, supposing there was no refusal, I should gently draw away the handkerchief, which my slight knowledge of human nature leads me to suppose the lady would be applying to her eyes at the moment, and steal a respectful kiss. I think I should kiss her, Mr Magnus; and at this particular point, I am decidedly of opinion that if the lady were going to take me at all, she would murmur into my ears a bashful acceptance."

Mr Magnus started; gazed on Mr Pickwick's intelligent face, for a short time in silence; and then (the dial pointing to the ten minutes past) shook him warmly by the hand, and rushed desperately from the room.

Mr Pickwick had taken a few strides to and fro; and the small hand of the clock following the latter part of his example, had arrived at the figure which indicates the half-hour, when the door suddenly opened. He turned round to meet Mr Peter Magnus, and encountered, in his stead, the joyous face of Mr Tupman, the serene countenance of Mr Winkle, and the intellectual lineaments of Mr Snodgrass. As Mr Pickwick greeted them, Mr Peter Magnus tripped into the room.

"My friends, the gentleman I was speaking of – Mr Magnus," said Mr Pickwick.

"Your servant, gentlemen," said Mr Magnus, evidently in a high state of excitement; "Mr Pickwick, allow me to speak to you one moment, sir."

As he said this, Mr Magnus harnessed his forefinger to Mr Pickwick's buttonhole, and, drawing him to a window recess, said –

"Congratulate me, Mr Pickwick; I followed your advice to the very letter."

"And it was all correct, was it?" inquired Mr Pickwick.

"It was, sir. Could not possibly have been better," replied Mr Magnus. "Mr Pickwick, she is mine."

"I congratulate you, with all my heart," replied Mr Pickwick, warmly shaking his new friend by the hand.

"You must see her, sir," said Mr Magnus; "this way, if you please. Excuse us for one instant, gentlemen." Hurrying on in this way, Mr Peter Magnus drew Mr Pickwick from the room. He paused at the next door in the passage, and tapped gently thereat.

"Come in," said a female voice. And in they went.

"Miss Witherfield," said Mr Magnus, "allow me to introduce my very particular friend, Mr Pickwick. Mr Pickwick, I beg to make you known to Miss Witherfield."

The lady was at the upper end of the room. As Mr Pickwick bowed, he took his spectacles from his waistcoat pocket, and put them on; then, uttering an exclamation of surprise, Mr Pickwick retreated several paces, and the lady, with a half-suppressed scream, hid her face in her hands, and dropped into a chair; whereupon Mr Peter Magnus was stricken motionless on the spot, and gazed from one to the other, with a countenance expressive of the extremities of horror and surprise.

This certainly was, to all appearance, very unaccountable behaviour; but the fact is, that Mr Pickwick no sooner put on his spectacles, than he at once recognised in the future Mrs Magnus the lady into whose room he had so unwarrantably intruded on the previous night; and the spectacles had no sooner crossed Mr Pickwick's nose, than the lady at once identified the countenance which she had seen surrounded by all the horrors of a nightcap. So the lady screamed, and Mr Pickwick started.

"Mr Pickwick!" exclaimed Mr Magnus, lost in astonishment, "what is the meaning of this, sir? What is the meaning of it, sir?" added Mr Magnus, in a threatening, and a louder tone.

"Sir," said Mr Pickwick, somewhat indignant at the very sudden manner in which Mr Peter Magnus had conjugated himself into the imperative mood, "I decline answering that question."

"You decline it, sir?" said Mr Magnus.

"I do, sir," replied Mr Pickwick; "I object to say anything which may compromise that lady, or awaken unpleasant recollections in her breast, without her consent and permission."

"Miss Witherfield," said Mr Peter Magnus, "do you know this person?"

"I have seen him," replied the middle-aged lady.

"Where?" inquired Mr Magnus, "where?"

"That," said the middle-aged lady, rising from her seat, and averting her head – "that I would not reveal for worlds."

"I understand you, ma'am," said Mr Pickwick, "and respect your delicacy; it shall never be revealed by *me*, depend upon it."

"Upon my word, ma'am," said Mr Magnus, "considering the situation in which I am placed with regard to yourself, you carry this matter off with tolerable coolness – tolerable coolness, ma'am."

"Cruel Mr Magnus!" said the middle-aged lady; here she wept very copiously indeed.

"Address your observations to me, sir," interposed Mr Pickwick; "I alone am to blame, if anybody be."

"Oh! you alone are to blame, are you, sir?" said Mr Magnus; "I see through this, sir. You repent of your determination now, do you?"

"My determination!" said Mr Pickwick.

"Your determination, sir. Oh! don't stare at me, sir," said Mr Magnus; "I recollect your words last night, sir. You came down here, sir, to expose the treachery and falsehood of an individual on whose truth and honour you had placed implicit reliance – eh?" Here Mr Peter Magnus indulged in a prolonged sneer; and, taking off his green spectacles, rolled his little eyes about, in a manner frightful to behold. "But you shall answer it, sir."

"Answer what?" said Mr Pickwick.

"Never mind, sir," replied Mr Magnus, striding up and down the room. "Never mind."

Mr Pickwick opened the room door, and abruptly called out, "Tupman, come here!"

Mr Tupman immediately presented himself, with a look of very considerable surprise.

"Tupman," said Mr Pickwick, "a secret of some delicacy, in which that lady is concerned, is the cause of a difference which has just arisen between this gentleman and myself. When I assure him, in your presence, that it has no relation to himself, and is not in any way connected with his affairs, I need hardly beg you to take notice that if he continue to dispute it I shall consider extremely insulting."

As Mr Pickwick said this, he looked encyclopedias at Mr Peter Magnus. Mr Pickwick's upright and honourable bearing would have carried conviction to any reasonable mind; but, unfortunately, at that particular moment, the mind of Mr Peter Magnus was in anything but reasonable order. Consequently, instead of receiving Mr Pickwick's explanation as he ought to have done, he proceeded to work himself into a red-hot, scorching, consuming passion, adding force to his declamation by striding to and fro, and pulling his hair – amusements which he would vary occasionally, by shaking his fist in Mr Pickwick's philanthropic countenance.

The consequence was, that words ran high, and voices higher; and at length Mr Magnus told Mr Pickwick he should hear from him; to which Mr Pickwick replied, with laudable politeness, that the sooner he heard from him the better; whereupon the middle-aged lady rushed in terror from the room, out of which Mr Tupman dragged Mr Pickwick, leaving Mr Peter Magnus to himself and meditation.

The more the middle-aged lady meditated, the more terrified she became; and at length she determined to repair to the house of the principal magistrate of the town, and request him to secure the persons of Mr Pickwick and Mr Tupman without delay. Filled with these reflections, the middle-aged lady arrayed herself in her bonnet and shawl, and repaired to the mayor's dwelling straightway.

Now George Nupkins, Esquire, the principal magistrate aforesaid, was sitting in his easy-chair, frowning with majesty, and boiling with rage, when a lady was announced on pressing, private, and particular business. Mr Nupkins looked calmly terrible, and commanded that the lady should be shown in and Miss Witherfield, interestingly agitated, was ushered in accordingly.

"Muzzle!" said the magistrate.

Muzzle was an undersized footman, with a long body and short legs. "Place a chair, and leave the room."

"Yes, your Worship."

"Now, ma'am, will you state your business?" said the magistrate.

"It is of a very painful kind, sir," said Miss Witherfield.

"Very likely, ma'am," said the magistrate. "Compose your feelings, ma'am and then tell me what legal business brings you here, ma'am."

"It is very distressing to me, sir, to give this information," said Miss Witherfield, "but I fear a duel is going to be fought here."

"Here, ma'am?" said the magistrate. "Where, ma'am?"

"In Ipswich."

"In Ipswich, ma'am! A duel in Ipswich!" said the magistrate, perfectly aghast at the notion. "Impossible, ma'am; nothing of the kind can be contemplated in this town."

"My information is, unfortunately, but too correct," said the middle-aged lady; "I was present at the quarrel."

"It's a most extraordinary thing," said the astounded magistrate. "Muzzle!"

"Yes, your Worship."

"Send Mr Jinks here, directly! Instantly."

"Yes, your Worship."

Muzzle retired; and a pale, sharp-nosed, half-fed, shabbily-clad clerk, of middle age, entered the room.

"Mr Jinks," said the magistrate. "This lady, Mr Jinks, has come here, to give information of an intended duel in this town."

The hungry-looking Jinks sighed, and, being ordered to take the lady's information, shambled to a seat, and proceeded to write it down.

"This man, Pickwick, is the principal, I understand?" said the magistrate, when the statement was finished.

"He is," said the middle-aged lady.

"And the other rioter – what's his name, Mr Jinks?"

"Tupman, sir."

"Tupman is the second?"

"Yes."

"The other principal, you say, has absconded, ma'am?"

"Yes," replied Miss Witherfield, with a short cough.

"Very well," said the magistrate. "These are two cut-throats from London, who have come down here to destroy his Majesty's population, thinking that at this distance from the capital, the arm of the law is weak and paralysed. They shall be made an example of. Draw up the warrants, Mr Jinks. Muzzle!"

"Yes, your Worship."

"Is Grummer downstairs?"

"Yes, your Worship."

"Send him up."

The obsequious Muzzle retired, and presently returned, introducing the elderly gentleman in the top-boots, who was chiefly remarkable for a bottle-nose, a hoarse voice, and a wandering eye.

"Nothing but vigorous measures will do in these times," said the magistrate, signing the warrants. "Grummer, you will bring these persons before me, this afternoon. You will find them at the Great White Horse. Muzzle!"

116

"Yes, your Worship."

"Show the lady out."

While these resolute and determined preparations for the conservation of the king's peace were pending, Mr Pickwick and his friends, wholly unconscious of the mighty events in progress, had sat quietly down to dinner; and very talkative and companionable they all were. Mr Pickwick was in the very act of relating his adventure of the preceding night, to the great amusement of his followers.

Mr Grummer's mode of proceeding was professional, but peculiar. His first act was to bolt the door on the inside; his second, to polish his head and countenance very carefully with a cotton handkerchief; his third, to place his hat, with the cotton handkerchief in it, on the nearest chair; and his fourth, to produce from the breast-pocket of his coat a short truncheon, surmounted by a brazen crown, with which he beckoned to Mr Pickwick with a grave and ghost-like air.

Mr Snodgrass was the first to break the astonished silence. He looked steadily at Mr Grummer for a brief space, and then said emphatically, "This is a private room, sir. A private room."

Mr Grummer shook his head, and replied, "No room's private to his Majesty when the street door's once passed. That's law. Some people maintains that an Englishman's house is his castle. That's gammon."

The Pickwickians gazed on each other with wondering eyes.

"Which is Mr Tupman?" inquired Mr Grummer. He had an intuitive perception of Mr Pickwick; he knew him at once.

"My name's Tupman," said that gentleman.

"My name's Law," said Mr Grummer.

"What?" said Mr Tupman.

"Law," replied Mr Grummer – "Law, civil power, and exekative; them's my titles; here's my authority. I apprehend you Pickwick! Tupman – the aforesaid."

"What do you mean by this insolence?" said Mr Tupman, starting up; "leave the room!"

"Hallo," said Mr Grummer, retreating very expeditiously to the door, and opening it an inch or two, "Dubbley."

"Well," said a deep voice from the passage.

"Come for'ard, Dubbley."

At the word of command, a dirty-faced man, something over six feet high, and stout in proportion, squeezed himself through the half-open door and entered the room.

"Is the other specials outside, Dubbley?" inquired Mr Grummer.

Mr Dubbley, who was a man of few words, nodded assent.

"Order in the diwision under your charge, Dubbley," said Mr Grummer.

Mr Dubbley did as he was desired; and half a dozen men, each with a short truncheon and a brass crown, flocked into the room.

Mr Grummer pocketed his staff, and looked at Mr Dubbley; Mr Dubbley pocketed his staff and looked at the division; the division pocketed their staves and looked at Messrs Tupman and Pickwick.

Mr Pickwick and his followers rose as one man.

"What is the meaning of this atrocious intrusion upon my privacy?" said Mr Pickwick.

"Who dares apprehend me?" said Mr Tupman.

"What do you want here, scoundrels?" said Mr Snodgrass.

Mr Winkle said nothing, but he fixed his eyes on Grummer, and bestowed a look upon him, which, if he had had any feeling, must have pierced his brain. As it was, however, it had no visible effect on him whatever.

When the executive perceived that Mr Pickwick and his friends were disposed to resist the authority of the law, they very significantly turned up their coat sleeves. This demonstration was not lost upon Mr Pickwick. He conferred a few moments with Mr Tupman apart, and then signified his readiness to proceed to the mayor's residence.

But Mr Pickwick resolutely protested against making his appearance in the public streets, surrounded and guarded by the officers of justice, like a common criminal. Mr Grummer as resolutely protested against walking on the opposite side of the way, and taking Mr Pickwick's parole that he would go straight to the magistrate's; and both Mr Pickwick and Mr Tupman as strenuously objected to the expense of a post-coach. The dispute ran high, and the dilemma lasted long; and just as the executive were on the point of overcoming Mr Pickwick's objection to walking to the magistrate's, it was recollected that there stood in the inn yard, an old sedan-chair, which would hold Mr Pickwick and Mr Tupman, at least as conveniently as a modern post-chaise. The chair was hired, and brought into the hall; Mr Pickwick and Mr Tupman squeezed themselves inside, and pulled down the blinds; a couple of chairmen were speedily found; and the procession started in grand order.

The specials surrounded the body of the vehicle; Mr Grummer and Mr Dubbley marched triumphantly in front; Mr Snodgrass and Mr Winkle walked arm-in-arm behind; and the unsoaped of Ipswich brought up the rear.

Mr Weller, habited in his morning jacket, with the black calico sleeves, beheld a crowd pouring down the street, surrounding an object which had very much the appearance of a sedan-chair. Mr Grummer passed, and Mr Dubbley passed, and the sedan passed, and the bodyguard of specials passed, and Sam was suddenly stopped by the unexpected appearance of Mr Winkle and Mr Snodgrass.

"What's the row, gen'l'm'n?" cried Sam. "Who have they got in this here watch-box in mournin'?"

Both gentlemen replied together, and, though the words were inaudible, Sam saw by the motion of the two pairs of lips that they had uttered the magic word "Pickwick." This was enough. In another minute Mr Weller had made his way through the crowd, stopped the chairmen, and confronted the portly Grummer.

"Hallo, old gen'l'm'n!" said Sam. "Who have you got in this here conweyance?"

"Stand back," said Mr Grummer, whose dignity had been wondrously augmented by a little popularity.

"Knock him down, if he don't," said Mr Dubbley.

"Stand back!" said the outraged Mr Grummer. By way of adding force to the command, he thrust the brass emblem of royalty into Sam's neckcloth with one hand, and seized Sam's collar with the other – a compliment which Mr Weller returned by knocking him down out of hand.

Mr Winkle animated by this display of Mr Weller's valour, no sooner saw Mr Grummer fall than he made a terrific onslaught on a small boy who stood next him; whereupon Mr Snodgrass, in a truly Christian spirit, announced in a very loud tone that he was going to begin, and proceeded to take off his coat with the utmost deliberation. He was immediately surrounded and secured; and it is but common justice both to him and Mr Winkle to say, that they did not make the slightest attempt to rescue either themselves or Mr Weller; who, after a most vigorous resistance, was overpowered by numbers and taken prisoner. The procession then reformed and the march was re-commenced.

CHAPTER 15

Showing, Among a Variety of Pleasant Matters, How Majestic and Impartial Mr Nupkins Was; and How Mr Weller Returned Mr Job Trotter's Shuttlecock as Heavily as it Came – With Another Matter, Which Will be Found in its Place

Mr Pickwick and his friends were conducted into the hall, hence, having been previously announced by Muzzle, and ordered in by Mr Nupkins, they were ushered into the worshipful presence of that public-spirited officer.

"Now, Grummer, who is that person?" said Mr Nupkins, pointing to Mr Pickwick, who, as the spokesman of his friends, stood hat in hand, bowing with the utmost politeness and respect.

"This here's Pickvick, your Wash-up," said Grummer.

Weller thrust Grummer aside, and addressed the magistrate with pleasant familiarity, "This here is S. Pickvick, Esquire; this here's Mr Tupman; that 'ere's Mr Snodgrass; and farder on, next him on the t'other side, Mr Winkle – all wery nice gen'l'm'n, sir, as you'll be wery happy to have the acquaintance on; so the sooner you commits these here officers o' yourn to the tread-mill for a month or two, the sooner we shall begin to be on a pleasant understanding."

At the conclusion of this address, Mr Weller brushed his hat with his right elbow, and nodded benignly to Jinks, who had heard him throughout with unspeakable awe.

"Who is this man, Grummer?" said the magistrate.

"Wery desp'rate ch'racter, your Wash-up," replied Grummer. "He attempted to rescue the prisoners, and assaulted the officers; so we took him into custody, and brought him here."

"You did quite right," replied the magistrate. "He is evidently a desperate ruffian."

"He is my servant, sir," said Mr Pickwick angrily.

"Oh! he is your servant, is he?" said Mr Nupkins. "A conspiracy to defeat the ends of justice, and murder its officers. Pickwick's servant. Put that down, Mr Jinks."

Mr Jinks did so.

"What's your name, fellow?" thundered Mr Nupkins.

120

"Veller," replied Sam.

"Put down his name, Mr Jinks," said the magistrate.

"Two L's, old feller," said Sam.

"Where do you live?" said the magistrate.

"Vere ever I can," replied Sam.

"Put down that, Mr Jinks," said the magistrate, who was fast rising into a rage.

"Score it under," said Sam.

"He is a vagabond, Mr Jinks," said the magistrate. "He is a vagabond on his own statement, – is he not, Mr Jinks?"

"Certainly, sir."

"Then I'll commit him – I'll commit him as such," said Mr Nupkins. Mr Jinks retired to his end of the table; and the magistrate, with a preparatory cough, drew himself up in his chair, and was proceeding to commence his address, when Mr Pickwick interposed.

"I beg your pardon, sir, for interrupting you," said Mr Pickwick; "but before you proceed to express any opinion you may have formed I must claim my right to be heard so far as I am personally concerned."

"Hold your tongue, sir," said the magistrate peremptorily.

"I must submit to you, sir – " said Mr Pickwick.

"Hold your tongue, sir," interposed the magistrate, "or I shall order an officer to remove you."

"You may order your officers to do whatever you please, sir," said Mr Pickwick; "but I shall take the liberty, sir, of claiming my right to be heard, until I am removed by force."

"Pickvick and principle!" exclaimed Mr Weller, in a very audible voice.

"Sam, be quiet," said Mr Pickwick.

"Dumb as a drum vith a hole in it, sir," replied Sam.

Mr Nupkins looked at Mr Pickwick with a gaze of intense astonishment, and was apparently about to return a very angry reply, when Mr Jinks pulled him by the sleeve, and whispered something in his ear. Jinks was evidently remonstrating. At length the magistrate, gulping down, with a very bad grace, his disinclination to hear anything more, turned to Mr Pickwick, and said sharply, "What do you want to say?"

"First," said Mr Pickwick, sending a look through his spectacles, under which even Nupkins quailed, "first, I wish to know what I and my friend have been brought here for?"

"Must I tell him?" whispered the magistrate to Jinks.

"I think you had better, sir," whispered Jinks to the magistrate.

"An information has been sworn before me," said the magistrate, "that it is apprehended you are going to fight a duel, and that the other man, Tupman, is your aider and abettor in it. Therefore – eh, Mr Jinks?"

"Certainly, sir."

"Therefore, I call upon you both, to – I think that's the course, Mr Jinks?"

"Certainly, sir."

"To – to – what, Mr Jinks?" said the magistrate pettishly.

"To find bail, sir."

"Yes. Therefore, I call upon you both – as I was about to say when I was interrupted by my clerk – to find bail."

"Good bail," whispered Mr Jinks.

"I shall require good bail," said the magistrate.

"Town's-people," whispered Jinks.

"They must be towns-people," said the magistrate.

"Fifty pounds each," whispered Jinks, "and householders, of course."

"I shall require two sureties of fifty pounds each," said the magistrate aloud, with great dignity, "and they must be householders, of course."

"But bless my heart, sir," said Mr Pickwick, who, together with Mr Tupman, was all amazement and indignation; "we are perfect strangers in this town. I have as little knowledge of any householders here, as I have intention of fighting a duel with anybody."

"I dare say," replied the magistrate, "I dare say – don't you, Mr Jinks?"

"Certainly, sir."

"Have you anything more to say?" inquired the magistrate.

Mr Pickwick had a great deal more to say, which he would no doubt have said, very little to his own advantage, or the magistrate's satisfaction, if he had not, the moment he ceased speaking, been pulled by the sleeve by Mr Weller, with whom he was immediately engaged in so earnest a conversation, that he suffered the magistrate's inquiry to pass wholly unnoticed.

Mr Nupkins was not the man to ask a question of the kind twice over; and so, with another preparatory cough, he proceeded to pronounce his decision. He should fine Weller two pounds for the first assault, and three pounds for the second. He should fine Winkle two pounds and Snodgrass one pound, besides requiring them to enter into their own recognisances to keep the peace towards all his Majesty's subjects, and especially towards his liege servant, Daniel Grummer. Pickwick and Tupman he had already held to bail.

Immediately on the magistrate ceasing to speak, Mr Pickwick, with a smile mantling on his again good-humoured countenance, stepped forward, and said –

"I beg the magistrate's pardon, but may I request a few minutes' private conversation with him, on a matter of deep importance to himself?"

"What?" said the magistrate.

Mr Pickwick repeated his request.

"This is a most extraordinary request," said the magistrate. "A private interview?"

"A private interview," replied Mr Pickwick firmly; "only, as a part of the information which I wish to communicate is derived from my servant, I should wish him to be present."

The magistrate looked at Mr Jinks; Mr Jinks looked at the magistrate; the officers looked at each other in amazement. Mr Nupkins debated the matter within himself for a few seconds, and then, rising from his chair, and requesting Mr Pickwick and Sam to follow him, led the way into a small room which opened into the justice-parlour.

"I will come to the point at once, sir," said Mr Pickwick; "it affects yourself and your credit materially. I have every reason to believe, sir, that you are harbouring in your house a gross impostor!"

"Two," interrupted Sam. "Mulberry agin all natur, for tears and willainny!"

"Sam," said Mr Pickwick, "if I am to render myself intelligible to this gentleman, I must beg you to control your feelings."

"Wery sorry, sir," replied Mr Weller; "but when I think o' that 'ere Job, I can't help opening the walve a inch or two."

"In one word, sir," said Mr Pickwick, "is my servant right in suspecting that a certain Captain Fitz-Marshall is in the habit of visiting here? Because," added Mr Pickwick, as he saw that Mr Nupkins was about to offer a very indignant interruption, "because if he be, I know that person to be a – "

"Hush, hush," said Mr Nupkins, closing the door. "Know him to be what, sir?"

"An unprincipled adventurer – a dishonourable character – a man who preys upon society, and makes easily-deceived people his dupes, sir; his absurd, his foolish, his wretched dupes, sir," said the excited Mr Pickwick.

"Dear me," said Mr Nupkins, turning very red, and altering his whole manner directly. "Dear me, Mr – "

"Pickvick," said Sam.

"Pickwick," said the magistrate, "dear me, Mr Pickwick – pray take a seat – you cannot mean this? Captain Fitz-Marshall!"

"Don't call him a cap'en," said Sam, "nor Fitz-Marshall neither; he ain't neither one nor t'other. He's a strolling actor, he is, and his name's Jingle; and if ever there was a wolf in a mulberry suit, that 'ere Job Trotter's him."

"It is very true, sir," said Mr Pickwick, replying to the magistrate's look of amazement; "my only business in this town, is to expose the person of whom we now speak."

Mr Pickwick proceeded to pour into the horror-stricken ear of Mr Nupkins, an abridged account of all Mr Jingle's atrocities. He related how he had first met him; how he had eloped with Miss Wardle; how he had cheerfully resigned the lady for a pecuniary consideration; how he had entrapped himself into a lady's boarding-school at midnight; and how he (Mr Pickwick) now felt it his duty to expose his assumption of his present name and rank.

As the narrative proceeded, all the warm blood in the body of Mr Nupkins tingled up into the very tips of his ears. He had picked up the captain at a neighbouring race-course. Charmed with his long list of aristocratic acquaintance, his extensive travel, and his fashionable demeanour, Mrs Nupkins and Miss Nupkins had exhibited Captain Fitz-Marshall, and quoted Captain Fitz-Marshall, and hurled Captain Fitz-Marshall at the devoted heads of their select circle of acquaintance, until their bosom friends, were ready to burst with jealousy and despair. Heavens! What would their friends, the Porkenhams say! What would be the triumph of Mr Sidney Porkenham when he found that his addresses had been slighted for such a rival! How should he, Nupkins, meet the eye of old Porkenham at the next quarter-sessions!

"But after all," said Mr Nupkins, brightening for a moment, after a long pause; "after all, this is a mere statement. Captain Fitz-Marshall is a man of very engaging manners, and, I dare say, has many enemies. What proof have you of the truth of these representations?"

"Confront me with him," said Mr Pickwick, "that is all I ask, and all I require. Confront him with me and my friends here; you will want no further proof."

"Why," said Mr Nupkins, "that might be very easily done, for he will be here to-night, and then there would be no occasion to make the matter public, just – just – for the young man's own sake, you know. I – I – should like to consult Mrs Nupkins on the propriety of the step, in the first instance, though. At all events, Mr Pickwick, we must despatch this legal business before we can do anything else. Pray step back into the next room."

Into the next room they went.

"Grummer," said the magistrate, in an awful voice.

"Your Wash-up," replied Grummer, with the smile of a favourite.

"Come, come, sir," said the magistrate sternly, "don't let me see any of this levity here. It is very unbecoming, and I can assure you that you have very little to smile at. Was the account you gave me just now strictly true? Now be careful, sir!"

"Your Wash-up," stammered Grummer, "I – "

"Oh, you are confused, are you?" said the magistrate. "Mr Jinks, you observe this confusion?"

"Certainly, sir," replied Jinks.

"Now," said the magistrate, "repeat your statement, Grummer, and again I warn you to be careful. Mr Jinks, take his words down."

The unfortunate Grummer proceeded to re-state his complaint, but, what between Mr Jinks's taking down his words, and the magistrate's taking them up, his natural tendency to rambling, and his extreme confusion, he managed to get involved, in something under three minutes, in such a mass of entanglement and contradiction, that Mr Nupkins at once declared he didn't believe him. So the fines were remitted, and Mr Jinks found a couple of bail in no time.

When Mr Nupkins sought Mrs Nupkins, and detailed the communication which had been made by Mr Pickwick, Mrs Nupkins suddenly recollected that she had always expected something of the kind; that she had always said it would be so; that her advice was never taken; that she really did not know what Mr Nupkins supposed she was; and so forth.

"The idea!" said Miss Nupkins, forcing a tear of very scanty proportions into the corner of each eye; "the idea of my being made such a fool of!"

"Ah! you may thank your papa, my dear," said Mrs Nupkins; "how I have begged that man to inquire into the captain's family connections. "

"My love," said Mr Nupkins, "you professed yourself very fond of Captain Fitz-Marshall. You have constantly asked him here, my dear, and you have lost no opportunity of introducing him elsewhere."

"Didn't I say so, Henrietta?" cried Mrs Nupkins, appealing to her daughter with the air of a much-injured female. "Didn't I say that your papa would turn round and lay all this at my door? Didn't I say so?"

Here Mrs Nupkins sobbed.

"Oh, pa!" remonstrated Miss Nupkins. And here she sobbed too.

"Isn't it too much, when he has brought all this disgrace and ridicule upon us, to taunt me with being the cause of it?" exclaimed Mrs Nupkins.

Mrs Nupkins's tears continued to gush forth, with great velocity, until she had gained a little time to think the matter over; when she decided, in her own mind, that the best thing to do would be to ask Mr Pickwick and his friends to remain until the captain's arrival, and then to give Mr Pickwick the opportunity he sought.

So Mr Pickwick and his friends, having washed off all marks of their late encounter, were introduced to the ladies, and soon afterwards to their dinner; and Mr Weller, whom the magistrate, with his peculiar sagacity, had discovered in half an hour to be one of the finest fellows alive, was consigned to the care and guardianship of Mr Muzzle, who was specially enjoined to take him below, and make much of him.

"This way, sir, if you please, this way." Preceding Mr Weller, with the utmost politeness, Mr Muzzle conducted him into the kitchen.

"Mary," said Mr Muzzle to the pretty servant-girl, "this is Mr Weller; a gentleman as master has sent down, to be made as comfortable as possible."

"And your master's a knowin' hand, and has just sent me to the right place," said Mr Weller, with a glance of admiration at Mary.

"Lor, Mr Weller!" said Mary blushing.

"Well, I never!" ejaculated the cook.

"Bless me, cook, I forgot you," said Mr Muzzle. "Mr Weller, let me introduce you."

Mr Weller's easy manners and conversational powers had such irresistible influence with his new friends, that before the dinner was half over, they were on a footing of perfect intimacy, and in possession of a full account of the delinquency of Job Trotter.

"I never could a-bear that Job," said Mary.

"No more you never ought to, my dear," replied Mr Weller.

"Why not?" inquired Mary.

"Cos ugliness and svindlin' never ought to be formiliar with elegance and virtew," replied Mr Weller.

Here Mary laughed, and said the cook had made her; and the cook laughed, and said she hadn't.

"I ha'n't got a glass," said Mary.

"Drink with me, my dear," said Mr Weller. "Put your lips to this here tumbler, and then I can kiss you by deputy."

"For shame, Mr Weller!" said Mary.

"What's a shame, my dear?"

"Talkin' in that way."

"Nonsense; it ain't no harm. It's natur; ain't it, cook?"

Mr Weller was in the height of his attentions to the pretty house-maid; Mr Muzzle was busy doing the honours of the table; and the cook had just paused to laugh, in the very act of raising a huge morsel to her lips; when the kitchen door opened, and in walked Mr Job Trotter. But the statement is not distinguished by our usual scrupulous adherence to fact. The door opened and Mr Trotter appeared. He would have walked in, and was in the very act of doing so, indeed, when catching sight of Mr Weller, he involuntarily shrank back a pace or two, and stood gazing on the unexpected scene before him, perfectly motionless with amazement and terror.

"Here he is!" said Sam, rising with great glee. "Why we were that wery moment a-speaking o' you. How are you? Where have you been? Come in."

Laying his hand on the mulberry collar of the unresisting Job, Mr Weller dragged him into the kitchen; and, locking the door, handed the key to Mr Muzzle, who very coolly buttoned it up in a side pocket.

"Well, here's a game!" cried Sam. "Only think o' my master havin' the pleasure o' meeting yourn upstairs, and me havin' the joy o' meetin' you down here. Well, I am so glad to see you. How happy you look. It's quite a treat to see you; ain't it, Mr Muzzle?"

"Quite," said Mr Muzzle.

"So cheerful he is!" said Sam.

"In such good spirits!" said Muzzle.

"And so glad to see us – that makes it so much more comfortable," said Sam. "Sit down; sit down."

Mr Trotter suffered himself to be forced into a chair by the fireside. He cast his small eyes, first on Mr Weller, and then on Mr Muzzle, but said nothing.

"Well, now," said Sam, "afore these here ladies, I should jest like to ask you, as a sort of curiosity, whether you don't consider yourself as nice and well-behaved a young gen'l'm'n, as ever used a pink check pocket-handkerchief?"

"And as was ever a-going to be married to a cook," said that lady indignantly.

"And leave off his evil ways, and set up in the chandlery line arterwards," said the housemaid.

"Well, then," said Mr Muzzle, "I'm very sorry to have to explain myself before ladies, but the urgency of the case will be my excuse. The back kitchen's empty, sir. If you will step in there, sir, Mr Weller will see fair, and we can have mutual satisfaction till the bell rings. Follow me, sir!"

As Mr Muzzle uttered these words, he took a step or two towards the door; and, by way of saving time, began to pull off his coat as he walked along. Now, the cook no sooner heard the concluding words of this desperate challenge, and saw Mr Muzzle about to put it into execution, than she uttered a loud and piercing shriek; and rushing on Mr Job Trotter, who rose from his chair on the instant, tore and buffeted his large flat face, with an energy peculiar to excited females, and twining her hands in his long black hair, tore about enough to make five or six dozen of the very largest-sized mourning-rings. Having accomplished this feat with all the ardour which her devoted love for Mr Muzzle inspired, she staggered back; and being a lady of very excitable and delicate feelings, she instantly fell under the dresser, and fainted away.

At this moment, the bell rang.

"That's for you, Job Trotter," said Sam; and before Mr Trotter could offer remonstrance or reply – even before he had time to stanch the wounds inflicted by the insensible lady – Sam seized one arm and Mr Muzzle the other, and one pulling before, and the other pushing behind, they conveyed him upstairs, and into the parlour.

It was an impressive tableau. Alfred Jingle, Esquire, alias Captain Fitz-Marshall, was standing near the door with his hat in his hand, and a smile on his face, wholly unmoved by his very unpleasant situation. Confronting him, stood Mr Pickwick, who had evidently been inculcating some high moral lesson; for his left hand was beneath his coat tail, and his right extended in air, as was his wont when delivering himself of an impressive address.

At a little distance, stood Mr Tupman with indignant countenance, carefully held back by his two younger friends; at the farther end of the room were Mr Nupkins, Mrs Nupkins, and Miss Nupkins, gloomily grand and savagely vexed.

"What prevents me," said Mr Nupkins, with magisterial dignity, as Job was brought in – "what prevents me from detaining these men as rogues and impostors? It is a foolish mercy. What prevents me?"

"Pride, old fellow, pride," replied Jingle, quite at his ease. "Wouldn't do – no go – caught a captain, eh? – ha! ha! very good – husband for daughter – biter bit – make it public – not for worlds – look stupid – very!"

"Wretch," said Mr Nupkins, "we scorn your base insinuations."

"I always hated him," added Henrietta.

"Oh, of course," said Jingle. "Tall young man – old lover – Sidney Porkenham – rich – fine fellow – not so rich as captain, though, eh? – turn him away – off with him – anything for captain – nothing like captain anywhere – all the girls – raving mad – eh, Job, eh?"

Here Mr Jingle laughed very heartily; and Job, rubbing his hands with delight, uttered the first sound he had given vent to since he entered the house – a low, noiseless chuckle, which seemed to intimate that he enjoyed his laugh too much, to let any of it escape in sound.

"Mr Nupkins," said the elder lady, "this is not a fit conversation for the servants to overhear. Let these wretches be removed."

"Certainly, my dear," said Mr Nupkins. "Muzzle!"

"Your Worship."

"Open the front door."

"Yes, your Worship."

"Leave the house!" said Mr Nupkins, waving his hand emphatically.

Jingle smiled, and moved towards the door.

"Stay!" said Mr Pickwick.

Jingle stopped.

"I might," said Mr Pickwick, "have taken a much greater revenge for the treatment I have experienced at your hands, and that of your hypocritical friend there." Job Trotter bowed with great politeness, and laid his hand upon his heart. "I say," said Mr Pickwick, growing gradually angry, "that I might have taken a greater revenge, but I content myself with exposing you, which I consider a duty I owe to society. This is a leniency, sir, which I hope you will remember."

When Mr Pickwick arrived at this point, Job Trotter, with facetious gravity, applied his hand to his ear, as if desirous not to lose a syllable he uttered.

"And I have only to add, sir," said Mr Pickwick, now thoroughly angry, "that I consider you a rascal, and a – a – ruffian – and – and worse than any man I ever saw, or heard of, except that pious and sanctified vagabond in the mulberry livery."

"Ha! ha!" said Jingle, "good fellow, Pickwick – fine heart – stout old boy – but must *not* be passionate – bad thing, very – bye, bye – see you again some day – keep up your spirits – now, Job – trot!"

With these words, Mr Jingle stuck on his hat in the old fashion, and strode out of the room. Job Trotter paused, looked round, smiled and then with a bow of mock solemnity to Mr Pickwick, and a wink to Mr Weller, the audacious slyness of which baffles all description, followed the footsteps of his hopeful master.

"Sam," said Mr Pickwick, as Mr Weller was following.

"Sir."

"Stay here."

Mr Weller seemed uncertain.

"Stay here," repeated Mr Pickwick.

"Mayn't I polish that 'ere Job off, in the front garden?" said Mr Weller.

"Certainly not," replied Mr Pickwick.

"Mayn't I kick him out o' the gate, sir?" said Mr Weller.

"Not on any account," replied his master.

For the first time since his engagement, Mr Weller looked, for a moment, discontented and unhappy. But his countenance immediately cleared up; for the wily Mr Muzzle, by concealing himself behind the street door, and rushing violently out, at the right instant, contrived with great dexterity to overturn both Mr Jingle and his attendant, down the flight of steps, into the tubs that stood beneath.

"Having discharged my duty, sir," said Mr Pickwick to Mr Nupkins, "I will, with my friends, bid you farewell. While we thank you for such hospitality as we have received, permit me to assure you, in our joint names, that we should not have accepted it, or have consented to extricate ourselves in this way, from our previous dilemma, had we not been impelled by a strong sense of duty. We return to London to-morrow. Your secret is safe with us."

Having thus entered his protest against their treatment of the morning, Mr Pickwick bowed low to the ladies, and notwithstanding the solicitations of the family, left the room with his friends.

"Get your hat, Sam," said Mr Pickwick.

"It's below stairs, sir," said Sam, and he ran down after it.

Now, there was nobody in the kitchen, but the pretty housemaid; and as Sam's hat was mislaid, he had to look for it, and the pretty housemaid lighted him. They had to look all over the place for the hat. The pretty housemaid, in her anxiety to find it, went down on her knees, and turned over all the things that were heaped together in a little corner by the door. It was an awkward corner. You couldn't get at it without shutting the door first.

"Here it is," said the pretty housemaid. "This is it, ain't it?"

"Let me look," said Sam.

The pretty housemaid had stood the candle on the floor; and, as it gave a very dim light, Sam was obliged to go down on his knees before he could see whether it really was his own hat or not. It was a remarkably small corner, and so – it was nobody's fault but the man's who built the house – Sam and the pretty housemaid were necessarily very close together.

"Yes, this is it," said Sam. "Good-bye!"

"Good-bye!" said the pretty housemaid.

"Good-bye!" said Sam; and as he said it, he dropped the hat that had cost so much trouble in looking for.

"How awkward you are," said the pretty housemaid. "You'll lose it again, if you don't take care."

So just to prevent his losing it again, she put it on for him.

Whether it was that the pretty housemaid's face looked prettier still, when it was raised towards Sam's, or whether it was the accidental consequence of their being so near to each other, is matter of uncertainty to this day; but Sam kissed her.

"You don't mean to say you did that on purpose," said the pretty housemaid, blushing.

"No, I didn't then," said Sam; "but I will now."

So he kissed her again.

"Sam!" said Mr Pickwick, calling over the banisters.

"Coming, sir," replied Sam, running upstairs.

"How long you have been!" said Mr Pickwick.

"There was something behind the door, sir, which perwented our getting it open, for ever so long, sir," replied Sam.

And this was the first passage of Mr Weller's first love.

CHAPTER 16

A Good-humoured Christmas Chapter, Containing an Account of a Wedding, and Some Other Sports Beside: Which Although in their Way, Even as Good Customs as Marriage Itself, are Not Quite So Religiously Kept Up, in these Degenerate Times

As brisk as bees, if not altogether as light as fairies, did the four Pickwickians assemble on the morning of the twenty-second day of December. Christmas was close at hand; it was the season of hospitality, merriment, and open-heartedness. Gay and merry was the time; and right gay and merry were at least four of the numerous hearts that were gladdened by its coming.

Such was the progress of Mr Pickwick and his friends on their way to Dingley Dell; and at three o'clock that afternoon they all stood high and dry, safe and sound, hale and hearty, upon the steps of the Blue Lion. Mr Pickwick was busily engaged in counting the barrels of oysters and superintending the disinterment of the cod-fish, when he felt himself gently pulled by the skirts of the coat. Looking round, he discovered that the individual who resorted to this mode of catching his attention was no other than Mr Wardle's favourite page, better known by the distinguishing appellation of the fat boy.

"Aha!" said Mr Pickwick.

"Aha!" said the fat boy.

132

As he said it, he glanced from the cod-fish to the oyster-barrels, and chuckled joyously. He was fatter than ever.

"Well, you look rosy enough, my young friend," said Mr Pickwick.

"I've been asleep, right in front of the tap-room fire," replied the fat boy, who had heated himself to the colour of a new chimney-pot, in the course of an hour's nap. "Master sent me over with the shay-cart, to carry your luggage up to the house. He'd ha' sent some saddle-horses, but he thought you'd rather walk, being a cold day."

"Yes, we would rather walk. Here, Sam!"

"Sir," said Mr Weller.

"Help Mr Wardle's servant to put the packages into the cart, and then ride on with him. We will walk forward at once."

Having given this direction, and settled with the coachman, Mr Pickwick and his three friends struck into the footpath across the fields, and walked briskly away, leaving Mr Weller and the fat boy confronted together for the first time. Sam looked at the fat boy with great astonishment, but without saying a word; and began to stow the luggage rapidly away in the cart, while the fat boy stood quietly by, and seemed to think it a very interesting sort of thing to see Mr Weller working by himself.

"There," said Sam, throwing in the last carpet-bag, "there they are!"

"Yes," said the fat boy, in a very satisfied tone, "there they are."

"Vell," said Sam, "Do you ever drink anythin'?"

"I likes eating better," replied the boy.

"Ah," said Sam, "I should ha' s'posed that; but what I mean is, should you like a drop of anythin' as'd warm you?"

"Sometimes," replied the boy; "and I likes a drop of something, when it's good."

"Oh, you do, do you?" said Sam, "come this way, then!"

The Blue Lion tap was soon gained, and the fat boy swallowed a glass of liquor without so much as winking – a feat which considerably advanced him in Mr Weller's good opinion. Mr Weller having transacted a similar piece of business on his own account, they got into the cart.

"Can you drive?" said the fat boy.

"I should rayther think so," replied Sam.

"There, then," said the fat boy, putting the reins in his hand, and pointing up a lane, "it's as straight as you can go; you can't miss it."

With these words, the fat boy laid himself affectionately down by the side of the cod-fish, and, placing an oyster-barrel under his head for a pillow, fell asleep instantaneously.

"Well," said Sam, "of all the cool boys ever I set my eyes on, this here young gen'l'm'n is the coolest. Come, wake up, young dropsy!"

But as young dropsy evinced no symptoms of returning animation, Sam Weller sat himself down in front of the cart, and starting the old horse with a jerk of the rein, jogged steadily on, towards the Manor Farm.

Meanwhile, Mr Pickwick and his friends having walked their blood into active circulation, proceeded cheerfully on. The paths were hard; the grass was crisp and frosty; the air had a fine, dry, bracing coldness; and the rapid approach of the grey twilight made them look forward with pleasant anticipation to the comforts which awaited them at their hospitable entertainer's.

As they turned into a lane they had to cross, the sound of many voices burst upon their ears; and before they had even had time to form a guess to whom they belonged, they walked into the very centre of the party who were expecting their arrival.

First, there was Wardle himself, looking, if that were possible, more jolly than ever; then there were Bella and her faithful Trundle; and, lastly, there were Emily and some eight or ten young ladies, who had all come down to the wedding, which was to take place next day, and they were, one and all, startling the fields and lanes, far and wide, with their frolic and laughter.

In two minutes thereafter, Mr Pickwick was joking with the young ladies who wouldn't come over the stile while he looked -- or who, having pretty feet and unexceptionable ankles, preferred standing on the top rail for five minutes or so, declaring that they were too frightened to move. It is worthy of remark, too, that Mr Snodgrass offered Emily far more assistance than the absolute terrors of the stile (although it was full three feet high, and had only a couple of stepping-stones) would seem to require; while one black-eyed young lady in a very nice little pair of boots with fur round the top, was observed to scream very loudly, when Mr Winkle offered to help her over.

But if they were social and happy outside the house, what was the warmth and cordiality of their reception when they reached the farm! The very servants grinned with pleasure at sight of Mr Pickwick; and Emma bestowed a half-demure, half-impudent, and all-pretty look of recognition, on Mr Tupman.

The old lady was seated with customary state in the front parlour, but she was rather cross, and, by consequence, most particularly deaf.

"Mother," said Wardle, "Mr Pickwick. You recollect him?"

"Never mind," replied the old lady, with great dignity. "Don't trouble Mr Pickwick about an old creetur like me. Nobody cares about me now, and it's very nat'ral they shouldn't." Here the old lady tossed her head, and smoothed down her lavender-coloured silk dress with trembling hands.

"Come, come, ma'am," said Mr Pickwick, "I can't let you cut an old friend in this way. I have come down expressly to have a long talk, and another rubber with you; and we'll show these boys and girls how to dance a minuet, before they're eight-and-forty hours older."

The good old lady heard this, for her lip quivered but she was not quite brought round yet. So, she smoothed down the lavender-coloured dress again, and turning to Mr Pickwick said, "Ah, Mr Pickwick, young people was very different, when I was a girl."

"No doubt of that, ma'am," said Mr Pickwick, "and that's the reason why I would make much of the few that have any traces of the old stock" -- and saying this, Mr Pickwick gently pulled Bella towards him, and bestowing a kiss upon her forehead, bade her sit down on the little stool at her grandmother's feet.

She was fairly melted so she threw herself on her grand-daughter's neck, and all the little ill-humour evaporated in a gush of silent tears.

A happy party they were, that night. Sedate and solemn were the score of rubbers in which Mr Pickwick and the old lady played together; uproarious was the mirth of the round table. Long after the ladies had retired, did the hot elder wine, well qualified with brandy and spice, go round, and round, and round again; and sound was the sleep and pleasant were the dreams that followed. It is a remarkable fact that those of Mr Snodgrass bore constant reference to Emily Wardle; and that the principal figure in Mr Winkle's visions was a young lady with black eyes, and arch smile, and a pair of remarkably nice boots with fur round the tops.

Mr Pickwick was awakened early in the morning, by a hum of voices and a pattering of feet, sufficient to rouse even the fat boy from his heavy slumbers. He sat up in bed and listened. The female servants and female visitors were running constantly to and fro; and there were such multitudinous demands for hot water, such repeated outcries for needles and thread, and so many half-suppressed entreaties of "Oh, do come and tie me, there's a dear!" that Mr Pickwick in his innocence began to imagine that something dreadful must have occurred – when he grew more awake, and remembered the wedding. The occasion being an important one, he dressed himself with peculiar care, and descended to the breakfast-room.

There were all the female servants in a brand new uniform of pink muslin gowns with white bows in their caps, running about the house in a state of excitement and agitation which it would be impossible to describe. The old lady was dressed out in a brocaded gown, which had not seen the light for twenty years.

Mr Trundle was in high feather and spirits, but a little nervous withal. The hearty old landlord was trying to look very cheerful and unconcerned, but failing signally in the attempt.

All the girls were in tears and white muslin, except a select two or three, who were being honoured with a private view of the bride and bridesmaids, upstairs.

All the Pickwickians were in most blooming array; and there was a terrific roaring on the grass in front of the house, occasioned by all the men, boys, and hobbledehoys attached to the farm, each of whom had got a white bow in his button-hole, and all of whom were cheering with might and main; being incited and stimulated by the example of Mr Samuel Weller, who had managed to become mighty popular already, and was as much at home as if he had been born on the land.

A wedding is a licensed subject to joke upon, but there really is no great joke in the matter after all. Let us briefly say, then, that the ceremony was performed by the old clergyman, in the parish church of Dingley Dell, and that Mr Pickwick's name is attached to the register, still preserved in the vestry thereof; that the young lady with the black eyes signed her name in a very unsteady and tremulous manner; that Emily's signature, as the other bridesmaid, is nearly illegible; that it all went off in very admirable style; that the young ladies generally thought it far less shocking than they had expected; and that although the owner of the black eyes and the arch smile informed Mr Wardle that she was sure she could never submit to anything so dreadful, we have the very best reasons for thinking she was mistaken. Then, the old church bell rang as gaily as it could, and they all returned to breakfast.

"Wardle," said Mr Pickwick, almost as soon as they were all seated, "a glass of wine in honour of this happy occasion!"

"I shall be delighted, my boy," said Wardle. "Joe – damn that boy, he's gone to sleep."

"No, I ain't, sir," replied the fat boy, starting up from a remote corner, where, like the patron saint of fat boys – the immortal Horner – he had been devouring a Christmas pie. "Fill Mr Pickwick's glass."

"Yes, sir."

The fat boy filled Mr Pickwick's glass, and then retired behind his master's chair, from whence he watched the progress of the choice morsels from the dishes to the mouths of the company, with a kind of dark and gloomy joy that was most impressive.

"God bless you, old fellow!" said Mr Pickwick.

"Same to you, my boy," replied Wardle; and they pledged each other, heartily.

"Mrs Wardle," said Mr Pickwick, "we old folks must have a glass of wine together, in honour of this joyful event."

The old lady was in a state of great grandeur just then, for she was sitting at the top of the table in the brocaded gown, with her newly-married grand-daughter on one side, and Mr Pickwick on the other, to do the carving. Mr Pickwick had not spoken in a very loud tone, but she understood him at once, and drank off a full glass of wine to his long life and happiness. Then the cake was cut, and passed through the ring; the young ladies saved pieces to put under their pillows to dream of their future husbands on; and a great deal of blushing and merriment was thereby occasioned.

Mr Pickwick expressed his heartfelt delight at every additional suggestion; and his eyes beamed with hilarity and cheerfulness.

"Ladies and gentlemen," said Mr Pickwick, suddenly rising.

"Hear, hear! Hear, hear! Hear, hear!" cried Mr Weller, in the excitement of his feelings.

"Call in all the servants," cried old Wardle, interposing to prevent the public rebuke which Mr Weller would otherwise have received from his master. "Give them a glass of wine each to drink the toast in. Now, Pickwick."

"My dear friends," resumed Mr Pickwick, "I am going to propose the health of the bride and bridegroom – God bless 'em (cheers and tears). My young friend, Trundle, I believe to be a very excellent and manly fellow; and his wife I know to be a very amiable and lovely girl, well qualified to transfer to another sphere of action the happiness which for twenty years she has diffused around her, in her father's house. I wish," added Mr Pickwick – "I was young enough to be her sister's husband (cheers), but, failing that, I am happy to be old enough to be her father. The bride's father, our good friend there, is a noble person, and I am proud to know him. So, let us drink their healths, and wish them prolonged life, and every blessing!"

Mr Pickwick concluded amidst a whirlwind of applause. Mr Wardle proposed Mr Pickwick; Mr Pickwick proposed the old lady. Mr Snodgrass proposed Mr Wardle; Mr Wardle proposed Mr Snodgrass. One of the poor relations proposed Mr Tupman, and the other poor relation proposed Mr Winkle; all was happiness and festivity, until the mysterious disappearance of both the poor relations beneath the table, warned the party that it was time to adjourn.

At dinner they met again, after a five-and-twenty mile walk, undertaken by the males at Wardle's recommendation, to get rid of the effects of the wine at breakfast. The dinner was as hearty an affair as the breakfast, and was quite as noisy, without the tears. Then came the dessert and some more toasts. Then came the tea and coffee; and then, the ball.

The best sitting-room at Manor Farm was a good, long, dark-panelled room with a high chimney-piece, and a capacious chimney. At the upper end of the room, seated in a shady bower of holly and evergreens were the two best fiddlers, and the only harp, in all Muggleton. In all sorts of recesses, and on all kinds of brackets, stood massive old silver candlesticks with four branches each. The carpet was up, the candles burned bright, the fire blazed and crackled on the hearth, and merry voices and light-hearted laughter rang through the room.

If anything could have added to the interest of this agreeable scene, it would have been the remarkable fact of Mr Pickwick's appearing without his gaiters, for the first time within the memory of his oldest friends.

"You mean to dance?" said Wardle.

"Of course I do," replied Mr Pickwick. "Don't you see I am dressed for the purpose?" Mr Pickwick called attention to his speckled silk stockings, and smartly tied pumps.

"*You* in silk stockings!" exclaimed Mr Tupman jocosely.

"And why not, sir – why not?" said Mr Pickwick, turning warmly upon him.

"Oh, of course there is no reason why you shouldn't wear them," responded Mr Tupman.

"I imagine not, sir – I imagine not," said Mr Pickwick, in a very peremptory tone.

Mr Tupman had contemplated a laugh, but he found it was a serious matter; so he looked grave, and said they were a pretty pattern.

"I hope they are," said Mr Pickwick, fixing his eyes upon his friend. "You see nothing extraordinary in the stockings, as stockings, I trust, sir?"

"Certainly not. Oh, certainly not," replied Mr Tupman. He walked away; and Mr Pickwick's countenance resumed its customary benign expression.

"We are all ready, I believe," said Mr Pickwick, who was stationed with the old lady at the top of the dance, and had already made four false starts, in his excessive anxiety to commence.

"Then begin at once," said Wardle. "Now!"

Up struck the two fiddles and the one harp, and off went Mr Pickwick into hands across, when there was a general clapping of hands, and a cry of "stop, stop!"

"What's the matter?" said Mr Pickwick, who was only brought to, by the fiddles and harp desisting, and could have been stopped by no other earthly power, if the house had been on fire.

"Where's Arabella Allen?" cried a dozen voices.

"And Winkle?" added Mr Tupman.

"Here we are!" exclaimed the gentleman, emerging with his pretty companion from the corner; as he did so, it would have been hard to tell which was the redder in the face, he or the young lady with the black eyes.

"What an extraordinary thing it is, Winkle," said Mr Pickwick, rather pettishly, "that you couldn't have taken your place before."

"Not at all extraordinary," said Mr Winkle.

"Well," said Mr Pickwick, with a very expressive smile, as his eyes rested on Arabella, "well, I don't know that it *was* extraordinary, either, after all."

However, there was no time to think more about the matter, for the fiddles and harp began in real earnest. Long before Mr Pickwick was weary of dancing, the newly-married couple had retired from the scene. There was a glorious supper downstairs, notwithstanding, and a good long sitting after it; and when Mr Pickwick awoke, late the next morning, he had a confused recollection of having, severally and confidentially, invited somewhere about five-and-forty people to dine with him at the George and Vulture, the very first time they came to London; which Mr Pickwick rightly considered a pretty certain indication of his having taken something besides exercise, on the previous night.

"And so your family has games in the kitchen to-night, my dear, has they?" inquired Sam of Emma.

"Yes, Mr Weller," replied Emma; "we always have on Christmas Eve. Master wouldn't neglect to keep it up on any account."

"Your master's a wery pretty notion of keeping anythin' up, my dear," said Mr Weller; "I never see such a sensible sort of man as he is, or such a reg'lar gen'l'm'n."

"Oh, that he is!" said the fat boy, joining in the conversation; "don't he breed nice pork!"

"Oh, you've woke up, at last, have you?" said Sam.

The fat boy nodded. And they all three repaired to the large kitchen, in which the family were by this time assembled, according to annual custom on Christmas Eve, observed by old Wardle's forefathers from time immemorial.

From the centre of the ceiling of this kitchen, old Wardle had just suspended, with his own hands, a huge branch of mistletoe, and this same branch of mistletoe instantaneously gave rise to a scene of general and most delightful struggling and confusion; in the midst of which, Mr Pickwick took the old lady by the hand, led her beneath the mystic branch, and saluted her in all courtesy and decorum. Mr Winkle kissed the young lady with the black eyes, and Mr Snodgrass kissed Emily; and Mr Weller, not being particular about the form of being under the mistletoe, kissed Emma and the other female servants, just as he caught them.

Wardle stood with his back to the fire, surveying the whole scene, with the utmost satisfaction; and the fat boy took the opportunity of appropriating to his own use, and summarily devouring, a particularly fine mince-pie, that had been carefully put by for somebody else.

Now, the screaming had subsided, and faces were in a glow, and curls in a tangle, and before Mr Pickwick distinctly knew what was the matter, he was surrounded by the whole body of young ladies and kissed by every one of them.

It was a pleasant thing to see Mr Pickwick in the centre of the group, now pulled this way, and then that, and first kissed on the chin, and then on the nose, and then on the spectacles, and to hear the peals of laughter which were raised on every side; but it was a still more pleasant thing to see Mr Pickwick, blinded shortly afterwards with a silk handkerchief, falling up against the wall, and scrambling into corners, and going through all the mysteries of blind-man's buff, with the utmost relish for the game, until at last he caught one of the poor relations, and then had to evade the blind-man himself, which he did with a nimbleness and agility that elicited the admiration and applause of all beholders.

When they all tired of blind-man's buff, there was a great game at snap-dragon, and when fingers enough were burned with that, and all the raisins were gone, they sat down by the huge fire of blazing logs to a substantial supper, and a mighty bowl of wassail, something smaller than an ordinary wash-house copper, in which the hot apples were hissing and bubbling with a rich look, and a jolly sound, that were perfectly irresistible.

"This," said Mr Pickwick, looking round him, "this is, indeed, comfort."

CHAPTER 17

How the Pickwickians Made and Cultivated the Acquaintance of a Couple of Nice Young Men Belonging to One of the Liberal Professions; How They Disported Themselves on the Ice; and How Their Visit Came to a Conclusion

"Well, Sam," said Mr Pickwick, as that favoured servitor entered his bed-chamber, with his warm water, on the morning of Christmas Day, "still frosty?"

"Water in the wash-hand basin's a mask o' ice, sir," responded Sam.

"Severe weather, Sam," observed Mr Pickwick.

"Fine time for them as is well wropped up, as the Polar Bear said to himself, ven he was practising his skating," replied Mr Weller.

"I shall be down in a quarter of an hour, Sam," said Mr Pickwick, untying his nightcap.

"Wery good, sir," replied Sam. "There's a couple o' sawbones downstairs."

"A couple of what!" exclaimed Mr Pickwick, sitting up in bed.

"A couple o' sawbones," said Sam.

"What's a sawbones?" inquired Mr Pickwick, not quite certain whether it was a live animal, or something to eat.

"What! Don't you know what a sawbones is, sir?" inquired Mr Weller. "I thought everybody know'd as a sawbones was a surgeon."

"Oh, a surgeon, eh?" said Mr Pickwick, with a smile.

"Just that, sir," replied Sam. "These here ones as is below, though, ain't reg'lar thoroughbred sawbones; they're only in trainin'."

"In other words they're medical students, I suppose?" said Mr Pickwick. Sam Weller nodded assent.

"I am glad of it," said Mr Pickwick, casting his nightcap energetically on the counterpane. "They are fine fellows – very fine fellows; with judgements matured by observation and reflection; and tastes refined by reading and study. I am very glad of it."

"They're a-smokin' cigars by the kitchen fire," said Sam.

"Ah!" observed Mr Pickwick, rubbing his hands, "overflowing with kindly feelings and animal spirits. Just what I like to see."

"And one on 'em," said Sam, not noticing his master's interruption, "one on 'em's got his legs on the table, and is a-drinking brandy neat, vile the t'other one has got a barrel o' oysters atween his knees, which he's a-openin' like steam, and as fast as he eats 'em, he takes a aim vith the shells at young dropsy, who's a sittin' down fast asleep, in the chimbley corner."

"Eccentricities of genius, Sam," said Mr Pickwick. "You may retire."

Sam did retire accordingly. Mr Pickwick at the expiration of the quarter of an hour, went down to breakfast.

"Here he is at last!" said old Mr Wardle. "Pickwick, this is Miss Allen's brother, Mr Benjamin Allen. Ben we call him, and so may you, if you like. This gentleman is his very particular friend, Mr – "

"Mr Bob Sawyer," interposed Mr Benjamin Allen; whereupon Mr Bob Sawyer and Mr Benjamin Allen laughed in concert.

Mr Pickwick bowed to Bob Sawyer, and Bob Sawyer bowed to Mr Pickwick.

"Splendid morning, gentlemen," said Mr Pickwick.

Mr Bob Sawyer slightly nodded his assent to the proposition, and asked Mr Benjamin Allen for the mustard.

"Peg away, Bob," said Mr Allen, to his companion, encouragingly.

"Nothing like dissecting, to give one an appetite," said Mr Bob Sawyer, looking round the table.

Mr Pickwick slightly shuddered.

"By the bye, Bob," said Mr Allen, "have you finished that leg yet?"

"Nearly," replied Sawyer, helping himself to half a fowl as he spoke. "It's a very muscular one for a child's."

"Is it?" inquired Mr Allen carelessly.

"Very," said Bob Sawyer, with his mouth full.

"I've put my name down for an arm at our place," said Mr Allen.

"Hush, hush, gentlemen, pray," said Mr Pickwick, "I hear the ladies."

As Mr Pickwick spoke, the ladies, gallantly escorted by Messrs Snodgrass, Winkle, and Tupman, returned from an early walk.

"Why, Ben!" said Arabella, in a tone which expressed more surprise than pleasure at the sight of her brother.

"Come to take you home to-morrow," replied Benjamin.

Mr Winkle turned pale.

"Don't you see Bob Sawyer, Arabella?" inquired Mr Benjamin Allen, somewhat reproachfully. Arabella gracefully held out her hand, in acknowledgment of Bob Sawyer's presence. A thrill of hatred struck to Mr Winkle's heart, as Bob Sawyer inflicted on the proffered hand a perceptible squeeze.

"Ben, dear!" said Arabella, blushing; "have – have – you been introduced to Mr Winkle?"

"I have not been, but I shall be very happy to be, Arabella," replied her brother gravely. Here Mr Allen bowed grimly to Mr Winkle, while Mr Winkle and Mr Bob Sawyer glanced mutual distrust out of the corners of their eyes.

"Now," said Wardle, after a substantial lunch, with the agreeable items of strong beer and cherry-brandy, had been done ample justice to, "what say you to an hour on the ice? We shall have plenty of time."

"Capital!" said Mr Benjamin Allen.

"Prime!" ejaculated Mr Bob Sawyer.

"You skate, of course, Winkle?" said Wardle.

"Ye-yes; oh, yes," replied Mr Winkle. "I – I – am rather out of practice."

"Oh, *do* skate, Mr Winkle," said Arabella. "I like to see it so much."

"I should be very happy, I'm sure," said Mr Winkle, reddening; "but I have no skates."

This objection was at once overruled. Trundle had a couple of pair, and the fat boy announced that there were half a dozen more downstairs; whereat Mr Winkle expressed exquisite delight, and looked exquisitely uncomfortable.

Old Wardle led the way to a pretty large sheet of ice; and the fat boy and Mr Weller, having shovelled and swept away the snow which had fallen on it during the night, Mr Bob Sawyer adjusted his skates with a dexterity which to Mr Winkle was perfectly marvellous, and described circles with his left leg, and cut figures of eight, and inscribed upon the ice, without once stopping for breath, a great many other pleasant and astonishing devices, to the excessive satisfaction of Mr Pickwick, Mr Tupman, and the ladies.

All this time, Mr Winkle, with his face and hands blue with the cold, had been forcing a gimlet into the sole of his feet, and putting his skates on, with the points behind, and getting the straps into a very complicated and entangled state, with the assistance of Mr Snodgrass, who knew rather less about skates than a Hindoo. At length, however, with the assistance of Mr Weller, the unfortunate skates were firmly screwed and buckled on, and Mr Winkle was raised to his feet.

"Now, then, sir," said Sam, in an encouraging tone; "off with you, and show 'em how to do it."

"Stop, Sam, stop!" said Mr Winkle, trembling violently, and clutching hold of Sam's arms with the grasp of a drowning man. "How slippery it is, Sam!"

"Not an uncommon thing upon ice, sir," replied Mr Weller. "Hold up, sir!"

This last observation of Mr Weller's bore reference to a demonstration Mr Winkle made at the instant, of a frantic desire to throw his feet in the air, and dash the back of his head on the ice.

"These – these – are very awkward skates; ain't they, Sam?" inquired Mr Winkle, staggering.

"I'm afeerd there's a orkard gen'l'm'n in 'em, sir," replied Sam.

"Now, Winkle," cried Mr Pickwick, quite unconscious that there was anything the matter. "Come; the ladies are all anxiety."

"Yes, yes," replied Mr Winkle, with a ghastly smile. "I'm coming."

"Just a-goin' to begin," said Sam, endeavouring to disengage himself. "Now, sir, start off!"

"Stop an instant, Sam," gasped Mr Winkle, clinging most affectionately to Mr Weller. "I find I've got a couple of coats at home that I don't want, Sam. You may have them, Sam."

"Thank'ee, sir," replied Mr Weller.

"Never mind touching your hat, Sam," said Mr Winkle hastily. "You needn't take your hand away to do that. I meant to have given you five shillings this morning for a Christmas box, Sam. I'll give it you this afternoon, Sam."

"You're wery good, sir," replied Mr Weller.

"Just hold me at first, Sam; will you?" said Mr Winkle. "There – that's right. I shall soon get in the way of it, Sam. Not too fast, Sam; not too fast."

Mr Winkle, stooping forward, with his body half doubled up, was being assisted over the ice by Mr Weller, in a very singular and un-swan-like manner, when Mr Pickwick most innocently shouted from the opposite bank –

"Sam!"

"Sir?"

"Here. I want you."

"Let go, sir," said Sam. "Don't you hear the governor a-callin'?"

With a violent effort, Mr Weller disengaged himself from the grasp of the agonised Pickwickian, and, in so doing, administered a considerable impetus to the unhappy Mr Winkle. With an accuracy which no degree of dexterity or practice could have insured, that unfortunate gentleman bore swiftly down into the centre of the reel, at the very moment when Mr Bob Sawyer was performing a flourish of unparalleled beauty. Mr Winkle struck wildly against him, and with a loud crash they both fell heavily down.

Mr Pickwick ran to the spot. Bob Sawyer had risen to his feet, but

Mr Winkle was far too wise to do anything of the kind, in skates. He was seated on the ice, making spasmodic efforts to smile; but anguish was depicted on every lineament of his countenance.

"Are you hurt?" inquired Mr Benjamin Allen, with great anxiety.

"Not much," said Mr Winkle, rubbing his back very hard.

"I wish you'd let me bleed you," said Mr Benjamin, with great eagerness.

"No, thank you," replied Mr Winkle hurriedly.

"I really think you had better," said Allen.

"Thank you," replied Mr Winkle; "I'd rather not."

"What do you think, Mr Pickwick?" inquired Bob Sawyer.

Mr Pickwick was excited and indignant. He beckoned to Mr Weller, and said in a stern voice, "Take his skates off."

"No; but really I had scarcely begun," remonstrated Mr Winkle.

"Take his skates off," repeated Mr Pickwick firmly.

The command was not to be resisted. Mr Winkle allowed Sam to obey it, in silence.

"Lift him up," said Mr Pickwick. Sam assisted him to rise. Mr Pickwick retired a few paces apart from the bystanders; and, beckoning his friend to approach, fixed a searching look upon him, and uttered in a low, but distinct and emphatic tone, these remarkable words –

"You're a humbug, sir."

"A what?" said Mr Winkle, starting.

"A humbug, sir. I will speak plainer, if you wish it. An impostor, sir."

With those words, Mr Pickwick turned slowly on his heel, and rejoined his friends.

"Do you slide?" Wardle demanded of him.

"I used to do so, on the gutters, when I was a boy," replied Mr Pickwick.

"Try it now," said Wardle.

"Oh, do, please, Mr Pickwick!" cried all the ladies.

"I should be very happy to afford you any amusement," replied Mr Pickwick, "but I haven't done such a thing these thirty years."

"Pooh! pooh! Nonsense!" said Wardle, dragging off his skates with the impetuosity which characterised all his proceedings. "Here; I'll keep you company; come along!" And away went the good-tempered old fellow down the slide, with a rapidity which came very close upon Mr Weller, and beat the fat boy all to nothing.

Mr Pickwick paused, considered, pulled off his gloves and put them in his hat; took two or three short runs, baulked himself as often, and at last took another run, and went slowly and gravely down the slide, with his feet about a yard and a quarter apart, amidst the gratified shouts of all the spectators.

"Keep the pot a-bilin', sir!" said Sam; and down went Wardle again, and then Mr Pickwick, and then Sam, and then Mr Winkle, and then Mr Bob Sawyer, and then the fat boy, and then Mr Snodgrass, following closely upon each other's heels, and running after each other with as much eagerness as if their future prospects in life depended on their expedition. The sport was at its height, the sliding was at the quickest, the laughter was at the loudest, when a sharp smart crack was heard. There was a quick rush towards the bank, a wild scream from the ladies, and a shout from Mr Tupman. A large mass of ice disappeared; the water bubbled up over it; Mr Pickwick's hat, gloves, and handkerchief were floating on the surface; and this was all of Mr Pickwick that anybody could see.

Dismay and anguish were depicted on every countenance; the males turned pale, and the females fainted; Mr Snodgrass and Mr Winkle grasped each other by the hand, and gazed at the spot where their leader had gone down, with frenzied eagerness; while Mr Tupman, by way of rendering the promptest assistance, and at the same time conveying to any persons who might be within hearing, the clearest possible notion of the catastrophe, ran off across the country at his utmost speed, screaming "Fire!" with all his might.

It was at this moment, when old Wardle and Sam Weller were approaching the hole with cautious steps, and Mr Benjamin Allen was holding a hurried consultation with Mr Bob Sawyer on the advisability of bleeding the company generally, as an improving little bit of professional practice – it was at this very moment, that a face, head, and shoulders, emerged from beneath the water, and disclosed the features and spectacles of Mr Pickwick.

"Keep yourself up for an instant – for only one instant!" bawled Mr Snodgrass.

"Yes, do; let me implore you – for my sake!" roared Mr Winkle, deeply affected.

"Do you feel the bottom there, old fellow?" said Wardle.

"Yes, certainly," replied Mr Pickwick, wringing the water from his head and face, and gasping for breath. "I fell upon my back. I couldn't get on my feet at first."

The clay upon so much of Mr Pickwick's coat as was yet visible, bore testimony to the accuracy of this statement; and as the fears of the spectators were still further relieved by the fat boy's suddenly recollecting that the water was nowhere more than five feet deep, prodigies of valour were performed to get him out. After a vast quantity of splashing, and cracking, and struggling, Mr Pickwick was at length fairly extricated from his unpleasant position, and once more stood on dry land.

"Oh, he'll catch his death of cold," said Emily.

"Dear old thing!" said Arabella. "Let me wrap this shawl round you, Mr Pickwick."

"Ah, that's the best thing you can do," said Wardle; "and when you've got it on, run home as fast as your legs can carry you, and jump into bed directly."

A dozen shawls were offered on the instant. Three or four of the thickest having been selected, Mr Pickwick was wrapped up, and started off, under the guidance of Mr Weller; presenting the singular phenomenon of an elderly gentleman, dripping wet, and without a hat, with his arms bound down to his sides, skimming over the ground, without any clearly-defined purpose, at the rate of six good English miles an hour.

Mr Pickwick paused not an instant until he was snug in bed. Sam Weller lighted a blazing fire in the room, and took up his dinner; a bowl of punch was carried up afterwards, and a grand carouse held in honour of his safety. Old Wardle would not hear of his rising, so they made the bed the chair, and Mr Pickwick presided. A second and a third bowl were ordered in; and when Mr Pickwick awoke next morning, there was not a symptom of rheumatism about him; which proves, as Mr Bob Sawyer very justly observed, that there is nothing like hot punch in such cases; and that if ever hot punch did fail to act as a preventive, it was merely because the patient fell into the vulgar error of not taking enough of it.

The jovial party broke up next morning. Breakings-up are capital things in our school-days, but in after life they are painful enough. The different members of the party dispersed to their several homes; Mr Pickwick and his friends once more took their seats on the top of the

Muggleton coach; and Arabella Allen repaired to her place of destination, wherever it might have been, under the care and guardianship of her brother Benjamin, and his most intimate and particular friend, Mr Bob Sawyer.

We feel that in this place we lay ourself open to the inquiry whether Mr Winkle was whispering, during this brief conversation, to Arabella Allen; and if so, what he said; and furthermore, whether Mr Snodgrass was conversing apart with Emily Wardle; and if so, what *he* said. To this, we reply, that whatever they might have said to the ladies, they said nothing at all to Mr Pickwick or Mr Tupman for eight-and-twenty miles, and that they sighed very often, refused ale and brandy, and looked gloomy. If our observant lady readers can deduce any satisfactory inferences from these facts, we beg them by all means to do so.

CHAPTER 18

Which is All About the Law, and Sundry Great Authorities Learned Therein

About half-past seven o'clock in the evening, some ten days or a fortnight after Mr Pickwick and his friends returned to London, there hurried into one of the offices of law, an individual in a brown coat and brass buttons. He produced from his coat pockets a long and narrow strip of parchment, on which the presiding functionary impressed an illegible black stamp. He then drew forth four scraps of paper, of similar dimensions, each containing a printed copy of the strip of parchment with blanks for a name; and having filled up the blanks, put all the five documents in his pocket, and hurried away.

The man in the brown coat, with the documents in his pocket, was Mr Jackson, of the house of Dodson & Fogg, Freeman's Court, Cornhill. Instead of returning to the office whence he came, however, he bent his steps direct to Sun Court, and walking straight into the George and Vulture, demanded to know whether one Mr Pickwick was within.

"Call Mr Pickwick's servant, Tom," said the barmaid of the George and Vulture.

"Don't trouble yourself," said Mr Jackson. "I've come on business. If you'll show me Mr Pickwick's room I'll step up myself."

"What name, sir?" said the waiter.

"Jackson," replied the clerk.

The waiter stepped upstairs to announce Mr Jackson; but Mr Jackson saved him the trouble by following close at his heels, and walking into the apartment before he could articulate a syllable.

Mr Pickwick had, that day, invited his three friends to dinner; they were all seated round the fire, drinking their wine, when Mr Jackson presented himself, as above described.

"How de do, sir?" said Mr Jackson, nodding to Mr Pickwick.

That gentleman bowed, and looked somewhat surprised.

"I have called from Dodson and Fogg's," said Mr Jackson, in an explanatory tone.

Mr Pickwick roused at the name. "I refer you to my attorney, sir; Mr Perker, of Gray's Inn," said he. "Waiter, show this gentleman out."

"Beg your pardon, Mr Pickwick," said Jackson, deliberately depositing his hat on the floor, and drawing from his pocket the strip of parchment. "But personal service, by clerk or agent, in these cases, you know, Mr Pickwick – nothing like caution, sir, in all legal forms – eh?"

Here Mr Jackson cast his eye on the parchment; and, resting his hands on the table, and looking round with a winning and persuasive smile, said, "Now, come; don't let's have no words about such a little matter as this. Which of you gentlemen's name's Snodgrass?"

At this inquiry, Mr Snodgrass gave such a very undisguised and palpable start, that no further reply was needed.

"Ah! I thought so," said Mr Jackson, more affably than before. "I've a little something to trouble you with, sir."

"Me!" exclaimed Mr Snodgrass.

"It's only a subpoena in Bardell and Pickwick on behalf of the plaintiff," replied Jackson, singling out one of the slips of paper, and producing a shilling from his waistcoat pocket. "It'll come on fourteenth of Febooary, we expect. That's yours, Mr Snodgrass." As Jackson said this, he presented the parchment before the eyes of Mr Snodgrass, and slipped the paper and the shilling into his hand.

Mr Tupman had witnessed this process in silent astonishment, when Jackson, turning sharply upon him, said –

"I think I ain't mistaken when I say your name's Tupman, am I?"

Mr Tupman looked at Mr Pickwick; but, perceiving no encouragement in that gentleman's widely opened eyes to deny his name, said –

"Yes, my name is Tupman, sir."

"And that other gentleman's Mr Winkle, I think?" said Jackson.

Mr Winkle faltered out a reply in the affirmative; and both gentlemen were forthwith invested with a slip of paper, and a shilling each, by the dexterous Mr Jackson.

"Now," said Jackson, "I'm afraid you'll think me rather troublesome, but I want somebody else, if it ain't inconvenient. I have Samuel Weller's name here, Mr Pickwick."

"Send my servant here, waiter," said Mr Pickwick. The waiter retired, considerably astonished, and Mr Pickwick motioned Jackson to a seat.

There was a painful pause, which was at length broken by the innocent defendant.

"I suppose, sir," said Mr Pickwick, his indignation rising while he spoke – "I suppose, sir, that it is the intention of your employers to seek to criminate me upon the testimony of my own friends?"

Mr Jackson struck his forefinger several times against the left side of his nose, to intimate that he was not there to disclose the secrets of the prison house, and playfully rejoined –

"Not knowin', can't say."

"For what other reason, sir," pursued Mr Pickwick, "are these subpoenas served upon them, if not for this?"

"Very good plant, Mr Pickwick," replied Jackson, slowly shaking his head. "But it won't do. No harm in trying, but there's little to be got out of me." Here Mr Jackson smiled once more upon the company. "No, no, Mr Pickwick," said Jackson, in conclusion; "Perker's people must guess what we've served these subpoenas for. If they can't, they must wait till the action comes on, and then they'll find out."

Mr Pickwick bestowed a look of excessive disgust on his unwelcome visitor, and would probably have hurled some tremendous anathema at the heads of Messrs Dodson and Fogg, had not Sam's entrance at the instant interrupted him.

"Samuel Weller?" said Mr Jackson, inquiringly.

"Vun o' the truest things as you've said for many a long year," replied Sam, in a most composed manner.

"Here's a subpoena for you, Mr Weller," said Jackson.

"What's that in English?" inquired Sam.

"Here's the original," said Jackson, declining the required explanation.

"Which?" said Sam.

"This," replied Jackson, shaking the parchment.

"Oh, that's the 'rig'nal, is it?" said Sam. "Well, I'm wery glad I've seen the 'rig'nal, 'cos it's a gratifyin' sort o' thing, and eases vun's mind so much."

"And here's the shilling," said Jackson. "It's from Dodson and Fogg's."

"And it's uncommon handsome o' Dodson and Fogg, as knows so little of me, to come down vith a present," said Sam.

Mr Jackson seemed rather puzzled by Sam's proceedings; but, as he had served the subpoenas, had nothing more to say and so returned to the office to report progress.

Mr Pickwick slept little that night; his memory had received a very disagreeable refresher on the subject of Mrs Bardell's action. He breakfasted betimes next morning, and, desiring Sam to accompany him, set forth towards Gray's Inn Square.

"This action, Sam," said Mr Pickwick, "is expected to come on on the fourteenth of next month."

"Remarkable coincidence that 'ere, sir," replied Sam.

"Why remarkable, Sam?" inquired Mr Pickwick.

"Walentine's day, sir," responded Sam; "reg'lar good day for a breach o' promise trial."

Mr Weller's smile awakened no gleam of mirth in his master's countenance. Mr Pickwick turned abruptly round, and led the way in silence to Mr Perker's chambers, where the clerk led the way to his principal's private room, and announced Mr Pickwick.

"Ah, my dear sir," said little Mr Perker, bustling up from his chair. "Well, my dear sir, and what's the news about your matter, eh? Anything more about our friends in Freeman's Court? They've not been sleeping, I know that. Ah, they're very smart fellows; very smart, indeed."

As the little man concluded, he took an emphatic pinch of snuff, as a tribute to the smartness of Messrs Dodson and Fogg.

"They are great scoundrels," said Mr Pickwick.

"Aye, aye," said the little man; "that's a matter of opinion, you know, because of course you can't be expected to view these subjects with a professional eye. Well, we've done everything that's necessary. I have retained Serjeant Snubbin."

"Is he a good man?" inquired Mr Pickwick.

"Good man!" replied Perker; "bless your heart and soul, my dear Sir, Serjeant Snubbin is at the very top of his profession. Gets treble the business of any man in court – engaged in every case. You needn't mention it abroad; but we say – we of the profession – that Serjeant Snubbin leads the court by the nose."

The little man took another pinch of snuff as he made this communication, and nodded mysteriously to Mr Pickwick.

"They have subpoena'd my three friends," said Mr Pickwick.

"Ah! of course they would," replied Perker. "Important witnesses; saw you in a delicate situation."

"But she fainted of her own accord," said Mr Pickwick. "She threw herself into my arms."

"Very likely, my dear sir," replied Perker; "very likely and very natural. Nothing more so, my dear sir, nothing. But who's to prove it?"

"They have subpoena'd my servant, too," said Mr Pickwick.

"Of course, my dear sir; of course. I knew they would. I could have told you that, a month ago."

"And what do they want him to prove?" asked Mr Pickwick, after two or three minutes' silence.

"That you sent him up to the plaintiff's to make some offer of a compromise, I suppose," replied Perker. "It don't matter much, though; I don't think many counsel could get a great deal out of *him*."

"I don't think they could," said Mr Pickwick, smiling, despite his vexation, at the idea of Sam's appearance as a witness. "What course do we pursue?"

"We have only one to adopt, my dear sir," replied Perker; "cross-examine the witnesses; trust to Snubbin's eloquence; throw dust in the eyes of the judge; throw ourselves on the jury."

"And suppose the verdict is against me?" said Mr Pickwick.

Mr Perker smiled, took a very long pinch of snuff, stirred the fire, shrugged his shoulders, and remained expressively silent.

"You mean that in that case I must pay the damages?" said Mr Pickwick, who had watched this telegraphic answer with considerable sternness.

Perker gave the fire another very unnecessary poke, and said, "I am afraid so."

"Then I beg to announce to you my unalterable determination to pay no damages whatever," said Mr Pickwick, most emphatically. "None, Perker. Not a pound, not a penny of my money, shall find its way into the pockets of Dodson and Fogg. That is my deliberate and irrevocable determination." Mr Pickwick gave a heavy blow on the table before him, in confirmation of the irrevocability of his intention.

"Very well, my dear sir, very well," said Perker. "You know best, of course."

"Of course," replied Mr Pickwick hastily. "Where does Serjeant Snubbin live?"

"In Lincoln's Inn Old Square," replied Perker.

"I should like to see him," said Mr Pickwick.

"See Serjeant Snubbin, my dear sir!" rejoined Perker, in utter amazement. "Pooh, pooh, my dear sir, impossible. See Serjeant Snubbin! Bless you, my dear sir, such a thing was never heard of, without a consultation fee being previously paid, and a consultation fixed. It couldn't be done, my dear sir; it couldn't be done."

Mr Pickwick, however, had made up his mind not only that it could be done, but that it should be done; and the consequence was, that within ten minutes after he had received the assurance that the thing was impossible, he was conducted by his solicitor into the office of the great Serjeant Snubbin himself.

Mr Serjeant Snubbins was a lantern-faced, sallow-complexioned man, of about five-and-forty, or he might be fifty. The marks of hair-powder on his coat-collar, and the ill-washed and worse tied white neckerchief round his throat, showed that he had not found leisure since he left the court to make any alteration in his dress; while the slovenly style of the remainder of his costume warranted the inference that his personal appearance would not have been very much improved if he had.

The Serjeant was writing when his clients entered; he bowed abstractedly when Mr Pickwick was introduced by his solicitor; and then, motioning them to a seat, put his pen carefully in the inkstand, nursed his left leg, and waited to be spoken to.

"Mr Pickwick is the defendant in Bardell and Pickwick, Serjeant Snubbin," said Perker.

"I am retained in that, am I?" said the Serjeant.

"You are, sir," replied Perker.

The Serjeant nodded his head, and waited for something else.

"Mr Pickwick was anxious to call upon you, Serjeant Snubbin," said Perker, "to state to you, before you entered upon the case, that he denies there being any ground or pretence whatever for the action against him; and that unless he came into court with clean hands, and without the most conscientious conviction that he was right in resisting the plaintiff's demand, he would not be there at all. I believe I state your views correctly; do I not, my dear sir?" said the little man, turning to Mr Pickwick.

"Quite so," replied that gentleman.

Mr Serjeant Snubbin unfolded his glasses, raised them to his eyes; and, after looking at Mr Pickwick for a few seconds with great curiosity, turned to Mr Perker, and said, smiling slightly as he spoke –

"Has Mr Pickwick a strong case?"

The attorney shrugged his shoulders.

"Do you propose calling witnesses?"

"No."

The smile on the Serjeant's countenance became more defined; he rocked his leg with increased violence; and, throwing himself back in his easy-chair, coughed dubiously. These tokens of the Serjeant's presentiments on the subject, slight as they were, were not lost on Mr Pickwick.

"Sir," Mr Pickwick began, "conscious as I am, sir, of the disadvantage of making such a declaration to you, under such circumstances, I have come here, because I wish you distinctly to understand, that I am innocent of the falsehood laid to my charge. Sir, I must beg to add, that unless you sincerely believe this, I would rather be deprived of the aid of your talents than have the advantage of them."

Long before the close of this address the Serjeant had relapsed into a state of abstraction. After some minutes, however, during which he had reassumed his pen, he appeared to be again aware of the presence of his clients; raising his head from the paper, he said, rather snappishly –

"Who is with me in this case?"

"Mr Phunky, Serjeant Snubbin," replied the attorney.

"Phunky – Phunky," said the Serjeant, "I never heard the name before. He must be a very young man."

"Yes, he is a very young man," replied the attorney. "Let me see – he has not been at the Bar eight years yet."

"Ah, I thought not," said the Serjeant, in that sort of pitying tone in which ordinary folks would speak of a very helpless little child. "Clerk, send round to Mr Phunky, and say I should be glad if he'd step here, a moment."

The clerk departed to execute his commission; and Serjeant Snubbin relapsed into abstraction until Mr Phunky himself was introduced. Although an infant barrister, he was a full-grown man. He had a very nervous manner, and a painful hesitation in his speech; it did not appear to be a natural defect, but seemed rather the result of timidity. He was overawed by the Serjeant, and profoundly courteous to the attorney.

"I have not had the pleasure of seeing you before, Mr Phunky," said Serjeant Snubbin, with haughty condescension.

Mr Phunky bowed. He had had the pleasure of seeing the Serjeant, and of envying him too, with all a poor man's envy, for eight years and a quarter.

"You are with me in this case, I understand?" said the Serjeant.

If Mr Phunky had been a rich man, he would have instantly sent for his clerk to remind him; if he had been a wise one, he would have applied his forefinger to his forehead, and endeavoured to recollect, whether, in the multiplicity of his engagements, he had undertaken this one or not; but as he was neither rich nor wise (in this sense, at all events) he turned red, and bowed.

"Have you read the papers, Mr Phunky?" inquired the Serjeant.

Here again, Mr Phunky should have professed to have forgotten all about the merits of the case; but as he had read such papers as had been laid before him in the course of the action, and had thought of nothing else, waking or sleeping, throughout the two months during which he had been retained as Mr Serjeant Snubbin's junior, he turned a deeper red and bowed again.

"This is Mr Pickwick," said the Serjeant, waving his pen in the direction in which that gentleman was standing.

Mr Phunky bowed to Mr Pickwick, with a reverence which a first client must ever awaken; and again inclined his head towards his leader.

"Perhaps you will take Mr Pickwick away," said the Serjeant, "and – and – and – hear anything Mr Pickwick may wish to communicate. We shall have a consultation, of course." With that hint that he had been interrupted quite long enough, Mr Serjeant Snubbin, who had been gradually growing more and more abstracted, applied his glass to his eyes for an instant, bowed slightly round, and was once more deeply immersed in the case before him.

Mr Phunky would not hear of passing through any door until Mr Pickwick and his solicitor had passed through before him, so it was some time before they got into the Square; and when they did reach it, they walked up and down, and held a long conference, the result of which was, that it was a very difficult matter to say how the verdict would go; that nobody could presume to calculate on the issue of an action; that it was very lucky they had prevented the other party from getting Serjeant Snubbin; and other topics of doubt and consolation, common in such a position of affairs.

Mr Weller was then roused by his master from a sweet sleep of an hour's duration; and, bidding adieu to Lowten, they returned to the city.

CHAPTER 19

Is Wholly Devoted to a Full and Faithful Report of the Memorable Trial of Bardell Against Pickwick

"I wonder what the foreman of the jury, whoever he'll be, has got for breakfast," said Mr Snodgrass, by way of keeping up a conversation on the eventful morning of the fourteenth of February.

"Ah!" said Perker, "I hope he's got a good one."

"Why so?" inquired Mr Pickwick.

"Highly important – very important, my dear sir," replied Perker. "A good, contented, well-breakfasted juryman is a capital thing to get hold of. Discontented or hungry jurymen, my dear sir, always find for the plaintiff."

"Bless my heart," said Mr Pickwick, looking very blank, "what do they do that for?"

"Why, I don't know," replied the little man coolly; "saves time, I suppose." The little man looked at his watch. "Time we were off, my dear sir; breach of promise trial-court is generally full in such cases. You had better ring for a coach, my dear sir, or we shall be rather late."

Mr Pickwick immediately rang the bell, and a coach having been procured, the four Pickwickians and Mr Perker ensconced themselves therein, and drove to Guildhall; Sam Weller, Mr Lowten, and the blue bag, following in a cab.

"Lowten," said Perker, when they reached the outer hall of the court, "put Mr Pickwick's friends in the students' box; Mr Pickwick himself had better sit by me. This way, my dear sir, this way." Taking Mr Pickwick by the coat sleeve, the little man led him to the low seat just beneath the desks of the King's Counsel.

There were already a pretty large sprinkling of spectators in the gallery, and a numerous muster of gentlemen in wigs, in the barristers' seats. To the great wonderment of Mr Pickwick, they were divided into little groups, who were chatting and discussing the news of the day in the most unfeeling manner possible – just as if no trial at all were coming on.

A bow from Mr Phunky, as he entered, and took his seat behind the row appropriated to the King's Counsel, attracted Mr Pickwick's attention; and he had scarcely returned it, when Mr Serjeant Snubbin appeared, followed by Mr Mallard, who half hid behind a large crimson bag, which he placed on his table, and, after shaking hands with Perker, withdrew. Then there entered two or three more Serjeants; and among them, one with a fat body and a red face, who nodded in a friendly manner to Mr Serjeant Snubbin, and said it was a fine morning.

"Who's that red-faced man, who said it was a fine morning, and nodded to our counsel?" whispered Mr Pickwick.

"Mr Serjeant Buzfuz," replied Perker. "He's opposed to us; he leads on the other side. That gentleman behind him is Mr Skimpin, his junior."

He was interrupted by a general rising of the barristers, and a loud cry of "Silence!" from the officers of the court. Looking round, Mr Pickwick found that this was caused by the entrance of the judge.

The judge had no sooner taken his seat, than the officer on the floor of the court called out "Silence!" in a commanding tone, upon which another officer in the gallery cried "Silence!" in an angry manner, whereupon three or four more ushers shouted "Silence!" in a voice of indignant remonstrance. This being done, a gentleman in black, who sat below the judge, proceeded to call over the names of the jury; and after a great deal of bawling, it was discovered that only ten special jurymen were present.

Upon this, the gentleman in black then proceeded to press into the special jury, two of the common jurymen; and a greengrocer and a chemist were caught directly.

Immediately afterwards Mrs Bardell, supported by Mrs Cluppins, was led in, and placed, in a drooping state, at the other end of the seat on which Mr Pickwick sat. Mrs Sanders then appeared, leading in Master Bardell. At sight of her child, Mrs Bardell kissed him in a frantic manner; then relapsing into a state of hysterical imbecility, the good lady requested to be informed where she was. In reply to this, Mrs Cluppins and Mrs Sanders turned their heads away and wept, while Messrs Dodson and Fogg entreated the plaintiff to compose herself. Serjeant Buzfuz rubbed his eyes very hard with a large white handkerchief, and gave an appealing look towards the jury, while the judge was visibly affected, and several of the beholders tried to cough down their emotion.

"Very good notion that indeed," whispered Perker to Mr Pickwick. "Capital fellows those Dodson and Fogg; excellent ideas of effect, my dear sir, excellent."

"Bardell and Pickwick," cried the gentleman in black, calling on the case, which stood first on the list.

"I am for the plaintiff, my Lord," said Mr Serjeant Buzfuz.

"Who is with you, Brother Buzfuz?" said the judge. Mr Skimpin bowed, to intimate that he was.

"I appear for the defendant, my Lord," said Mr Serjeant Snubbin.

"Anybody with you, Brother Snubbin?" inquired the court.

"Mr Phunky, my Lord," replied Serjeant Snubbin.

"Serjeant Buzfuz and Mr Skimpin for the plaintiff," said the judge, writing down the names in his note-book, and reading as he wrote; "for the defendant, Serjeant Snubbin and Mr Monkey."

"Beg your Lordship's pardon, Phunky."

"Oh, very good," said the judge; "I never had the pleasure of hearing the gentleman's name before."

The ushers again called silence, and Mr Skimpin proceeded to "open the case"; and the case appeared to have very little inside it when he had opened it, for he kept such particulars as he knew, completely to himself, and sat down, after a lapse of three minutes, leaving the jury in precisely the same advanced stage of wisdom as they were in before.

Serjeant Buzfuz then rose with all the majesty and dignity which the grave nature of the proceedings demanded, and having whispered to Dodson, and conferred briefly with Fogg, pulled his gown over his shoulders, settled his wig, and addressed the jury.

Serjeant Buzfuz began by saying, that never, in the whole course of his professional experience had he approached a case with feelings of such deep emotion, or with such a heavy sense of the responsibility imposed upon him – a responsibility, he would say, which he could never have supported, were he not buoyed up and sustained by a conviction that the cause of his much-injured and most oppressed client, must prevail with the high-minded and intelligent dozen of men whom he now saw in that box before him.

A visible effect was produced immediately, several jurymen beginning to take voluminous notes with the utmost eagerness.

"The plaintiff, gentlemen," continued Serjeant Buzfuz, in a soft and melancholy voice, "the plaintiff is a widow; yes, gentlemen, a widow. The late Mr Bardell, after enjoying, for many years, the esteem and confidence of his sovereign, as one of the guardians of his royal revenues, glided almost imperceptibly from the world."

At this pathetic description of the decease of Mr Bardell, who had been knocked on the head with a quart-pot in a public-house cellar, the learned serjeant's voice faltered, and he proceeded, with emotion –

"Some time before his death, he had stamped his likeness upon a little boy. With this little boy Mrs Bardell shrank from the world, and courted the retirement and tranquillity of Goswell Street; and here she placed in her front parlour window a written placard, bearing this inscription – 'Apartments furnished for a single gentleman. Inquire within.'" Here Serjeant Buzfuz paused, while several gentlemen of the jury took a note of the document.

"There is no date to that, is there?" inquired a juror.

"There is no date, gentlemen," replied Serjeant Buzfuz; "but I am instructed to say that it was put in the plaintiff's parlour window just this time three years. I entreat the attention of the jury to the wording of this document – 'Apartments furnished for a single gentleman'! Mrs Bardell's opinions of the opposite sex, gentlemen, were derived from a long contemplation of the inestimable qualities of her lost husband. Actuated by this beautiful and touching impulse the lonely and desolate widow furnished her first floor, caught her innocent boy to her maternal bosom, and put the bill up in her parlour window. Before the bill had been in the parlour window three days – three days, gentlemen – a being, erect upon two legs, and bearing all the outward semblance of a man, and not of a monster, knocked at the door of Mrs Bardell's house. He inquired within – he took the lodgings; and on the very next day he entered into possession of them. This man was Pickwick – Pickwick, the defendant."

Serjeant Buzfuz, who had proceeded with such volubility that his face was perfectly crimson, here paused for breath. The silence awoke Mr Justice Stareleigh, who immediately wrote down something with a pen without any ink in it, and looked unusually profound, to impress the jury with the belief that he always thought most deeply with his eyes shut. Serjeant Buzfuz proceeded –

"Of this man Pickwick I will say little; the subject presents but few attractions; and I, gentlemen, am not the man, nor are you, gentlemen, the men, to delight in the contemplation of revolting heartlessness, and of systematic villainy."

Here Mr Pickwick, who had been writhing in silence for some time, gave a violent start, as if some vague idea of assaulting Serjeant Buzfuz. An admonitory gesture from Perker restrained him, and he listened to the learned gentleman's continuation with a look of indignation.

"I say systematic villainy, gentlemen," said Serjeant Buzfuz, looking through Mr Pickwick, and talking *at* him; "let me tell the defendant Pickwick, if he be in court, as I am informed he is, that it would have been more decent in him, and in better taste, if he had stopped away. Let me tell him, gentlemen, that any gestures of dissent in which he may indulge in this court will not go down with you; and let me tell him further, as my Lord will tell you, gentlemen, that a counsel, in the discharge of his duty to his client, is neither to be intimidated nor bullied, nor put down; and that any attempt to do either the one or the other will recoil on the head of the attempter, be his name Pickwick, or Noakes, or Stoakes, or Stiles, or Brown, or Thompson."

This little divergence from the subject in hand, had, of course, the intended effect of turning all eyes to Mr Pickwick.

Serjeant Buzfuz, having partially recovered from the state of moral elevation into which he had lashed himself, resumed –

"I shall show you, gentlemen, that for two years, Pickwick continued to reside constantly, and without interruption or intermission, at Mrs Bardell's house. I shall show you that Mrs Bardell, during the whole of that time, waited on him, attended to his comforts, cooked his meals, looked out his linen for the washerwoman, darned, aired, and prepared it for wear, and, in short, enjoyed his fullest trust and confidence. I shall show you that, on many occasions, he gave halfpence, and on some occasions even sixpences, to her little boy; and I shall prove to you, that on one occasion he patted the boy on the head, and made use of the remarkable expression, 'How should you like to have another father?' I shall prove to you, gentlemen, that about a year ago, Pickwick suddenly began to absent himself from home, during long intervals, as if with the intention of gradually breaking off from my client; but that on one occasion, when he returned from the country, he distinctly and in terms, offered her marriage: previously, however, taking special care that there would be no witness to their solemn contract; and I am in a situation to prove to you, on the testimony of three of his own friends – most unwilling witnesses, gentlemen – that on that morning he was discovered by them holding the plaintiff in his arms, and soothing her agitation by his caresses and endearments."

A visible impression was produced upon the auditors by this part of the learned Serjeant's address. Drawing forth two very small scraps of paper, he proceeded –

"And now, gentlemen, but one word more. Two letters have passed between these parties, letters which are admitted to be in the handwriting of the defendant, and which speak volumes, indeed. They are covert, sly, underhanded communications, letters that must be viewed with a cautious and suspicious eye – letters that were evidently intended at the time, by Pickwick, to mislead and delude any third parties into whose hands they might fall. Let me read the first: 'Garraways, twelve o'clock. Dear Mrs B. – Chops and tomato sauce. Yours, *Pickwick*.' Gentlemen, what does this mean? Chops and tomato sauce. Yours, Pickwick! Chops! Gracious heavens! and tomato sauce! Gentlemen, is the happiness of a sensitive and confiding female to be trifled away, by such shallow artifices as these? The next has no date whatever, which is in itself suspicious. 'Dear

Mrs B., I shall not be at home till to-morrow. Slow coach.' And then follows this very remarkable expression. 'Don't trouble yourself about the warming-pan.' The warming-pan! Why, gentlemen, who *does* trouble himself about a warming-pan? Why is Mrs Bardell so earnestly entreated not to agitate herself about this warming-pan, unless (as is no doubt the case) it is a mere cover for hidden fire – a mere substitute for some endearing word or promise, artfully contrived by Pickwick with a view to his contemplated desertion? And what does this allusion to the slow coach mean? For aught I know, it may be a reference to Pickwick himself, who has most unquestionably been a criminally slow coach during the whole of this transaction, but whose speed will now be very unexpectedly accelerated, and whose wheels, gentlemen, as he will find to his cost, will very soon be greased by you!"

Mr Serjeant Buzfuz paused in this place, to see whether the jury smiled at his joke; but as nobody took it, the learned Serjeant considered it advisable to undergo a slight relapse into the dismals before he concluded.

"But enough of this, gentlemen," said Mr Serjeant Buzfuz, "it is difficult to smile with an aching heart. My client's hopes and prospects are ruined, and it is no figure of speech to say that her occupation is gone indeed. All is gloom and silence in the house; even the voice of the child is hushed; his infant sports are disregarded when his mother weeps. But Pickwick, gentlemen, Pickwick, the ruthless destroyer of this domestic oasis in the desert of Goswell Street – Pickwick, who comes before you to-day with his heartless tomato sauce and warming-pans – Pickwick still rears his head with unblushing effrontery, and gazes without a sigh on the ruin he has made. Damages, gentlemen – heavy damages is the only punishment with which you can visit him; the only recompense you can award to my client. And for those damages she now appeals to an enlightened, a high-minded, a right-feeling, a conscientious, a dispassionate, a sympathising, a contemplative jury of her civilised countrymen." With this beautiful peroration, Mr Serjeant Buzfuz sat down, and Mr Justice Stareleigh woke up.

"Nathaniel Winkle!" said Mr Skimpin.

"Here!" replied a feeble voice. Mr Winkle entered the witness-box, and having been duly sworn, bowed to the judge with considerable deference.

Mr Winkle was then examined by Mr Skimpin, who, being a promising young man of two or three-and-forty, was of course anxious to confuse a witness who was notoriously predisposed in favour of the other side, as much as he could.

"Now, sir," said Mr Skimpin, "have the goodness to let his Lordship know what your name is, will you?"

"Winkle," replied the witness.

"What's your Christian name, sir?" angrily inquired the little judge.

"Nathaniel, sir."

"Daniel – any other name?"

"Nathaniel, sir – my Lord, I mean."

"Nathaniel Daniel, or Daniel Nathaniel?"

"No, my Lord, only Nathaniel – not Daniel at all."

"What did you tell me it was Daniel for, then, sir?" inquired the judge.

"I didn't, my Lord," replied Mr Winkle.

"You did, sir," replied the judge, with a severe frown. "How could I have got Daniel on my notes, unless you told me so, sir?"

This argument was, of course, unanswerable.

"Mr Winkle has rather a short memory, my Lord," interposed Mr Skimpin, with another glance at the jury. "We shall find means to refresh it before we have quite done with him, I dare say."

"You had better be careful, sir," said the little judge, with a sinister look at the witness.

Poor Mr Winkle bowed, and endeavoured to feign an easiness of manner, which, in his then state of confusion, gave him rather the air of a disconcerted pickpocket.

"Now, Mr Winkle," said Mr Skimpin, "attend to me, if you please, sir. I believe you are a particular friend of Mr Pickwick, the defendant, are you not?"

"I have known Mr Pickwick now, as well as I recollect at this moment, nearly – "

"Pray, Mr Winkle, do not evade the question. Are you, or are you not, a particular friend of the defendant's?"

"I was just about to say, that – "

"Will you, or will you not, answer my question, sir?"

"If you don't answer the question, you'll be committed, sir," interposed the little judge, looking over his note-book.

"Come, sir," said Mr Skimpin, "yes or no, if you please."

"Yes, I am," replied Mr Winkle.

"Yes, you are. And why couldn't you say that at once, sir? Perhaps you know the plaintiff too? Eh, Mr Winkle?"

"I don't know her; I've seen her."

"Oh, you don't know her, but you've seen her? Now, have the goodness to tell the gentlemen of the jury what you mean by that, Mr Winkle."

"I mean that I am not intimate with her, but I have seen her when I went to call on Mr Pickwick, in Goswell Street."

"Pray, Mr Winkle, do you remember calling on the defendant Pickwick at these apartments in the plaintiff's house in Goswell Street, on one particular morning, in the month of July last?"

"Yes, I do."

"Were you accompanied on that occasion by a friend of the name of Tupman, and another by the name of Snodgrass?"

"Yes, I was."

"Are they here?"

"Yes, they are," replied Mr Winkle, looking very earnestly towards the spot where his friends were stationed.

"Pray attend to me, Mr Winkle, and never mind your friends," said Mr Skimpin, with another expressive look at the jury. "They must tell their stories without any previous consultation with you, if none has yet taken place (another look at the jury). Now, sir, tell the gentlemen of the jury what you saw on entering the defendant's room, on this particular morning. Come; out with it, sir; we must have it, sooner or later."

"The defendant, Mr Pickwick, was holding the plaintiff in his arms, with his hands clasping her waist," replied Mr Winkle with natural hesitation, "and the plaintiff appeared to have fainted away."

"Did you hear the defendant say anything?"

"I heard him call Mrs Bardell a good creature, and I heard him ask her to compose herself, for what a situation it was, if anybody should come, or words to that effect."

"Now, Mr Winkle, I have only one more question to ask you, and I beg you to bear in mind his Lordship's caution. Will you undertake to swear that Pickwick, the defendant, did not say on the occasion in question – 'My dear Mrs Bardell, you're a good creature; compose yourself to this situation, for to this situation you must come,' or words to that effect?"

"I – I didn't understand him so, certainly," said Mr Winkle, astounded on this ingenious dove-tailing of the few words he had heard. "I was on the staircase, and couldn't hear distinctly; the impression on my mind is – "

"The gentlemen of the jury want none of the impressions on your mind, Mr Winkle, which I fear would be of little service to honest, straightforward men," interposed Mr Skimpin. "You were on the staircase, and didn't distinctly hear; but you will not swear that Pickwick did not make use of the expressions I have quoted? Do I understand that?"

"No, I will not," replied Mr Winkle; and down sat Mr Skimpin with a triumphant countenance.

Mr Pickwick's case had not gone off in a particularly happy a manner, up to this point. But as it could afford to be placed in a rather better light, Mr Phunky rose for the purpose of getting something important out of Mr Winkle in cross-examination. Whether he did get anything important out of him, will immediately appear.

"I believe, Mr Winkle," said Mr Phunky, "that Mr Pickwick is not a young man?"

"Oh, no," replied Mr Winkle; "old enough to be my father."

"You have told my learned friend that you have known Mr Pickwick a long time. Had you ever any reason to suppose or believe that he was about to be married?"

"Oh, no; certainly not;" replied Mr Winkle with so much eagerness, that Mr Phunky ought to have got him out of the box with all possible dispatch. Lawyers hold that there are two kinds of particularly bad witnesses – a reluctant witness, and a too-willing witness; it was Mr Winkle's fate to figure in both characters.

"I will even go further than this, Mr Winkle," continued Mr Phunky, in a most smooth and complacent manner. "Did you ever see anything in Mr Pickwick's manner and conduct towards the opposite sex, to induce you to believe that he ever contemplated matrimony of late years, in any case?"

"Oh, no; certainly not," replied Mr Winkle.

"You have never known anything in his behaviour towards Mrs Bardell, or any other female, in the least degree suspicious?" said Mr Phunky, preparing to sit down; for Serjeant Snubbin was winking at him.

"N-n-no," replied Mr Winkle, "except on one trifling occasion, which, I have no doubt, might be easily explained."

Now, if the unfortunate Mr Phunky had sat down when Serjeant Snubbin had winked at him, or if Serjeant Buzfuz had stopped this irregular cross-examination at the outset (which he knew better than to do; observing Mr Winkle's anxiety), this unfortunate admission would not have been elicited. The moment the words fell from Mr Winkle's lips, Mr Phunky sat down, and Serjeant Snubbin rather hastily told him he might leave the box, which Mr Winkle prepared to do with great readiness, when Serjeant Buzfuz stopped him.

"Stay, Mr Winkle, stay!" said Serjeant Buzfuz, "will your Lordship have the goodness to ask him, what this one instance of suspicious behaviour towards females on the part of this gentleman, who is old enough to be his father, was?"

"You hear what the learned counsel says, sir," observed the judge, turning to the miserable and agonised Mr Winkle. "Describe the occasion to which you refer."

"My Lord," said Mr Winkle, trembling with anxiety, "I – I'd rather not."

"Perhaps so," said the little judge; "but you must."

Amid the profound silence of the whole court, Mr Winkle faltered out, that the trifling circumstance of suspicion was Mr Pickwick's being found in a lady's sleeping-apartment at midnight; which had terminated, he believed, in the breaking off of the projected marriage of the lady in question, and had led, he knew, to the whole party being forcibly carried before George Nupkins, Esq., magistrate and justice of the peace, for the borough of Ipswich!

"You may leave the box, sir," said Serjeant Snubbin. Mr Winkle did leave the box, and rushed with delirious haste to the George and Vulture, where he was discovered some hours after, by the waiter, groaning in a hollow and dismal manner, with his head buried beneath the sofa cushions.

Tracy Tupman, and Augustus Snodgrass, were severally called into the box; both corroborated the testimony of their unhappy friend; and each was driven to the verge of desperation by excessive badgering.

Susannah Sanders was then called, and examined by Serjeant Buzfuz, and cross-examined by Serjeant Snubbin. Had always said and believed that Pickwick would marry Mrs Bardell; knew that Mrs Bardell's being engaged to Pickwick was the current topic of conversation in the neighbourhood, after the fainting in July. Had heard Pickwick ask the little boy how he should like to have another father. Thought Mrs Bardell fainted away on the morning in July, because Pickwick asked her to name the day and believed that everybody as called herself a lady would do the same, under similar circumstances.

Serjeant Buzfuz now rose with more importance than he had yet exhibited, if that were possible, and vociferated; "Call Samuel Weller."

It was quite unnecessary to call Samuel Weller; for Samuel Weller stepped briskly into the box the instant his name was pronounced; and placing his hat on the floor, and his arms on the rail, took a bird's-eye view of the Bar, and a comprehensive survey of the Bench, with a remarkably cheerful and lively aspect.

"What's your name, sir?" inquired the judge.

"Sam Weller, my Lord," replied that gentleman.

"Do you spell it with a 'V' or a 'W'?" inquired the judge.

"That depends upon the taste and fancy of the speller, my Lord," replied Sam; "I never had occasion to spell it more than once or twice in my life, but I spells it with a 'V'."

"Now, Mr Weller," said Serjeant Buzfuz. "I believe you are in the service of Mr Pickwick, the defendant in this case? Speak up, if you please, Mr Weller."

"I mean to speak up, sir," replied Sam; "I am in the service o' that 'ere gen'l'man, and a wery good service it is."

"Do you recollect anything particular happening on the morning when you were first engaged by the defendant; eh, Mr Weller?" said Serjeant Buzfuz.

"Yes, I do, sir," replied Sam.

"Have the goodness to tell the jury what it was."

"I had a reg'lar new fit out o' clothes that mornin', gen'l'men of the jury," said Sam, "and that was a wery partickler circumstance vith me in those days."

Hereupon there was a general laugh; and the little judge, looking with an angry countenance over his desk, said, "You had better be careful, sir."

"So Mr Pickwick said at the time, my Lord," replied Sam; "and I was wery careful o' that 'ere suit o' clothes; wery careful indeed, my Lord."

The judge looked sternly at Sam for full two minutes, but Sam's features were so perfectly calm and serene that the judge said nothing, and motioned Serjeant Buzfuz to proceed.

"Do you mean to tell me, Mr Weller," said Serjeant Buzfuz, folding his arms emphatically, and turning half-round to the jury, as if in mute assurance that he would bother the witness yet – "do you mean to tell me, Mr Weller, that you saw nothing of this fainting on the part of the plaintiff in the arms of the defendant, which you have heard described by the witnesses?"

"Certainly not," replied Sam; "I was in the passage till they called me up, and then the old lady was not there."

"Now, attend, Mr Weller," said Serjeant Buzfuz, dipping a large pen into the inkstand before him, for the purpose of frightening Sam with a show of taking down his answer. "You were in the passage, and yet saw nothing of what was going forward. Have you a pair of eyes, Mr Weller?"

"Yes, I have a pair of eyes," replied Sam, "and that's just it. If they wos a pair o' patent double million magnifyin' gas microscopes of hextra power, p'raps I might be able to see through a flight o' stairs and a deal door; but bein' only eyes, you see, my wision 's limited."

At this answer, which was delivered without the slightest appearance of irritation, and with the most complete simplicity and equanimity of manner, the spectators tittered, the little judge smiled, and Serjeant Buzfuz looked particularly foolish.

After a short consultation with Dodson and Fogg, the learned Serjeant again turned towards Sam, and said, with a painful effort to conceal his vexation, "Now, Mr Weller, I'll ask you a question on another point, if you please."

"If you please, sir," rejoined Sam, with the utmost good-humour.

"Do you remember going up to Mrs Bardell's house, one night in November last?"

"Oh, yes, wery well."

"Oh, you do remember that, Mr Weller," said Serjeant Buzfuz, recovering his spirits; "I thought we should get at something at last."

"I rayther thought that, too, sir," replied Sam; and at this the spectators tittered again.

"Well; I suppose you went up to have a little talk about this trial – eh, Mr Weller?" said Serjeant Buzfuz, looking knowingly at the jury.

"I went up to pay the rent; but we did get a-talkin' about the trial," replied Sam.

"Oh, you did get a-talking about the trial," said Serjeant Buzfuz, brightening up with the anticipation of some important discovery. "Now, what passed about the trial; will you have the goodness to tell us, Mr Weller?"

"Vith all the pleasure in life, sir," replied Sam. "Arter a few unimportant obserwations the ladies gets into a very great state o' admiration at the honourable conduct of Mr Dodson and Fogg – them two gen'l'men as is settin' near you now." This, of course, drew general attention to Dodson and Fogg, who looked as virtuous as possible.

"The attorneys for the plaintiff," said Mr Serjeant Buzfuz. "Well! They spoke in high praise of the honourable conduct of Messrs Dodson and Fogg, the attorneys for the plaintiff, did they?"

"Yes," said Sam, "they said what a wery gen'rous thing it was o' them to have taken up the case on spec, and to charge nothing at all for costs, unless they got 'em out of Mr Pickwick."

At this very unexpected reply, the spectators tittered again, and Dodson and Fogg, turning very red, leaned over to Serjeant Buzfuz, and in a hurried manner whispered something in his ear.

"You are quite right," said Serjeant Buzfuz aloud, with affected composure. "It's perfectly useless, my Lord, attempting to get at any evidence through the impenetrable stupidity of this witness. I will not trouble the court by asking him any more questions. Stand down, sir."

"Would any other gen'l'man like to ask me anythin'?" inquired Sam, taking up his hat, and looking round most deliberately.

"Not I, Mr Weller, thank you," said Serjeant Snubbin, laughing.

"You may go down, sir," said Serjeant Buzfuz, waving his hand impatiently. Sam went down accordingly, after doing Messrs Dodson and Fogg's case as much harm as he conveniently could, and saying just as little respecting Mr Pickwick as might be, which was precisely the object he had had in view all along.

"I have no objection to admit, my Lord," said Serjeant Snubbin, "if it will save the examination of another witness, that Mr Pickwick has retired from business, and is a gentleman of considerable independent property."

"Very well," said Serjeant Buzfuz, putting in the two letters to be read, "then that's my case, my Lord."

Serjeant Snubbin then addressed the jury on behalf of the defendant; and a very long and a very emphatic address he delivered, in which he

170

bestowed the highest possible praises on the conduct and character of Mr Pickwick. He attempted to show that the letters which had been exhibited, merely related to Mr Pickwick's dinner, or to the preparations for receiving him in his apartments on his return from some country excursion. It is sufficient to add in general terms, that he did the best he could for Mr Pickwick; and the best, as everybody knows, could do no more.

Mr Justice Stareleigh summed up, in the old-established and most approved form. He read as much of his notes to the jury as he could decipher on so short a notice, and made running-comments on the evidence as he went along. If Mrs Bardell were right, it was perfectly clear that Mr Pickwick was wrong, and if they thought the evidence worthy of credence they would believe it, and, if they didn't, why, they wouldn't. If they were satisfied that a breach of promise of marriage had been committed they would find for the plaintiff with such damages as they thought proper; and if, on the other hand, it appeared to them that no promise of marriage had ever been given, they would find for the defendant with no damages at all. The jury then retired to their private room to talk the matter over, and the judge retired to *his* private room, to refresh himself with a mutton chop and a glass of sherry.

An anxious quarter of a hour elapsed; the jury came back; the judge was fetched in. Mr Pickwick put on his spectacles, and gazed at the foreman with an agitated countenance and a quickly-beating heart.

"Gentlemen," said the individual in black, "are you all agreed upon your verdict?"

"We are," replied the foreman.

"Do you find for the plaintiff, gentlemen, or for the defendant?"

"For the plaintiff."

"With what damages, gentlemen?"

"Seven hundred and fifty pounds."

Mr Pickwick took off his spectacles, carefully wiped the glasses, folded them into their case, and put them in his pocket; then, having drawn on his gloves with great nicety, and stared at the foreman all the while, he mechanically followed Mr Perker and the blue bag out of court.

They stopped in a side room while Perker paid the court fees; and here, Mr Pickwick was joined by his friends. Here, too, he encountered Messrs Dodson and Fogg, rubbing their hands with every token of outward satisfaction.

"Well, gentlemen," said Mr Pickwick.

"Well, sir," said Dodson, for self and partner.

"You imagine you'll get your costs, don't you, gentlemen?" said Mr Pickwick.

Fogg said they thought it rather probable. Dodson smiled, and said they'd try.

"You may try, and try, and try again, Messrs Dodson and Fogg," said Mr Pickwick vehemently, "but not one farthing of costs or damages do you ever get from me, if I spend the rest of my existence in a debtor's prison."

"Ha! ha!" laughed Dodson. "You'll think better of that, before next term, Mr Pickwick."

"He, he, he! We'll soon see about that, Mr Pickwick," grinned Fogg.

Speechless with indignation, Mr Pickwick allowed himself to be led by his solicitor and friends to the door, and there assisted into a hackney-coach, which had been fetched for the purpose, by the ever-watchful Sam Weller. Sam had put up the steps, and was preparing to jump upon the box, when he felt himself gently touched on the shoulder; and, looking round, his father stood before him. The old gentleman's countenance wore a mournful expression, as he shook his head gravely, and said, in warning accents –

"I know'd what 'ud come o' this here mode o' doin' bisness. Oh, Sammy, Sammy, vy worn't there a alleybi!"

CHAPTER 20

Introduces Mr Pickwick to a New and Not
Uninteresting Scene in the Great Drama of Life

Trinity Term commenced. On the expiration of its first week, Mr Pickwick and his friends, former gentleman, attended of course by Sam, straightway repaired to his old quarters at the George and Vulture.

On the third morning after their arrival, just as all the clocks in the city were striking nine individually, and somewhere about nine hundred and ninety-nine collectively, Sam was taking the air in George Yard, when a queer sort of fresh-painted vehicle drove up, out of which there jumped a queer sort of gentleman. He was dressed in a particularly gorgeous manner, with plenty of articles of jewellery about him all about three sizes larger than those which are usually worn by gentlemen – and a rough great-coat to crown the whole. It had not escaped Sam's attention that, when this person dismounted, a shabby-looking man in a brown great-coat shorn of divers buttons, who had been previously slinking about, on the opposite side of the way, crossed over, and remained stationary close by. Having something more than a suspicion of the object of the gentleman's visit, Sam preceded him to the George and Vulture, and, turning sharp round, planted himself in the centre of the doorway.

"Now, my fine fellow!" said the man in the rough coat, in an imperious tone, attempting at the same time to push his way past.

"Now, sir, wot's the matter?" replied Sam, returning the push with compound interest.

"Come, none of this, my man; this won't do with me," said the owner of the rough coat, raising his voice, and turning white.

"Here, Smouch!"

"Well, wot's amiss here?" growled the man in the brown coat, who had been gradually sneaking up the court during this short dialogue.

"Only some insolence of this young man's," said the principal, giving Sam another push.

"Come, none o' this gammon," growled Smouch, giving him another, and a harder one.

This last push had the effect which it was intended by the experienced Mr Smouch to produce; for while Sam was grinding that gentleman's body against the door-post, the principal crept past, and made his way to the bar, whither Sam, after bandying a few epithetical remarks with Mr Smouch, followed at once.

"Good-morning, my dear," said the principal, addressing the young lady at the bar, "which is Mr Pickwick's room, my dear?"

"Show him up," said the barmaid to a waiter, without deigning another look at the exquisite, in reply to his inquiry.

The waiter led the way upstairs as he was desired, and the man in the rough coat followed, with Sam behind him. Mr Smouch, who was troubled with a hoarse cough, remained below, and expectorated in the passage.

Mr Pickwick was fast asleep in bed, when his early visitor, followed by Sam, entered the room. The noise they made, in so doing, awoke him.

"Shaving-water, Sam," said Mr Pickwick, from within the curtains.

"Shave you directly, Mr Pickwick," said the visitor, drawing one of them back from the bed's head. "I've got an execution against you, at the suit of Bardell. – Here's the warrant. – Common Pleas. – Here's my card. I suppose you'll come over to my house." Giving Mr Pickwick a friendly tap on the shoulder, the sheriff's officer (for such he was) threw his card on the counterpane, and pulled a gold toothpick from his waistcoat pocket.

"Namby's the name," said the sheriff's deputy, as Mr Pickwick took his spectacles from under the pillow, and put them on, to read the card. "Namby, Bell Alley, Coleman Street."

Mr Namby soon after called up Smouch. Having informed him that the capture was made, and that he was to wait for the prisoner until he should have finished dressing, Namby then swaggered out, and drove away. Smouch, requesting Mr Pickwick in a surly manner "to be as alive as he could, for it was a busy time," drew up a chair by the door and sat there, until he had finished dressing. Sam was then despatched for a hackney-coach, and in it the triumvirate proceeded to Coleman Street.

The coach having turned into a very narrow and dark street, stopped before a house with iron bars to all the windows; the door-posts of which were graced by the name and title of "Namby, officer to the Sheriffs of London"; the inner gate having been opened by a gentleman who might have passed for a neglected twin-brother of Mr Smouch, and who was endowed with a large key for the purpose, Mr Pickwick was shown into the "coffee-room."

This coffee-room was a front parlour, the principal features of which were fresh sand and stale tobacco smoke. Mr Pickwick bowed to the three persons who were seated in it when he entered; and having despatched Sam for Perker, Mr Pickwick rang the bell, and was shown, at his own request, into a private room furnished with a carpet, table, chairs, sideboard and sofa, and ornamented with a looking-glass, and various old prints. Here he had the advantage of hearing Mrs Namby's performance on a square piano overhead, while the breakfast was getting ready; when it came, Mr Perker came too.

"Aha, my dear sir," said the little man, "nailed at last, eh? Come, come, I'm not sorry for it either, because now you'll see the absurdity of this conduct. I've noted down the amount of the taxed costs and damages and we had better settle at once and lose no time. What say you, my dear sir? Shall I draw a cheque, or will you?" The little man rubbed his hands with affected cheerfulness.

"Perker," said Mr Pickwick, "let me hear no more of this, I beg. I see no advantage in staying here, so I shall go to prison to-night."

"You can't go to Whitecross Street, my dear sir," said Perker. "Impossible! There are sixty beds in a ward; and the bolt's on, sixteen hours out of the four-and-twenty."

"I would rather go to some other place of confinement if I can," said Mr Pickwick. "If not, I must make the best I can of that."

"You can go to the Fleet, my dear sir, if you're determined to go somewhere," said Perker.

"That'll do," said Mr Pickwick. "I'll go there directly I have finished my breakfast."

"Stop, stop, my dear sir; not the least occasion for being in such a violent hurry to get into a place that most other men are as eager to get out of," said the good-natured little attorney. "We must have a habeas-corpus. There'll be no judge at chambers till four o'clock this afternoon. You must wait till then."

"Very good," said Mr Pickwick, with unmoved patience. "Then we will have a chop here, at two. See about it, Sam, and tell them to be punctual."

Mr Pickwick remaining firm, despite all the remonstrances and arguments of Perker, the chops appeared and disappeared in due course; he was then put into another hackney coach, and carried off to Chancery Lane.

The usual forms having been gone through, the body of Samuel Pickwick was soon afterwards confided to the custody of the tipstaff, to be taken to the warden of the Fleet Prison, and there detained until the amount of the damages and costs in the action of Bardell against Pickwick was fully paid and satisfied.

"And that," said Mr Pickwick, laughing, "will be a very long time. Sam, call another hackney-coach. Perker, my dear friend, good-bye."

"I shall go with you, and see you safe there," said Perker.

"Indeed," replied Mr Pickwick, "I would rather go without any other attendant than Sam. As soon as I get settled, I will write and let you know, and I shall expect you immediately. Until then, good-bye."

As Mr Pickwick said this, he got into the coach which had by this time arrived, followed by the tipstaff. Sam having stationed himself on the box, it rolled away. The hackney-coach jolted along Fleet Street, as hackney-coaches usually do. Mr Pickwick sat opposite the tipstaff; and the tipstaff sat with his hat between his knees, whistling a tune, and looking out of the coach window. They stopped at length, and Mr Pickwick alighted at the gate of the Fleet.

The tipstaff, just looking over his shoulder to see that his charge was following close at his heels, preceded Mr Pickwick into the prison; they passed through an open door into a lobby, from which a heavy gate, which was guarded by a stout turnkey with the key in his hand, led at once into the interior of the prison.

Here they stopped, while the tipstaff delivered his papers; and here Mr Pickwick was apprised that he would remain, until he had undergone the ceremony, known to the initiated as "sitting for your portrait."

Mr Pickwick sat himself down; when Mr Weller, who stationed himself at the back of the chair, whispered that the sitting was merely another term for undergoing an inspection by the different turnkeys, in order that they might know prisoners from visitors.

"Well, Sam," said Mr Pickwick, "then I wish the artists would come. This is rather a public place."

"There's a bird-cage, sir," says Sam. "Veels vithin veels, a prison in a prison. Ain't it, sir?"

As Mr Weller made this philosophical remark, Mr Pickwick was aware that his sitting had commenced. The stout turnkey sat down, and looked at him carelessly, from time to time, while a long thin man thrust his hands beneath his coat tails, and planting himself opposite, took a good long view of him. A third rather surly-looking gentleman, who was disposing of the last remnant of a crust and butter when he came in, stationed himself close to Mr Pickwick; and, resting his hands on his hips, inspected him narrowly; while two others mixed with the group, and studied his features with most intent and thoughtful faces.

At length the likeness was completed, and Mr Pickwick was informed that he might now proceed into the prison.

"Where am I to sleep to-night?" inquired Mr Pickwick.

"Why, I don't rightly know about to-night," replied the stout turnkey. "You'll be chummed on somebody to-morrow, and then you'll be all snug and comfortable. The first night's generally rather unsettled, but you'll be set all squares to-morrow."

After some discussion, it was discovered that one of the turnkeys had a bed to let, which Mr Pickwick could have for that night. He gladly agreed to hire it.

"If you'll come with me, I'll show it you at once," said the man. "It ain't a large 'un; but it's an out-and-outer to sleep in. This way, sir."

They passed through the inner gate, and descended a short flight of steps. The key was turned after them; and Mr Pickwick found himself, for the first time in his life, within the walls of a debtors' prison.

CHAPTER 21

What Befell Mr Pickwick When He Got Into the Fleet; What Prisoners He Saw There, and How He Passed the Night

Mr Tom Roker, the gentleman who had accompanied Mr Pickwick into the prison, turned sharp to the right when he got to the bottom of the little flight of steps, and led the way, through an iron gate and up another short flight of steps, into a long narrow gallery, dirty and low, paved with stone, and very dimly lighted by a window at each remote end.

"This," said the gentleman, looking carelessly over his shoulder to Mr Pickwick – "this here is the hall flight."

"Oh," replied Mr Pickwick, looking down a dark and filthy staircase, which appeared to lead to a range of damp and gloomy stone vaults, beneath the ground, "and those, I suppose, are the little cellars where the prisoners keep their small quantities of coals. Unpleasant places to have to go down to; but very convenient, I dare say."

"Yes, I shouldn't wonder if they was convenient," replied the gentleman, "seeing that a few people live there, pretty snug. That's the Fair, that is."

"My friend," said Mr Pickwick, "you don't really mean to say that human beings live down in those wretched dungeons?"

"Don't I?" replied Mr Roker, with indignant astonishment; "why shouldn't I?"

"Live! – live down there!" exclaimed Mr Pickwick.

"Live down there! Yes, and die down there, too, very often!" replied

Mr Roker; "and what of that? Yes, and a wery good place it is to live in, ain't it?"

Mr Roker then proceeded to mount another staircase, as dirty as that which led to the place which has just been the subject of discussion, closely followed by Mr Pickwick and Sam.

"There," said Mr Roker, when they reached another gallery of the same dimensions as the one below, "this is the coffee-room flight; the one above's the third, and the one above that's the top; and the room where you're a-going to sleep to-night is the warden's room, and it's this way – come on."

Having said all this in a breath, Mr Roker mounted another flight of stairs with Mr Pickwick and Sam Weller following at his heels. The guide led the way into a small passage at the extreme end, opened a door, and disclosed an apartment of an appearance by no means inviting, containing eight or nine iron bedsteads.

"There," said Mr Roker, holding the door open, and looking triumphantly round at Mr Pickwick, "there's a room!"

Mr Pickwick's face, however, betokened a very trifling portion of satisfaction at the appearance of his lodging.

"There's a room, young man," observed Mr Roker.

"I see it," replied Sam, with a placid nod of the head.

"You wouldn't think to find such a room as this in the Farringdon Hotel, would you?" said Mr Roker, with a complacent smile.

Mr Weller proceeded to inquire which was the individual bedstead that Mr Roker had so flatteringly described as an out-and-outer to sleep in.

"That's it," replied Mr Roker, pointing to a very rusty one in a corner. "It would make any one go to sleep, that bedstead would, whether they wanted to or not."

"I should think," said Sam, eyeing the piece of furniture in question with a look of excessive disgust – "I should think poppies was nothing to it."

"Nothing at all," said Mr Roker.

"And I s'pose," said Sam, with a sidelong glance at his master, as if to see whether there were any symptoms of his determination being shaken by what passed, "I s'pose the other gen'l'men as sleeps here *are* gen'l'men."

"Nothing but it," said Mr Roker. "One of 'em takes his twelve pints of ale a day, and never leaves off smoking even at his meals."

"He must be a first-rater," said Sam.

"A1," replied Mr Roker.

Nothing daunted, even by this intelligence, Mr Pickwick smilingly announced his determination to test the powers of the narcotic bedstead for that night; and Mr Roker, after informing him that he could retire to rest at whatever hour he thought proper, without any further notice or formality, walked off, leaving him standing with Sam in the gallery.

Mr Pickwick slowly retraced his steps downstairs. After a few thoughtful turns in the Painted Ground, which, as it was now dark, was nearly deserted, he intimated to Mr Weller that he thought it high time for him to withdraw for the night; requesting him to seek a bed in some adjacent public-house, and return early in the morning, to make arrangements for the removal of his master's wardrobe from the George and Vulture.

There is no disguising the fact that Mr Pickwick felt very low-spirited and uncomfortable – not for lack of society, for the prison was very full, and a bottle of wine would at once have purchased the utmost good-fellowship of a few choice spirits, without any more formal ceremony of introduction; but he was alone in the coarse, vulgar crowd, and felt the depression of spirits and sinking of heart, naturally consequent on the reflection that he was cooped and caged up, without a prospect of liberation. As to the idea of releasing himself by ministering to the sharpness of Dodson and Fogg, it never for an instant entered his thoughts.

In this frame of mind he turned again into the coffee-room gallery, and walked slowly to and fro. There was a perpetual slamming and banging of doors as the people went in and out; and the noise of their voices and footsteps echoed and re-echoed through the passages constantly. A young woman, with a child in her arms, who seemed scarcely able to crawl, from emaciation and misery, was walking up and down the passage in conversation with her husband, who had no other place to see her in. As they passed Mr Pickwick, he could hear the female sob bitterly; and once she burst into such a passion of grief, that she was compelled to lean against the wall for support, while the man took the child in his arms, and tried to soothe her. Mr Pickwick's heart was really too full to bear it, and he went upstairs to bed.

Now, although the warder's room was a very uncomfortable one it had at present the merit of being wholly deserted save by Mr Pickwick himself. So, he sat down at the foot of his little iron bedstead, and began to wonder how much a year the warder made out of the dirty room. After settling this point, he began to be conscious that he was getting sleepy; whereupon he took his nightcap out of the pocket in which he had had the precaution to stow it in the morning, and, leisurely undressing himself, got into bed and fell asleep.

CHAPTER 22

Illustrative, Like the Preceding One, of the Old Proverb, That Adversity Brings a Man Acquainted with Strange Bedfellows – Likewise Containing Mr Pickwick's Extraordinary and Startling Announcement to Mr Samuel Weller

After breakfasting in a small closet attached to the coffee-room, which bore the imposing title of the Snuggery, and, after despatching Mr Weller on some necessary errands, Mr Pickwick repaired to the lodge, to consult Mr Roker concerning his future accommodation.

"Accommodation, eh?" said that gentleman, consulting a large book. "Plenty of that, Mr Pickwick. Your chummage ticket will be on twenty-seven, in the third."

"Oh," said Mr Pickwick. "My what, did you say?"

"Your chummage ticket," replied Mr Roker; "you're up to that?"

"Not quite," replied Mr Pickwick, with a smile.

"Why," said Mr Roker, "it's as plain as Salisbury. You'll have a chummage ticket upon twenty-seven in the third, and them as is in the room will be your chums."

"Are there many of them?" inquired Mr Pickwick dubiously.

"Three," replied Mr Roker.

Mr Pickwick coughed.

Mr Roker, closed the book, and placing the small piece of paper in Mr Pickwick's hands. "That's the ticket, sir."

Very much perplexed by this summary disposition of this person, Mr Pickwick walked back into the prison, revolving in his mind what he had better do. After groping about in the gallery for some time, attempting in the dim light to decipher the numbers on the different doors, he at length appealed to a pot-boy, who happened to be pursuing his morning occupation of gleaning for pewter.

"Which is twenty-seven, my good fellow?" said Mr Pickwick.

"Five doors farther on," replied the pot-boy. "There's the likeness of a man being hung, and smoking the while, chalked outside the door."

Guided by this direction, Mr Pickwick proceeded slowly along the gallery until he encountered the "portrait of a gentleman," above described, upon whose countenance he tapped, with the knuckle of his forefinger – gently at first, and then audibly. After repeating this process several times without effect, he ventured to open the door and peep in.

There was only one man in the room, and he was leaning out of window as far as he could without overbalancing himself, endeavouring, with great perseverance, to spit upon the crown of the hat of a personal friend on the parade below. As neither speaking, coughing, sneezing, knocking, nor any other ordinary mode of attracting attention, made this person aware of the presence of a visitor, Mr Pickwick, after some delay, stepped up to the window, and pulled him gently by the coat tail. The individual brought in his head and shoulders with great swiftness, and surveying Mr Pickwick from head to foot, demanded in a surly tone what the – something beginning with a capital H – he wanted.

"I believe," said Mr Pickwick, consulting his ticket – "I believe this is twenty-seven in the third?"

"Well?" replied the gentleman.

"I have come here in consequence of receiving this bit of paper," rejoined Mr Pickwick.

"Hand it over," said the gentleman. Mr Pickwick complied.

"I think Roker might have chummed you somewhere else," said Mr Simpson after a very discontented sort of a pause.

Mr Pickwick thought so also; but, under all the circumstances, he considered it a matter of sound policy to be silent. Mr Simpson mused for a few moments after this, and then, thrusting his head out of the window, gave a shrill whistle, and pronounced some word aloud, several times.

In a few seconds, a gentleman, clothed in a professional blue jean frock and top-boots with circular toes, entered the room nearly out of breath, closely followed by another gentleman in very shabby black, and a sealskin cap. The latter gentleman had a very coarse red face, and looked like a drunken chaplain; which, indeed, he was. These two gentlemen having by turns perused Mr Pickwick's billet, and they looked at Mr Pickwick and each other in awkward silence.

"It's an aggravating thing, just as we got the beds so snug," said the chaplain, looking at three dirty mattresses, each rolled up in a blanket; which occupied one corner of the room during the day, and formed a kind of slab, on which were placed an old cracked basin, ewer, and soap-dish, of common yellow earthenware, with a blue flower – "very aggravating."

Mr Martin expressed the same opinion in rather stronger terms; Mr Simpson, after having let a variety of expletive adjectives loose upon society, tucked up his sleeves, and began to wash the greens for dinner.

While this was going on, Mr Pickwick had been eyeing the room, which was filthily dirty, and smelt intolerably close. There was no vestige of carpet, curtain, or blind. Remnants of loaves and pieces of cheese, and damp towels, and scrags of meat, and articles of wearing apparel, and mutilated crockery, and bellows without nozzles, and toasting-forks without prongs were scattered about the floor of a small apartment, which was the common sitting and sleeping room of three idle men.

"I really am so wholly ignorant of the rules of this place," said Mr Pickwick, "Can I live anywhere else?"

"*Can* you!" repeated Mr Martin, with a smile of pity.

"Well, if I knew as little of life as that, I'd eat my hat and swallow the buckle whole," said the clerical gentleman.

After this introductory preface, the three chums informed Mr Pickwick, in a breath, that money was, in the Fleet, just what money was out of it; that it would instantly procure him almost anything he desired; and that, supposing he had it, and had no objection to spend it, if he only signified his wish to have a room to himself, he might take possession of one, furnished and fitted in half an hour's time.

With this the parties separated, very much to their common satisfaction; Mr Pickwick once more retracing his steps to the lodge, and the three companions adjourning to the coffee-room, there to spend the five shillings which the clerical gentleman had, with admirable prudence and foresight, borrowed of him for the purpose.

"I knowed it!" said Mr Roker, with a chuckle, when Mr Pickwick stated the object with which he had returned. "I knowed you'd want a room for yourself, bless you! Let me see. You'll want some furniture. You'll hire that of me, I suppose? That's the reg'lar thing."

"With great pleasure," replied Mr Pickwick.

"There's a capital room up in the coffee-room flight, that belongs to a Chancery prisoner," said Mr Roker. "It'll stand you in a pound a week. I suppose you don't mind that?"

"Not at all," said Mr Pickwick.

"Just step there with me," said Roker, taking up his hat with great alacrity; "the matter's settled in five minutes. Lord! Why didn't you say at first that you was willing to come down handsome?"

The matter was soon arranged, as the turnkey had foretold. The Chancery prisoner had been there long enough to have lost his friends, fortune, home, and happiness, and to have acquired the right of having a room to himself. As he laboured, however, under the inconvenience of often wanting a morsel of bread, he eagerly listened to Mr Pickwick's proposal to rent the apartment, and agreed to yield him up the sole and undisturbed possession thereof, in consideration of the weekly payment of twenty shillings.

As they struck the bargain, Mr Pickwick surveyed him with a painful interest. He was a tall, gaunt, cadaverous man, in an old great-coat and slippers, with sunken cheeks, and a restless, eager eye. His lips were bloodless, and his bones sharp and thin.

"I am afraid, sir," said Mr Pickwick, laying his hand gently and compassionately on his arm – "I am afraid you will have to live in some noisy, crowded place. Now, pray, consider this room your own when you want quiet, or when any of your friends come to see you."

"Friends!" interposed the man, in a voice which rattled in his throat. "I could not be more forgotten or unheeded than I am here. I am a dead man; dead to society, without the pity they bestow on those whose souls have passed to judgement."

And pressing his withered hands together in a hasty and disordered manner, he shuffled from the room.

Mr Roker entered upon his arrangements with such expedition, that in a short time the room was furnished with a carpet, six chairs, a table, a sofa bedstead, a tea-kettle, and various small articles, on hire, at the very reasonable rate of seven-and-twenty shillings and sixpence per week.

"Now, is there anything more we can do for you?" inquired Mr Roker, looking round with great satisfaction, and gaily chinking the first week's hire in his closed fist.

"Why, yes," said Mr Pickwick, who had been musing deeply for some time. "Are there any people here who run on errands, and so forth?"

"Outside, do you mean?" inquired Mr Roker.

"Yes. I mean who are able to go outside. Not prisoners."

"Yes, there is," said Roker. "There's an unfortunate devil, who has got a friend on the poor side, that's glad to do anything of that sort. He's been running odd jobs, and that, for the last two months. Shall I send him?"

"If you please," rejoined Mr Pickwick. "Stay; no. The poor side, you say? I should like to see it. I'll go to him myself."

The poor side of a debtor's prison is, as its name imports, that in which the most miserable and abject class of debtors are confined. A prisoner having declared upon the poor side, pays neither rent nor chummage. His fees, upon entering and leaving the jail, are reduced in amount, and he becomes entitled to a share of some small quantities of food: to provide which, a few charitable persons have, from time to time, left trifling legacies in their wills. Not a week passes but some of these men must inevitably expire in the slow agonies of want, if they were not relieved by their fellow-prisoners.

Turning these things in his mind, as he mounted the narrow staircase at the foot of which Roker had left him, Mr Pickwick gradually worked himself to the boiling-over point; and so excited was he with his reflections on this subject, that he burst into the room to which he had been directed.

He had no sooner cast his eye on the figure of a man who was brooding over the dusty fire, than, letting his hat fall on the floor, he stood perfectly fixed and immovable with astonishment. Yes; in tattered garments, and without a coat; his common calico shirt, yellow and in rags; his hair hanging over his face; his features changed with suffering, and pinched with famine – there sat Mr Alfred Jingle; his head resting on his hands, his eyes fixed upon the fire, and his whole appearance denoting misery and dejection!

Mr Pickwick looked round him in amazement. The noise of someone stumbling hastily into the room, roused him. Turning his eyes towards the door, they encountered the new-comer; and in him, through his rags and dirt, he recognised the familiar features of Mr Job Trotter.

"Mr Pickwick!" exclaimed Job aloud.

"Eh?" said Jingle, starting from his seat. "Mr – ! So it is – queer place

– strange things – serves me right – very." Mr Jingle thrust his hands into the place where his trousers pockets used to be, and, dropping his chin upon his breast, sank back into his chair.

Mr Pickwick looked mildly at Jingle, and said –

"I should like to speak to you in private. Will you step out for an instant?"

"Certainly," said Jingle, rising hastily. "Can't step far – no danger of overwalking yourself here."

"You have forgotten your coat," said Mr Pickwick, as they walked out to the staircase, and closed the door after them.

"Gone, my dear sir – last coat – can't help it. Lived on a pair of boots – whole fortnight. Silk umbrella – ivory handle – week – fact – honour – ask Job – knows it."

"Oh," said Mr Pickwick; "I understand you. You have pawned your wardrobe."

"Everything – Job's too – all shirts gone – never mind – saves washing. Nothing soon – lie in bed – starve – die – inquest – poor prisoner – common necessaries – hush it up – gentlemen of the jury – keep it snug – natural death – coroner's order – workhouse funeral – serve him right – all over – drop the curtain."

Jingle delivered this singular summary of his prospects in life, with his accustomed volubility, and with various twitches of the countenance to counterfeit smiles. Mr Pickwick easily perceived that his recklessness was assumed, and looking him full, but not unkindly, in the face, saw that his eyes were moist with tears.

"Good fellow," said Jingle, pressing his hand, and turning his head away. "Ungrateful dog – boyish to cry – can't help it – bad fever – weak – ill – hungry. Deserved it all – but suffered much – very."

Wholly unable to keep up appearances any longer, and perhaps rendered worse by the effort he had made, the dejected stroller sat down on the stairs, and, covering his face with his hands, sobbed like a child.

"Come, come," said Mr Pickwick, with considerable emotion, "we will see what can be done, when I know all about the matter. Here, Job; where is that fellow?"

"Here, sir," replied Job, presenting himself on the staircase.

"Come here, sir," said Mr Pickwick, trying to look stern, with four large tears running down his waistcoat. "Take that, sir."

In the ordinary acceptation of such language, it should have been a blow. As the world runs, it ought to have been a sound, hearty cuff; for Mr Pickwick had been duped, deceived, and wronged by the destitute outcast who was now wholly in his power. Must we tell the truth? It was something from Mr Pickwick's waistcoat pocket, which chinked as it was given into Job's hand, and the giving of which, somehow or other imparted a sparkle to the eye, and a swelling to the heart, of our excellent old friend, as he hurried away.

Sam had returned when Mr Pickwick reached his own room, and was inspecting the arrangements that had been made for his comfort, with a kind of grim satisfaction which was very pleasant to look upon. Having a decided objection to his master's being there at all, Mr Weller appeared to consider it a high moral duty not to appear too much pleased with anything that was done, said, suggested, or proposed.

"Well, Sam," said Mr Pickwick.

"Well, sir," replied Mr Weller.

"Pretty comfortable now, eh, Sam?"

"Pretty vell, sir," responded Sam, looking round him in a disparaging manner.

"Have you seen Mr Tupman and our other friends?"

"Yes, I have seen 'em, sir, and they're a-comin' to-morrow, and wos wery much surprised to hear they warn't to come to-day," replied Sam.

"You have brought the things I wanted?"

Mr Weller in reply pointed to various packages which he had arranged, as neatly as he could, in a corner of the room.

"Very well, Sam," said Mr Pickwick, after a little hesitation; "listen to what I am going to say, Sam."

"Cert'nly, sir," rejoined Mr Weller; "fire away, sir."

"I have felt from the first, Sam," said Mr Pickwick, with much solemnity, "that this is not the place to bring a young man to."

"Nor an old 'un neither, sir," observed Mr Weller.

"You're quite right, Sam," said Mr Pickwick; "but old men may come here through their own heedlessness and young men may be brought here by the selfishness of those they serve. It is better for those young men, in every point of view, that they should not remain here. Do you understand me, Sam?"

"Vy no, sir, I do *not*," replied Mr Weller doggedly.

"Try, Sam," said Mr Pickwick.

"Vell, sir," rejoined Sam, after a short pause, "I think I see your drift; and if I do see your drift, it's my 'pinion that you're a-comin' it a great deal too strong, as the mail-coachman said to the snowstorm, ven it overtook him."

"Sam," said Mr Pickwick, "for a time you must leave me."

"Oh, for a time, eh, sir?" rejoined Mr Weller, rather sarcastically.

"Yes, for the time that I remain here," said Mr Pickwick. "Your wages I shall continue to pay. Any one of my three friends will be happy to take you, were it only out of respect to me. And if I ever do leave this place, Sam," added Mr Pickwick, with assumed cheerfulness – "if I do, I pledge you my word that you shall return to me instantly."

"Now I'll tell you wot it is, sir," said Mr Weller, in a grave and solemn voice. "This here sort o' thing won't do at all, so don't let's hear no more about it."

"I am serious, and resolved, Sam," said Mr Pickwick.

"You air, air you, sir?" inquired Mr Weller firmly. "Wery good, sir; then so am I."

Thus speaking, Mr Weller fixed his hat on his head with great precision, and abruptly left the room.

"Sam!" cried Mr Pickwick, calling after him, "Sam! Here!"

But the long gallery ceased to re-echo the sound of footsteps. Sam Weller was gone.

CHAPTER 23

In Which Mr Samuel Weller Begins to Devote his Energies to the Return Match Between Himself and Mr Trotter

But later in the following day, Sam, having been formally delivered into the warder's custody, to the intense astonishment of Roker, passed at once into the prison, walked straight to his master's room, and knocked at the door.

"Come in," said Mr Pickwick.

Sam appeared, pulled off his hat, and smiled.

"Ah, Sam, my good lad!" said Mr Pickwick, evidently delighted to see his humble friend again; "I had no intention of hurting your feelings yesterday, my faithful fellow, by what I said. Put down your hat, Sam, and let me explain my meaning, a little more at length."

"I'd rayther not now, sir," rejoined Sam.

"Why?" inquired Mr Pickwick.

"'Cause – " said Sam, hesitating.

"Because of what?" inquired Mr Pickwick. "Speak out, Sam."

"'Cause," rejoined Sam – "'cause I've got a little bisness as I want to do."

"What business?" inquired Mr Pickwick.

"Nothin' partickler, sir," replied Sam.

"Oh, if it's nothing particular," said Mr Pickwick, with a smile, "you can speak with me first."

"The fact is – " said Sam, stopping short.

"Well!" said Mr Pickwick. "Speak out, Sam."

"Why, the fact is," said Sam, with a desperate effort, "perhaps I'd better see arter my bed afore I do anythin' else."

"*Your bed!*" exclaimed Mr Pickwick, in astonishment.

"Yes, my bed, sir," replied Sam, "I'm a prisoner. I was arrested this here wery arternoon for debt."

"You arrested for debt!" exclaimed Mr Pickwick, sinking into a chair.

"Yes, for debt, sir," replied Sam. "And the man as puts me in, 'ull never let me out till you go yourself."

"Bless my heart and soul!" ejaculated Mr Pickwick. "What do you mean?"

"Wot I say, sir," rejoined Sam. "If it's forty years to come, I shall be a prisoner, and I'm very glad on it; and if it had been Newgate, it would ha' been just the same. Now the murder's out, and, damme, there's an end on it!"

With these words, which he repeated with great emphasis and violence, Sam Weller dashed his hat upon the ground, in a most unusual state of excitement; and then, folding his arms, looked firmly and fixedly in his master's face.

Mr Pickwick felt a great deal too much touched by the warmth of Sam's attachment, to be able to exhibit any manifestation of anger at the course he had adopted, in voluntarily consigning himself to a debtor's prison for an indefinite period.

"But consider, Sam," Mr Pickwick remonstrated, "the sum is so small that it can very easily be paid; and having made up my mind that you shall stop with me, you should recollect how much more useful you would be, if you could go outside the walls."

"I takes my determination on principle, sir," remarked Sam, "and you takes yours on the same ground." Mr Weller paused when he arrived at this point, and cast a comical look at his master out of the corners of his eyes.

Finding all gentle remonstrance useless, Mr Pickwick at length yielded a reluctant consent to his taking lodgings by the week, of a bald-headed cobbler, who rented a small slip room in one of the upper galleries. To this humble apartment Mr Weller moved a mattress and bedding, which he hired of Mr Roker; and, by the time he lay down upon it at night, was as much at home as if he had been bred in the prison, and his whole family had vegetated therein for three generations.

Mr Pickwick was sitting at breakfast, alone, next morning (Sam being busily engaged in the cobbler's room, polishing his master's shoes and brushing the black gaiters) when there came a knock at the door, which was followed by the appearance of the three Pickwickians.

"My dear friends," said Mr Pickwick, shaking hands alternately with Mr Tupman, Mr Winkle, and Mr Snodgrass, who were the three visitors in question, "I am delighted to see you."

The triumvirate were much affected. Mr Tupman shook his head deploringly, Mr Snodgrass drew forth his handkerchief, with undisguised emotion; and Mr Winkle retired to the window, and sniffed aloud.

"Mornin', gen'l'm'n," said Sam, entering at the moment with the shoes and gaiters. "Velcome to the college, gen'l'm'n."

"This foolish fellow," said Mr Pickwick, tapping Sam on the head as he knelt down to button up his master's gaiters – "this foolish fellow has got himself arrested, in order to be near me."

"What!" exclaimed the three friends.

"Yes, gen'l'm'n," said Sam, "I'm a prisoner, gen'l'm'n. Con-fined, as the lady said."

"A prisoner!" exclaimed Mr Winkle, with unaccountable vehemence.

"Hallo, sir!" responded Sam, looking up. "Wot's the matter, sir?"

"I had hoped, Sam, that – Nothing, nothing," said Mr Winkle precipitately.

There was something so very abrupt and unsettled in Mr Winkle's manner, that Mr Pickwick involuntarily looked at his two friends for an explanation.

"We don't know," said Mr Tupman, answering this mute appeal aloud. "He has been much excited for two days past, and his whole demeanour very unlike what it usually is. We feared there must be something the matter, but he resolutely denies it."

"No, no," said Mr Winkle, colouring beneath Mr Pickwick's gaze; "there is really nothing. I assure you there is nothing, my dear sir. It will be necessary for me to leave town, for a short time, on private business, and I had hoped to have prevailed upon you to allow Sam to accompany me."

Mr Pickwick looked more astonished than before.

"I think," faltered Mr Winkle, "that Sam would have had no objection to do so; but, of course, his being a prisoner here, renders it impossible. So I must go alone."

As Mr Winkle said these words, Mr Pickwick felt, with some astonishment, that Sam's fingers were trembling at the gaiters, as if he were rather surprised or startled. Sam looked up at Mr Winkle, too, though the glance they exchanged was instantaneous, they seemed to understand each other.

"Do you know anything of this, Sam?" said Mr Pickwick sharply.

"Wy, sir," responded Mr Weller; "I'm sure so far, that I've never heerd anythin' on the subject afore this moment. If I makes any guess about it," added Sam, looking at Mr Winkle, "I haven't got any right to say what it is, fear it should be a wrong 'un."

"I have no right to make any further inquiry into the private affairs of a friend, however intimate a friend," said Mr Pickwick, after a short silence; "at present let me merely say, that I do not understand this at all. There. We have had quite enough of the subject."

Thus expressing himself, Mr Pickwick led the conversation to different topics, and Mr Winkle gradually appeared more at ease, though still very far from being completely so. They had all so much to converse about, that the morning very quickly passed away; and when, at three o'clock, Mr Weller produced upon the little dining-table, a roast leg of mutton and an enormous meat-pie, with sundry dishes of vegetables, and pots of porter. The meat had been purchased, and dressed, and the pie made, and baked, at the prison cookery hard by. To these succeeded a bottle or two of very good wine, for which a messenger was despatched by Mr Pickwick to the Horn Coffee-house, in Doctors' Commons. The bottle or two, indeed, might be more properly described as a bottle or six, for by the time it was drunk, and tea over, the bell began to ring for strangers to withdraw.

But, if Mr Winkle's behaviour had been unaccountable in the morning, it became perfectly unearthly and solemn when, under the influence of his feelings, and his share of the bottle or six, he prepared to take leave of his friend. He lingered behind, until Mr Tupman and Mr Snodgrass had disappeared, and then fervently clenched Mr Pickwick's hand, with an expression of face in which deep and mighty resolve was fearfully blended with the very concentrated essence of gloom.

"Good-night, my dear sir!" said Mr Winkle between his set teeth.

"Bless you, my dear fellow!" replied the warm-hearted Mr Pickwick, as he returned the pressure of his young friend's hand.

There was another good-night, and another, and half a dozen more after that, and still Mr Winkle had fast hold of his friend's hand, and was looking into his face with the same strange expression.

"Is anything the matter?" said Mr Pickwick at last, when his arm was quite sore with shaking.

"Nothing," said Mr Winkle.

"Well then, good-night," said Mr Pickwick, attempting to disengage his hand.

"My friend, my benefactor, my honoured companion," murmured Mr Winkle, catching at his wrist. "Do not judge me harshly; do not, when you hear that, driven to extremity by hopeless obstacles, I – "

"Now then," said Mr Tupman, reappearing at the door. "Are you coming, or are we to be locked in?"

"Yes, yes, I am ready," replied Mr Winkle. And with a violent effort he tore himself away.

As Mr Pickwick was gazing down the passage after them in silent astonishment, Sam Weller appeared at the stair-head, and whispered for one moment in Mr Winkle's ear.

"Oh, certainly, depend upon me," said that gentleman aloud.

"Thank'ee, sir. You won't forget, sir?"

"Of course not," replied Mr Winkle.

"Wish you luck, sir," said Sam, touching his hat. "I should very much liked to ha' joined you, sir; but the gov'nor, o' course, is paramount."

"It is very much to your credit that you remain here," said Mr Winkle. With these words they disappeared down the stairs.

"Very extraordinary," said Mr Pickwick, going back into his room, and seating himself at the table in a musing attitude. "What can that young man be going to do?"

CHAPTER 24

Mr Pickwick Makes a Tour of the Diminutive World He Inhabits, and Resolves to Mix with It, in Future, as Little as Possible

A few mornings after his incarceration, Mr Samuel Weller, having arranged his master's room with all possible care, and seen him comfortably seated over his books and papers, withdrew to employ himself for an hour or two to come, as he best could. Having purchased the beer, and obtained, moreover, the day-but-one-before-yesterday's paper, he repaired to the skittle-ground, and seating himself on a bench, proceeded to enjoy himself in a very sedate and methodical manner, when Mr Pickwick accosted him.

"I see a prisoner we know coming this way, Sam," said Mr Pickwick, smiling. "You recollect the gentleman very well, I dare say, Sam,"

As Mr Pickwick spoke, Jingle walked up. He looked less miserable than before, being clad in a half-worn suit of clothes, which, with Mr Pickwick's assistance, had been released from the pawnbroker's. He wore clean linen too, and had had his hair cut. He was very pale and thin, however; and as he crept slowly up, leaning on a stick, it was easy to see that he had suffered severely from illness and want, and was still very weak. He took off his hat as Mr Pickwick saluted him, and seemed much humbled and abashed at the sight of Sam Weller.

Following close at his heels, came Mr Job Trotter, in the catalogue of whose vices, want of faith and attachment to his companion could at all events find no place. He was still ragged and squalid, but his face was not quite so hollow as on his first meeting with Mr Pickwick, a few days before. As he took off his hat to our benevolent old friend, he murmured some broken expressions of gratitude, and muttered something about having been saved from starving.

"Well, well," said Mr Pickwick, impatiently interrupting him, "you can follow with Sam. I want to speak to you, Mr Jingle. Here, give me your arm."

"No, no," replied Jingle; "won't indeed – rather not."

"Nonsense," said Mr Pickwick; "lean upon me, I desire, sir." Mr Pickwick cut the matter short by drawing the invalided stroller's arm through his, and leading him away, without saying another word about it.

During the whole of this time the countenance of Mr Samuel Weller had exhibited an expression of the most overwhelming and absorbing astonishment that the imagination can portray. After looking from Job to Jingle, and from Jingle to Job in profound silence, he softly ejaculated the words, "Well, I'm damn'd!" which he repeated at least a score of times.

Job kept his eyes fixed on the ground for some time until, looking stealthily up, said –

"How do you do, Mr Weller?"

"It *is* him!" exclaimed Sam; and having established Job's identity beyond all doubt, he smote his leg, and vented his feelings in a long, shrill whistle.

"Things has altered with me, sir," said Job.

"I should think they had," exclaimed Mr Weller, surveying his companion's rags with undisguised wonder. "This is rayther a change for the worse, Mr Trotter."

"It is indeed," replied Job, shaking his head. "There is no deception now, Mr Weller. Tears," said Job, with a look of momentary slyness – "tears are not the only proofs of distress, nor the best ones."

"No, they ain't," replied Sam expressively.

"They may be put on, Mr Weller," said Job.

"I know they may," said Sam; "some people, indeed, has 'em always ready laid on, and can pull out the plug wenever they likes."

"Yes," replied Job; "but these sort of things are not so easily counterfeited, Mr Weller, and it is a more painful process to get them up." As he spoke, he pointed to his sallow, sunken cheeks, and, drawing up his coat sleeve, disclosed an arm which looked as if the bone could be broken

193

at a touch, so sharp and brittle did it appear, beneath its thin covering of flesh.

"Wot have you been a-doin' to yourself?" said Sam, recoiling.

"Nothing," replied Job.

"Nothin'!" echoed Sam.

"I have been doin' nothing for many weeks past," said Job, "and eating and drinking almost as little."

Sam took one comprehensive glance at Mr Trotter's thin face and wretched apparel; and then, seizing him by the arm, commenced dragging him away with great violence.

"Where are you going, Mr Weller?" said Job, vainly struggling in the powerful grasp of his old enemy.

"Come on," said Sam; "come on!" He deigned no further explanation till they reached the tap, and then called for a pot of porter, which was speedily produced.

"Now," said Sam, "drink that up, ev'ry drop on it, and then turn the pot upside down, to let me see as you've took the medicine."

"But, my dear Mr Weller," remonstrated Job.

"Down vith it!" said Sam peremptorily.

Thus admonished, Mr Trotter raised the pot to his lips, and, by gentle and almost imperceptible degrees, tilted it into the air. He paused once, and only once, to draw a long breath, but without raising his face from the vessel, which, in a few moments thereafter, he held out at arm's length, bottom upward. Nothing fell upon the ground but a few particles of froth, which slowly detached themselves from the rim, and trickled lazily down.

"Well done!" said Sam. "How do you find yourself arter it?"

"Better, sir. I think I am better," responded Job.

"O' course you air," said Sam argumentatively. "It's like puttin' gas in a balloon. I can see with the naked eye that you gets stouter under the operation. Wot do you say to another o' the same dimensions?"

"I would rather not, I am much obliged to you, sir," replied Job – "much rather not."

"Vell, then, wot do you say to some wittles?" inquired Sam.

"Thanks to your worthy governor, sir," said Mr Trotter, "we have half a leg of mutton, baked, at a quarter before three, with the potatoes under it to save boiling."

"Wot! Has *he* been a-purwidin' for you?" asked Sam emphatically.

"He has, sir," replied Job. "More than that, Mr Weller; my master being very ill, he got us a room – we were in a kennel before – and paid for it, sir; and come to look at us, at night, when nobody should know. Mr Weller," said Job, with real tears in his eyes, for once, "I could serve that gentleman till I fell down dead at his feet."

"I say!" said Sam, "I'll trouble you, my friend! None o' that young feller. No man serves him but me but mark my vords, Job Trotter, he's a reg'lar thoroughbred angel; and let me see the man as wenturs to tell me he knows a better vun." With this defiance, Mr Weller buttoned up his change in a side pocket, and, with many confirmatory nods and gestures by the way, proceeded in search of the subject of discourse.

They found Mr Pickwick, in company with Jingle, talking very earnestly.

"Well," said Mr Pickwick, as Sam and his companion drew nigh, "you will see how your health becomes, and think about it meanwhile. Make the statement out for me when you feel yourself equal to the task, and I will discuss the subject with you when I have considered it. Now, go to your room. You are tired, and not strong enough to be out long."

Mr Alfred Jingle, without one spark of his old animation – with nothing even of the dismal gaiety which he had assumed when Mr Pickwick first stumbled on him in his misery – bowed low without speaking, and, motioning to Job not to follow him just yet, crept slowly away.

"Curious scene this, is it not, Sam?" said Mr Pickwick, looking good-humouredly round.

"Wery much so, sir," replied Sam. "Wonders 'ull never cease."

From this spot, Mr Pickwick wandered along all the galleries, up and down all the staircases, and once again round the whole area of the yard. There were the same squalor, the same turmoil and noise, the same general characteristics, in every corner; in the best and the worst alike. The whole place seemed restless and troubled; and the people were crowding and flitting to and fro, like the shadows in an uneasy dream.

"I have seen enough," said Mr Pickwick, as he threw himself into a chair in his little apartment. "My head aches with these scenes, and my heart too. Henceforth I will be a prisoner in my own room."

And Mr Pickwick steadfastly adhered to this determination. For three long months he remained shut up, all day; only stealing out at night to breathe the air, when the greater part of his fellow-prisoners were in bed or carousing in their rooms. His health was beginning to suffer from the closeness of the confinement, but neither the often-repeated entreaties of Perker and his friends, nor the still more frequently-repeated warnings and admonitions of Mr Samuel Weller, could induce him to alter one jot of his inflexible resolution.

CHAPTER 25

Records a Touching Act of Delicate Feeling, Not Unmixed with Pleasantry, Achieved and Performed by Messrs Dodson and Fogg

Mrs Bardell and her party walked forth in quest of a Hampstead stage. This was soon found, and in a couple of hours they all arrived safely in the Spaniards Tea-gardens, where the luckless Mr Raddle's very first act nearly occasioned his good lady a relapse; it being neither more nor less than to order tea for seven, whereas (as the ladies one and all remarked), what could have been easier than for Tommy to have drank out of anybody's cup – or everybody's, if that was all – when the waiter wasn't looking, which would have saved one head of tea, and the tea just as good!

However, there was no help for it, and the tea-tray came, with seven cups and saucers, and bread-and-butter on the same scale. Mrs Bardell was unanimously voted into the chair, and Mrs Rogers being stationed on her right hand, and Mrs Raddle on her left, the meal proceeded with great merriment and success.

"How sweet the country is, to be sure!" sighed Mrs Rogers; "I almost wish I lived in it always."

"Oh, you wouldn't like that, ma'am," replied Mrs Bardell, rather hastily; for it was not at all advisable, with reference to the lodgings, to encourage such notions; "you wouldn't like it, ma'am."

"Oh! I should think you was a deal too lively and sought after, to be content with the country, ma'am," said little Mrs Cluppins.

"Perhaps I am, ma'am. Perhaps I am," sighed the first-floor lodger.

"For lone people as have got nobody to care for them, or take care of them, or as have been hurt in their mind, or that kind of thing," observed

Mr Raddle, plucking up a little cheerfulness, and looking round, "the country is all very well. The country for a wounded spirit, they say."

Now, of all things in the world that the unfortunate man could have said, any would have been preferable to this. Of course Mrs Bardell burst into tears, and requested to be led from the table instantly; upon which the affectionate child began to cry too, most dismally.

"Would anybody believe, ma'am," exclaimed Mrs Raddle, turning fiercely to the first-floor lodger, "that a woman could be married to such a unmanly creetur, which can tamper with a woman's feelings as he does, every hour in the day, ma'am?"

"My dear," remonstrated Mr Raddle, "I didn't mean anything, my dear."

"You didn't mean!" repeated Mrs Raddle, with great scorn and contempt. "Go away. I can't bear the sight on you, you brute."

"You must not flurry yourself, Mary Ann," interposed Mrs Cluppins. "You really must consider yourself, my dear, which you never do. Now go away, Raddle, there's a good soul, or you'll only aggravate her."

"You had better take your tea by yourself, sir, indeed," said Mrs Rogers, again applying the smelling-bottle.

Mrs Sanders, who, according to custom, was very busy with the bread-and-butter, expressed the same opinion, and Mr Raddle quietly retired.

It was at this moment, that the sound of approaching wheels was heard, and that the ladies, looking up, saw a hackney-coach stop at the garden gate.

"More company!" said Mrs Sanders.

"It's a gentleman," said Mrs Raddle.

"Well, if it ain't Mr Jackson, the young man from Dodson and Fogg's!" cried Mrs Bardell. "Why, gracious! Surely Mr Pickwick can't have paid the damages."

"Or hoffered marriage!" said Mrs Cluppins.

"Dear me, how slow the gentleman is," exclaimed Mrs Rogers. "Why doesn't he make haste!"

As the lady spoke these words, Mr Jackson turned from the coach where he had been addressing some observations to a shabby man in black leggings, who had just emerged from the vehicle with a thick ash stick in his hand, and made his way to the place where the ladies were seated.

"Is anything the matter? Has anything taken place, Mr Jackson?" said Mrs Bardell eagerly.

"Nothing whatever, ma'am," replied Mr Jackson. "How de do, ladies? I have to ask pardon, ladies, for intruding – but the law, ladies – the law." With this apology Mr Jackson smiled and made a comprehensive bow.

Mrs Rogers whispered to Mrs Raddle that he was really an elegant young man.

"I called in Goswell Street," resumed Mr Jackson, "and hearing that you were here, from the slavey, took a coach and came on. Our people want you down in the city directly, Mrs Bardell."

"Lor!" ejaculated that lady, starting at the sudden nature of the communication.

"Yes," said Mr Jackson, biting his lip. "It's very important and pressing business, which can't be postponed on any account. Indeed, Dodson expressly said so to me, and so did Fogg. I've kept the coach on purpose for you to go back in."

"How very strange!" exclaimed Mrs Bardell.

The ladies agreed that it *was* very strange, but were unanimously of opinion that it must be very important, or Dodson and Fogg would never have sent; and further, that the business being urgent, she ought to repair to Dodson and Fogg's without any delay.

There was a certain degree of pride and importance about being wanted by one's lawyers in such a monstrous hurry, that was by no means displeasing to Mrs Bardell, especially as it might be reasonably supposed to enhance her consequence in the eyes of the first-floor lodger. She simpered a little, affected extreme vexation and hesitation, and at last arrived at the conclusion that she supposed she must go.

"But won't you refresh yourself after your walk, Mr Jackson?" said Mrs Bardell persuasively.

"Why, really there ain't much time to lose," replied Jackson; "and I've got a friend here," he continued, looking towards the man with the ash stick.

"Oh, ask your friend to come here, sir," said Mrs Bardell.

"Why, thank'ee, I'd rather not," said Mr Jackson, with some embarrassment of manner. "He's not much used to ladies' society, and it makes him bashful. If you'll order the waiter to deliver him anything short, he won't drink it off at once, won't he! – only try him!" Mr

Jackson's fingers wandered playfully round his nose at this portion of his discourse, to warn his hearers that he was speaking ironically.

The waiter was at once despatched to the bashful gentleman, and the bashful gentleman took something; Mr Jackson also took something, and the ladies took something, for hospitality's sake. Mr Jackson then said he was afraid it was time to go; upon which, Mrs Sanders, Mrs Cluppins, and Tommy (who it was arranged should accompany Mrs Bardell, leaving the others to Mr Raddle's protection), got into the coach.

"Isaac," said Jackson, as Mrs Bardell prepared to get in, looking up at the man with the ash stick, who was seated on the box, smoking a cigar.

"Well?"

"This is Mrs Bardell."

"Oh, I know'd that long ago," said the man.

Mrs Bardell got in, Mr Jackson got in after her, and away they drove. Mrs Bardell could not help ruminating on what Mr Jackson's friend had said. Shrewd creatures, those lawyers. Lord bless us, how they find people out!

"Sad thing about these costs of our people's, ain't it," said Jackson, when Mrs Cluppins and Mrs Sanders had fallen asleep; "your bill of costs, I mean."

"I'm very sorry they can't get them," replied Mrs Bardell. "But if you law gentlemen do these things on speculation, why you must get a loss now and then, you know."

"You gave them a *cognovit* for the amount of your costs, after the trial, I'm told!" said Jackson.

"Yes. Just as a matter of form," replied Mrs Bardell.

"Certainly," replied Jackson drily. "Quite a matter of form. Quite."

On they drove, and Mrs Bardell fell asleep. She was wakened, after some time, by the stopping of the coach.

"Bless us!" said the lady. "Are we at Freeman's Court?"

"We're not going quite so far," replied Jackson. "Have the goodness to step out."

Mrs Bardell, not yet thoroughly awake, complied. It was a curious place: a large wall, with a gate in the middle, and a gas-light burning inside.

"Now, ladies," cried the man with the ash stick, looking into the coach, and shaking Mrs Sanders to wake her, "Come!"

Rousing her friend, Mrs Sanders alighted. Mrs Bardell, leaning on

Jackson's arm, and leading Tommy by the hand, had already entered the porch. They followed. The room they turned into was even more odd-looking than the porch. Such a number of men standing about! And they stared so!

"What place is this?" inquired Mrs Bardell, pausing.

"Only one of our public offices," replied Jackson, hurrying her through a door, and looking round to see that the other women were following. "Look sharp, Isaac!"

"Safe and sound," replied the man with the ash stick. The door swung heavily after them, and they descended a small flight of steps.

"Here we are at last. All right and tight, Mrs Bardell!" said Jackson, looking exultingly round.

"What do you mean?" said Mrs Bardell, with a palpitating heart.

"Just this," replied Jackson, drawing her a little on one side; "don't be frightened, Mrs Bardell. There never was a more delicate man than Dodson, ma'am, or a more humane man than Fogg. It was their duty in the way of business, to take you in execution for them costs; but they were anxious to spare your feelings as much as they could. What a comfort it must be, to you, to think how it's been done! This is the Fleet, ma'am. Wish you good-night, Mrs Bardell. Good-night, Tommy!"

As Jackson hurried away in company with the man with the ash stick, another man, with a key in his hand, who had been looking on, led the bewildered female to a second short flight of steps leading to a doorway. Mrs Bardell screamed violently; Tommy roared; Mrs Cluppins shrunk within herself; and Mrs Sanders made off, without more ado. For there stood the injured Mr Pickwick, taking his nightly allowance of air; and beside him leant Samuel Weller, who, seeing Mrs Bardell, took his hat off with mock reverence, while his master turned indignantly on his heel.

"Don't bother the woman," said the turnkey to Weller; "she's just come in."

"A prisoner!" said Sam, quickly replacing his hat. "Who's the plaintives? What for? Speak up, old feller."

"Dodson and Fogg," replied the man; "execution on *cognovit* for costs."

"Here, Job, Job!" shouted Sam, dashing into the passage. "Run to Mr Perker's, Job. I want him directly. I see some good in this. Here's a game. Hooray! vere's the gov'nor?"

But there was no reply to these inquiries, for Job had started furiously off, the instant he received his commission, and Mrs Bardell had fainted in real downright earnest.

CHAPTER 26

Is Chiefly Devoted to Matters of Business, and the Temporal Advantage of Dodson and Fogg – Mr Winkle Reappears Under Extraordinary Circumstances – Mr Pickwick's Benevolence Proves Stronger than his Obstinacy

Mr Perker had had a dinner-party that day, as was testified by the appearance of lights in the drawing-room windows, the sound of an improved grand piano, and an improvable cabinet voice issuing therefrom, and a rather overpowering smell of meat which pervaded the steps and entry.

From this society, little Mr Perker detached himself, on his clerk being announced in a whisper; and repairing to the dining-room, there found Mr Lowten and Job Trotter looking very dim and shadowy by the light of a kitchen candle.

"Now, Lowten," said little Mr Perker, shutting the door, "what's the matter? No important letter come in a parcel, is there?"

"No, sir," replied Lowten. "This is a messenger from Mr Pickwick, sir."

"From Pickwick, eh?" said the little man, turning quickly to Job. "Well, what is it?"

"Dodson and Fogg have taken Mrs Bardell in execution for her costs, sir," said Job.

"No!" exclaimed Perker, putting his hands in his pockets, and reclining against the sideboard.

"Yes," said Job. "It seems they got a *cognovit* out of her, for the amount of 'em, directly after the trial."

"By Jove!" said Perker, taking both hands out of his pockets, and striking the knuckles of his right against the palm of his left, emphatically, "those are the cleverest scamps I ever had anything to do with!"

"The sharpest practitioners I ever knew, sir," observed Lowten.

"Sharp!" echoed Perker. "There's no knowing where to have them."

"Very true, sir, there is not," replied Lowten; and then, both master and man pondered for a few seconds, with animated countenances, as if they were reflecting upon one of the most beautiful and ingenious discoveries that the intellect of man had ever made. Perker nodded his head thoughtfully, and pulled out his watch.

"At ten precisely, I will be there," said the little man. "Will you take a glass of wine, Lowten?"

"No, thank you, sir."

"You mean yes, I think," said the little man, turning to the sideboard for a decanter and glasses.

As Lowten did mean yes, he said no more on the subject, but inquired of Job, in an audible whisper, whether the portrait of Perker, which hung opposite the fireplace, wasn't a wonderful likeness, to which Job of course replied that it was. The wine being by this time poured out, Lowten drank to Mrs Perker and the children, and Job to Perker. They showed themselves out. The attorney betook himself to his drawing-room, the clerk to the Magpie and Stump, and Job to Covent Garden Market to spend the night in a vegetable basket.

Punctually at the appointed hour next morning, the good-humoured little attorney tapped at Mr Pickwick's door, which was opened with great alacrity by Sam Weller.

"Mr Perker, sir," said Sam, announcing the visitor to Mr Pickwick, who was sitting at the window in a thoughtful attitude.

"Wery glad you've looked in accidentally, sir. I rather think the gov'nor wants to have a word and a half with you, sir."

Perker bestowed a look of intelligence on Sam, intimating that he understood he was not to say he had been sent for; and beckoning him to approach, whispered briefly in his ear.

"You don't mean that 'ere, sir?" said Sam, starting back in excessive surprise.

Perker nodded and smiled.

Mr Samuel Weller looked at the little lawyer, then at Mr Pickwick, then at the ceiling, then at Perker again; grinned, laughed outright, and finally, catching up his hat from the carpet, without further explanation, disappeared.

"What does this mean?" inquired Mr Pickwick, looking at Perker with astonishment. "What has put Sam into this extraordinary state?"

"Oh, nothing, nothing," replied Perker. "Come, my dear sir, draw up your chair to the table. I have a good deal to say to you."

"What papers are those?" inquired Mr Pickwick, as the little man deposited on the table a small bundle of documents tied with red tape.

"The papers in Bardell and Pickwick," replied Perker, undoing the knot with his teeth.

Mr Pickwick grated the legs of his chair against the ground; and throwing himself into it, folded his hands and looked sternly – if Mr Pickwick ever could look sternly – at his legal friend.

"You don't like to hear the name of the cause?" said the little man, still busying himself with the knot.

"No, I do not indeed," replied Mr Pickwick.

"Sorry for that," resumed Perker, "because it will form the subject of our conversation."

"I would rather that the subject should be never mentioned between us, Perker," interposed Mr Pickwick hastily.

"Pooh, pooh, my dear sir," said the little man, untying the bundle, and glancing eagerly at Mr Pickwick out of the corners of his eyes. "It must be mentioned. I have come here on purpose. Now, are you ready to hear what I have to say, my dear sir? No hurry; if you are not, I can wait. I have this morning's paper here. Your time shall be mine. There!" Hereupon, the little man threw one leg over the other, and made a show of beginning to read with great composure and application.

"Well, well," said Mr Pickwick, with a sigh, but softening into a smile at the same time. "Say what you have to say; it's the old story, I suppose?"

"With a difference, my dear sir; with a difference," rejoined Perker, deliberately folding up the paper and putting it into his pocket again. "Mrs Bardell, the plaintiff in the action, is within these walls, sir."

"I know it," was Mr Pickwick's reply,

"Very good," retorted Perker. "And you know how she comes here, I suppose; I mean on what grounds, and at whose suit?"

"Yes; at least I have heard Sam's account of the matter," said Mr Pickwick, with affected carelessness.

"Sam's account of the matter," replied Perker, "is, I will venture to say, a perfectly correct one. Well now, my dear sir, the first question I have to ask, is, whether this woman is to remain here?"

"To remain here!" echoed Mr Pickwick.

"To remain here, my dear sir," rejoined Perker, leaning back in his chair and looking steadily at his client.

"How can you ask me?" said that gentleman. "It rests with Dodson and Fogg; you know that very well."

"I know nothing of the kind," retorted Perker firmly. "It does *not* rest with Dodson and Fogg; you know the men, my dear sir, as well as I do. It rests solely, wholly, and entirely with you."

"With me!" ejaculated Mr Pickwick.

"I have seen the woman, this morning. By paying the costs, you can obtain a full release and discharge from the damages."

Before Mr Pickwick could reply there was a low murmuring of voices outside, and then a hesitating knock at the door.

"Beg your pardon, sir," rejoined Mr Weller. "But here's a lady here, sir, as says she's somethin' wery partickler to disclose."

"I can't see any lady," replied Mr Pickwick, whose mind was filled with visions of Mrs Bardell.

"I wouldn't make too sure o' that, sir," urged Mr Weller, shaking his head. "If you know'd who was near, sir."

"Who is it?" inquired Mr Pickwick.

"Will you see her, sir?" asked Mr Weller, holding the door in his hand as if he had some curious live animal on the other side.

"I suppose I must," said Mr Pickwick, looking at Perker.

"Well then, all in to begin!" cried Sam. "Sound the gong, draw up the curtain, and enter the two conspiraytors."

As Sam Weller spoke, he threw the door open, and there rushed tumultuously into the room, Mr Nathaniel Winkle, leading after him by the hand, the identical young lady who at Dingley Dell had worn the boots with the fur round the tops, and who, now a very pleasing compound of blushes and confusion, and lilac silk, and a smart bonnet, and a rich lace veil, looked prettier than ever.

"Miss Arabella Allen!" exclaimed Mr Pickwick, rising from his chair.

"No," replied Mr Winkle, dropping on his knees. "Mrs Winkle. Pardon, my dear friend, pardon!"

Mr Pickwick could scarcely believe the evidence of his senses, and perhaps would not have done so, but for the corroborative testimony afforded by the smiling countenance of Perker, and the bodily presence, in the background, of Sam and the pretty housemaid; who appeared to contemplate the proceedings with the liveliest satisfaction.

"Oh, Mr Pickwick!" said Arabella, in a low voice, as if alarmed at the silence. "Can you forgive my imprudence?"

Mr Pickwick returned no verbal response to this appeal; but he took off his spectacles in great haste, and seizing both the young lady's hands in his, kissed her a great number of times – perhaps a greater number than was absolutely necessary – and then, still retaining one of her hands, told Mr Winkle he was an audacious young dog, and bade him get up. This, Mr Winkle did; whereupon Mr Pickwick slapped him on the back several times, and then shook hands heartily with Perker, who, not to be behind-hand in the compliments of the occasion, saluted both the bride and the pretty housemaid with right good-will, and, having wrung Mr, Winkle's hand most cordially, wound up his demonstrations of joy.

"Mary, my dear, sit down," said Mr Pickwick, cutting short these compliments. "Now then; how long have you been married, eh?"

Arabella looked bashfully at her lord and master, who replied, "Only three days."

"Only three days, eh?" said Mr Pickwick. "Why, what have you been doing these three months?"

"Ah, to be sure!" interposed Perker; "come, account for this idleness. You see Mr Pickwick's only astonishment is, that it wasn't all over, months ago."

"Why the fact is," replied Mr Winkle, looking at his blushing young wife, "that I could not persuade Bella to run away, for a long time. And when I had persuaded her, it was a long time more before we could find an opportunity. Mary had to give a month's warning, too, before she could leave her place next door, and we couldn't possibly have done it without her assistance."

"Upon my word," exclaimed Mr Pickwick, who by this time had resumed his spectacles, and was looking from Arabella to Winkle, and from Winkle to Arabella, with as much delight depicted in his countenance as warmheartedness and kindly feeling can communicate to the human face – "upon my word! you seem to have been very systematic in your proceedings."

Mr Tupman and Mr Snodgrass arrived, most opportunely, in this stage of the pleadings, and as it was necessary to explain to them all that had occurred, the whole of the arguments were gone over again, after which everybody urged every argument in his own way, and at his own length. And, at last, Mr Pickwick, fairly argued and remonstrated out of all his resolutions, and being in imminent danger of being argued and remonstrated out of his wits, caught Arabella in his arms, and declaring that she was a very amiable creature, and that he didn't know how it was, but he had always been very fond of her from the first, said he could never find it in his heart to stand in the way of young people's happiness, and they might do with him as they pleased.

At three o'clock that afternoon, Mr Pickwick took a last look at his little room, and made his way, as well as he could, through the throng of debtors who pressed eagerly forward to shake him by the hand, until he reached the lodge steps. He turned here, to look about him, and his eye lightened as he did so. In all the crowd of wan, emaciated faces, he saw not one which was not happier for his sympathy and charity.

"Perker," said Mr Pickwick, beckoning one young man towards him, "this is Mr Jingle, whom I spoke to you about."

"Very good, my dear sir," replied Perker, looking hard at Jingle. "You will see me again, young man, to-morrow. I hope you may live to remember and feel deeply, what I shall have to communicate, sir."

Jingle bowed respectfully, trembled very much as he took Mr Pickwick's proffered hand, and withdrew.

"Job you know, I think?" said Mr Pickwick, presenting that gentleman.

"I know the rascal," replied Perker good-humouredly. "See after your friend, and be in the way to-morrow at one. Do you hear? Now, is there anything more?"

"Nothing," rejoined Mr Pickwick. "God bless you, my friends!"

As Mr Pickwick uttered this adieu, the crowd raised a loud shout. Many among them were pressing forward to shake him by the hand again, when he drew his arm through Perker's, and hurried from the prison, far more sad and melancholy, for the moment, than when he had first entered it. Alas! how many sad and unhappy beings had he left behind!

CHAPTER 27

Comprising the Final Exit of Mr Jingle and Job Trotter, with a Great Morning of Business in Gray's Inn Square – Concluding with a Double Knock at Mr Perker's Door

It still wanted ten minutes to the hour when Mr Pickwick ascended the staircase on which Perker's chambers were. The clerks had not arrived yet, and he beguiled the time by looking out of the staircase window. The healthy light of a fine October morning made even the dingy old houses brighten up a little; some of the dusty windows actually looking almost cheerful as the sun's rays gleamed upon them.

"You're early, Mr Pickwick," said a voice behind him.

"Ah, Mr Lowten," replied that gentleman, looking round, and recognising his old acquaintance. "Perker's been about that business of yours, by the bye."

"What business?" inquired Mr Pickwick. "Mrs Bardell's costs?"

"No, I don't mean that," replied Mr Lowten. "About getting that customer out of the Fleet, you know – about getting him to Demerara."

"Oh, Mr Jingle," said Mr Pickwick hastily. "Yes. Well?"

"Well, it's all arranged," said Lowten, mending his pen. "The agent at Liverpool said he had been obliged to you many times when you were in business, and he would be glad to take him on your recommendation."

"That's well," said Mr Pickwick. "I am delighted to hear it."

"But I say," resumed Lowten, scraping the back of the pen preparatory to making a fresh split, "what a soft chap that other is!"

"Which other?"

"Why, that servant, or friend, or whatever he is; you know, Trotter."

"Ah!" said Mr Pickwick, with a smile. "I always thought him the reverse."

"Well, and so did I, from what little I saw of him," replied Lowten, "it only shows how one may be deceived. What do you think of his going to Demerara, too?"

"What! And giving up what was offered him here!" exclaimed Mr Pickwick, with glistening eyes. "Foolish fellow."

The greeting between Mr Pickwick and his professional adviser was warm and cordial; the client was scarcely ensconced in the attorney's arm-chair, however, when a knock was heard at the door, and a voice inquired whether Mr Perker was within.

"Hark!" said Perker, "that's one of our vagabond friends – Jingle himself, my dear sir. Will you see him?"

"What do you think?" inquired Mr Pickwick, hesitating.

"Yes, I think you had better. Here, you sir, what's your name, walk in, will you?"

In compliance with this unceremonious invitation, Jingle and Job walked into the room, but, seeing Mr Pickwick, stopped short in some confusion.

"Well," said Perker, "don't you know that gentleman?"

"Good reason to," replied Mr Jingle, stepping forward. "Mr Pickwick – deepest obligations – life preserver – made a man of me – you shall never repent it, sir."

"I am happy to hear you say so," said Mr Pickwick. "You look much better."

"Thanks to you, sir – great change – Majesty's Fleet – unwholesome place – very," said Jingle, shaking his head. He was decently and cleanly dressed, and so was Job, who stood bolt upright behind him, staring at Mr Pickwick with a visage of iron.

"When do they go to Liverpool?" inquired Mr Pickwick, half aside to Perker.

"This evening, sir, at seven o'clock," said Job, taking one step forward. "By the heavy coach from the city, sir."

"Are your places taken?"

"They are, sir," replied Job.

"You have fully made up your mind to go?"

"I have sir," answered Job.

"Certainly," interposed Jingle, with great firmness. "Clear head – man of the world – quite right – perfectly." Here Mr Jingle paused, and striking the crown of his hat with great violence, passed his hand over his eyes, and sat down.

"He means to say," said Job, advancing a few paces, "that if he is not carried off by the fever, he will pay the money back again. If he lives, he will, Mr Pickwick. I will see it done. I know he will, sir," said Job, with energy. "I could undertake to swear it."

"Well, well," said Mr Pickwick, "you must be careful not to play any more desperate cricket matches, Mr Jingle, or to renew your acquaintance with Sir Thomas Blazo, and I have little doubt of your preserving your health."

"Well," said Perker, "Deliver this letter to the agent when you reach Liverpool, and now you had better leave Mr Pickwick and me alone, for we have other matters to talk over, and time is precious." As Perker said this, he looked towards the door, with an evident desire to render the leave-taking as brief as possible.

It was brief enough on Mr Jingle's part. He thanked the little attorney in a few hurried words and, turning to his benefactor, stood for a few seconds as if irresolute what to say or how to act. Job Trotter relieved his perplexity; for, with a humble and grateful bow to Mr Pickwick, he took his friend gently by the arm, and led him away.

"A worthy couple!" said Perker, as the door closed behind them.

"I hope they may become so," replied Mr Pickwick. "What do you think? Is there any chance of their permanent reformation?"

Perker shrugged his shoulders doubtfully.

They had no sooner arrived at this point, than a most violent and startling knocking was heard at the door; it was not an ordinary double-knock, but a constant and uninterrupted succession of the loudest single raps, as if the knocker were endowed with the perpetual motion, or the person outside had forgotten to leave off.

"Dear me, what's that?" exclaimed Perker, starting.

"I think it is a knock at the door," said Mr Pickwick, as if there could be the smallest doubt of the fact.

"Dear me!" said Perker, ringing his bell, "we shall alarm the inn. Make haste, Mr Lowten," Perker called out; "we shall have the panels beaten in."

Mr Lowten hurried to the door, and turning the handle, beheld the appearance which is described in the next chapter.

CHAPTER 28

Containing Some Particulars Relative to the Double Knock, and Other Matters: Among Which Certain Interesting Disclosures Relative to Mr Snodgrass and a Young Lady Are by no Means Irrelevant to this History

The object that presented itself to the eyes of the astonished clerk, was a boy – a wonderfully fat boy standing upright on the mat, with his eyes closed as if in sleep. He had never seen such a fat boy, in or out of a travelling caravan; and this, coupled with the calmness and repose of his appearance, so very different from what was reasonably to have been expected of the inflicter of such knocks, smote him with wonder.

"What the devil do you knock in that way for?" inquired the clerk angrily.

"Which way?" said the boy, in a slow and sleepy voice.

"Why, like forty hackney-coachmen," replied the clerk.

"Because master said, I wasn't to leave off knocking till they opened the door, for fear I should go to sleep," said the boy.

"Well," said the clerk, "what message have you brought?"

"He's downstairs," rejoined the boy.

"Who?"

"Master. He wants to know whether you're at home."

All further inquiries were superseded by the appearance of old Wardle, who, running upstairs and just recognising Lowten, passed at once into Mr Perker's room.

"Pickwick!" said the old gentleman. "Your hand, my boy! Why have I never heard until the day before yesterday of your suffering yourself to be cooped up in jail? And why did you let him do it, Perker?"

"I couldn't help it, my dear sir," replied Perker, with a smile and a pinch of snuff; "you know how obstinate he is?"

"Of course I do; of course I do," replied the old gentleman. "I am heartily glad to see him, notwithstanding. I will not lose sight of him again, in a hurry."

With these words, Wardle shook Mr Pickwick's hand once more, and, having done the same by Perker, threw himself into an arm-chair, his jolly red face shining again with smiles and health.

"Well!" said Wardle. "Here are pretty goings on – a pinch of your snuff, Perker, my boy – never were such times, eh?"

"What do you mean?" inquired Mr Pickwick.

"Mean!" replied Wardle. "Why, I think the girls are all running mad; that's no news, you'll say? Perhaps it's not; but it's true, for all that."

"You have not come up to London, of all places in the world, to tell us that, my dear sir, have you?" inquired Perker.

"No, not altogether," replied Wardle; "though it was the main cause of my coming. How's Arabella?"

"Very well," replied Mr Pickwick, "and will be delighted to see you, I am sure."

"Black-eyed little jilt!" replied Wardle. "I had a great idea of marrying her myself, one of these odd days. But I am glad of it too, very glad."

"How did the intelligence reach you?" asked Mr Pickwick.

"Oh, it came to my girls, of course," replied Wardle. "Arabella wrote, the day before yesterday. But this is not the best of it, it seems. This is only half the love-making and plotting that have been going forward. We have been walking on mines for the last six months, and they're sprung at last."

"What do you mean?" exclaimed Mr Pickwick, turning pale; "no other secret marriage, I hope?"

"No, no," replied old Wardle; "not so bad as that; no."

"How?" asked Mr Pickwick anxiously. "In what way?"

The old gentleman proceeded with his great disclosure in these words – "It must come out, sooner or later, the long and the short of it is, then, that Bella at last mustered up courage to tell me that Emily was very unhappy; that she and your young friend Snodgrass had been in constant correspondence and communication ever since last Christmas; inasmuch as I had always been rather kindly disposed to both of them, they had thought of asking whether I would have any objection to their being married. There now, Mr Pickwick, if you can make it convenient to reduce your eyes to their usual size again, and to let me hear what you think we ought to do, I shall feel rather obliged to you!"

The testy manner in which the hearty old gentleman uttered this last sentence was not wholly unwarranted; for Mr Pickwick's face had settled down into an expression of blank amazement and perplexity, quite curious to behold.

"Snodgrass! – since last Christmas!" were the first broken words that issued from the lips of the confounded gentleman.

"Since last Christmas," replied Wardle; "that's plain enough, and very bad spectacles we must have worn, not to have discovered it before."

"I don't understand it," said Mr Pickwick, ruminating; "I cannot really understand it."

"It's easy enough to understand it," replied the choleric old gentleman. "If you had been a younger man, you would have been in the secret long ago. Now the question is, what's to be done?"

"What have *you* done?" inquired Mr Pickwick.

"I!"

"I mean what did you do when your married daughter told you this?"

"Oh, I made a fool of myself of course," rejoined Wardle. "Went into a great passion and frightened my mother into a fit!"

"That was judicious," remarked Perker; "and what else?"

"I fretted and fumed all next day, and raised a great disturbance," rejoined the old gentleman. "At last I got tired of rendering myself unpleasant and making everybody miserable; so I hired a carriage at Muggleton, and, putting my own horses in it, came up to town, under pretence of bringing Emily to see Arabella."

"Miss Wardle is with you, then?" said Mr Pickwick.

"To be sure she is," replied Wardle. "She is at Osborne's Hotel in the Adelphi at this moment, unless your enterprising friend has run away with her since I came out this morning."

"You are reconciled then?" said Perker.

"Not a bit of it," answered Wardle; "she has been crying and moping ever since, except last night, between tea and supper, when she made a great parade of writing a letter that I pretended to take no notice of."

"You want my advice in this matter, I suppose?" said Perker, looking from the musing face of Mr Pickwick to the eager countenance of Wardle, and taking several consecutive pinches of his favourite stimulant.

"I suppose so," said Wardle, looking at Mr Pickwick.

"Certainly," replied that gentleman.

"Well then," said Perker, rising and pushing his chair back, "my advice is, that you both walk away together, or ride away, or get away by some means or other, and just talk this matter over between you. If you have not settled it by the next time I see you, I'll tell you what to do."

"This is satisfactory," said Wardle, hardly knowing whether to smile or be offended.

"Pooh, pooh, my dear sir," returned Perker. "I know you both a great deal better than you know yourselves. You have settled it already, to all intents and purposes."

Thus expressing himself, the little gentleman poked his snuff-box first into the chest of Mr Pickwick, and then into the waistcoat of Mr Wardle, upon which they all three laughed, especially the two last-named gentlemen, who at once shook hands again, without any obvious or particular reason.

CHAPTER 29

In Which The Pickwick Club is Finally Dissolved, and Everything Concluded to the Satisfaction of Everybody

For a whole week after the happy arrival of Mr Winkle from Birmingham, Mr Pickwick and Sam Weller were from home all day long, only returning just in time for dinner, and then wearing an air of mystery and importance quite foreign to their natures. It was evident that very grave and eventful proceedings were on foot; but various surmises were afloat, respecting their precise character.

Some (among whom was Mr Tupman) were disposed to think that Mr Pickwick contemplated a matrimonial alliance; but this idea the ladies most strenuously repudiated. Others rather inclined to the belief that he had projected some distant tour, and was at present occupied in effecting the preliminary arrangements; but this again was stoutly denied by Sam himself, who had unequivocally stated, when cross-examined by Mary, that no new journeys were to be undertaken. At length, when the brains of the whole party had been racked for six long days, by unavailing speculation, it was unanimously resolved that Mr Pickwick should be called upon to explain his conduct, and to state distinctly why he had thus absented himself from the society of his admiring friends.

With this view, Mr Wardle invited the full circle to dinner at the Adelphi; and the decanters having been thrice sent round, opened the business.

"We are all anxious to know," said the old gentleman, "what we have done to offend you, and to induce you to desert us and devote yourself to these solitary walks."

"Are you?" said Mr Pickwick. "If you will give me another glass of wine, I will satisfy your curiosity."

The decanters passed from hand to hand with unwonted briskness, and Mr Pickwick, looking round on the faces of his friends with a cheerful smile, proceeded –

"All the changes that have taken place among us," said Mr Pickwick, "I mean the marriage that *has* taken place, and the marriage that *will* take place, with the changes they involve, rendered it necessary for me to think, soberly and at once, upon my future plans. I determined on retiring to some quiet, pretty neighbourhood in the vicinity of London; I saw a house which exactly suited my fancy; I have taken it and furnished it. It is fully prepared for my reception, and I intend entering upon it at once, trusting that I may yet live to spend many quiet years in peaceful retirement."

Here Mr Pickwick paused, and a low murmur ran round the table.

"The house I have taken," said Mr Pickwick, "is at Dulwich. It has a large garden, and is situated in one of the most pleasant spots near London. Sam accompanies me there. I propose to consecrate this little retreat, by having a ceremony in which I take a great interest, performed there. I wish, if my friend Wardle entertains no objection, that his daughter should be married from my new house, on the day I take possession of it. The happiness of young people," said Mr Pickwick, a little moved, "has ever been the chief pleasure of my life. It will warm my heart to witness the happiness of those friends who are dearest to me, beneath my own roof."

Mr Pickwick paused again: Emily and Arabella sobbed audibly.

"I have communicated, both personally and by letter, with the club," resumed Mr Pickwick, "acquainting them with my intention. During our long absence, it has suffered much from internal dissentions; and the withdrawal of my name, coupled with this and other circumstances, has occasioned its dissolution. The Pickwick Club exists no longer.

"I shall never regret," said Mr Pickwick in a low voice, "having devoted the greater part of two years to mixing with different varieties and shades of human character, frivolous as my pursuit of novelty may have appeared to many. Numerous scenes of which I had no previous conception have dawned upon me – I hope to the enlargement of my mind, and the improvement of my understanding. If I have done but little good, I trust I have done less harm, and that none of my adventures will be other than a source of amusing and pleasant recollection to me in the decline of life. God bless you all!"

With these words, Mr Pickwick filled and drained a bumper with a trembling hand; and his eyes moistened as his friends rose with one accord, and pledged him from their hearts. And in the midst of all this, stood Mr Pickwick, his countenance lighted up with smiles, which the heart of no man, woman, or child, could resist: himself the happiest of the group: shaking hands, over and over again, with the same people, and when his own hands were not so employed, rubbing them with pleasure: turning round in a different direction at every fresh expression of gratification or curiosity, and inspiring everybody with his looks of gladness and delight.

Let us leave our old friend in one of those moments of unmixed happiness, of which, if we seek them, there are ever some, to cheer our transitory existence here.

Mr and Mrs Winkle, being fully received into favour by the old gentleman, were shortly afterwards installed in a newly-built house, not half a mile from Mr Pickwick's. Mr Winkle, being engaged in the city as agent or town correspondent of his father, exchanged his old costume for the ordinary dress of Englishmen, and presented all the external appearance of a civilised Christian ever afterwards.

Mr and Mrs Snodgrass settled at Dingley Dell, where they purchased and cultivated a small farm, more for occupation than profit. Mr Snodgrass, being occasionally abstracted and melancholy, is to this day reputed a great poet among his friends and acquaintance, although we do not find that he has ever written anything to encourage the belief.

Mr Tupman, when his friends married, and Mr Pickwick settled, took lodgings at Richmond, where he has ever since resided. He walks constantly on the terrace during the summer months, with a youthful and jaunty air, which has rendered him the admiration of the numerous elderly ladies of single condition, who reside in the vicinity. He has never proposed again.

Mrs Bardell let lodgings to many conversable single gentlemen, with great profit, but never brought any more actions for breach of promise of marriage. Her attorneys, Messrs Dodson and Fogg, continue in business, from which they realise a large income, and in which they are universally considered among the sharpest of the sharp.

Sam Weller kept his word, and remained unmarried, for two years. The old housekeeper dying at the end of that time, Mr Pickwick promoted Mary to the situation, on condition of her marrying Mr Weller at once, which she did without a murmur. From the circumstance of two sturdy little boys having been repeatedly seen at the gate of the back garden, there is reason to suppose that Sam has some family.

The elder Mr Weller drove a coach for twelve months, but being afflicted with the gout, was compelled to retire. The contents of the pocket-book had been so well invested for him, however, by Mr Pickwick, that he had a handsome independence to retire on, upon which he still lives at an excellent public-house near Shooter's Hill, where he is quite reverenced as an oracle, boasting very much of his intimacy with Mr Pickwick, and retaining a most unconquerable aversion to widows.

Mr Pickwick himself continued to reside in his new house, employing his leisure hours in arranging the memoranda which he afterwards presented to the secretary of the once famous club, or in hearing Sam Weller read aloud, with such remarks as suggested themselves to his mind, which never failed to afford Mr Pickwick great amusement. He was much troubled at first, by the numerous applications made to him by Mr Snodgrass, Mr Winkle, and Mr Trundle, to act as godfather to their offspring; but he has become used to it now, and officiates as a matter of course. He never had occasion to regret his bounty to Mr Jingle; for both that person and Job Trotter became, in time, worthy members of society, although they have always steadily objected to return to the scenes of their old haunts and temptations.

Mr Pickwick is somewhat infirm now; but he retains all his former juvenility of spirit, and may still be frequently seen, contemplating the pictures in the Dulwich Gallery, or enjoying a walk about the pleasant neighbourhood on a fine day. He is known by all the poor people about, who never fail to take their hats off, as he passes, with great respect. The children idolise him and so indeed does the whole neighbourhood. Every year he repairs to a large family merry-making at Mr Wardle's; on this, as on all other occasions, he is invariably attended by the faithful Sam, between whom and his master there exists a steady and reciprocal attachment which nothing but death will terminate.